HIS MATCHMAKING WALLFLOWER

JAYNE RIVERS

MAGGIE KENT

To every girl
who just wants to
be noticed

CHAPTER 1

London
June 1813

As soon as they arrived at the ball, Lady Charlotte Fitzgerald wanted to go home. For a self-confessed wall-flower, even the most anticipated event of the season—*especially* the most anticipated ball of the season—held little attraction.

The carriage came to a halt outside the summer residence of the Earl and Countess of Wembley, and Charlotte turned imploring eyes upon her brother.

"William, must I really go in? I have the beginnings of a terrible headache." She put the back of a silk-gloved hand to her forehead and adopted an expression she hoped made it appear that she might be about to swoon.

Her brother, William Fitzgerald, who'd become the Marquess of Ensley following their father's death several years ago, raised a dark eyebrow at her. "The Wembleys are expecting us. As is everyone else. I promised Henry that I would see him here."

Charlotte lowered her hand and reached for her fan to

disguise the sudden tremble in her fingers. "Oh, the Duke of Arundel is coming? I thought he had only just returned from his country estate and would be busy getting his affairs in order to attend the House of Lords."

"Of course Henry's here." William stepped down from the carriage and offered Charlotte his hand. "This is the most important ball of the season. Anyone who is anyone in the *ton* will be here."

As if she needed reminding of *that*. Suppressing a sigh, Charlotte placed her hand in William's and exited the carriage, squaring her shoulders under her light silken shawl, which the modiste had declared was just the thing for a midsummer ball.

As though Charlotte cared about fashion. The shawl, a softly muted pale green that matched her gown, was practical and thus suitable for a young lady who most emphatically did *not* appreciate being trussed up and put on display for all the marriageable young men of the season.

She told herself that the fluttering low down in her stomach was entirely due to her dislike of large social gatherings and most definitely not anything to do with the impending presence of the Duke of Arundel, her brother's best friend and a man she'd long admired.

They walked inside through an ornate arch flanked by gilded columns and were greeted by the footman, who took her brother's jacket and Charlotte's shawl. He ushered them over to the countess, who was greeting guests before they could descend the stairs into the ballroom. A tall woman with tightly pinned black hair and the sharp, dark eyes of a hawk, she gave William a wide smile, her gaze barely sliding over Charlotte.

"Countess," Charlotte murmured, dipping her knees as William swept into an exaggerated bow that made the countess flutter both her fan and her eyelashes.

Charlotte was used to being ignored at these events—she

preferred it, even—but some acknowledgement of her existence would be nice.

As her brother exchanged pleasantries, Charlotte looked
down and sucked in her breath. The Wembleys had transformed their ballroom into an exquisite scene. Maroon
velvet curtains hung at the windows, and a huge crystal
chandelier sparkled overhead. Shrubbery had been brought
inside to create a fresh atmosphere, boasting colorful blooms
that Charlotte had never seen in her own gardens, and the
oak floor had been polished until it shone.

The chatter and laughter of the assembled ladies and
gentleman floated up to her as William finished conversing
and started down the stairs. Still holding her breath, she
followed him, concentrating on not tripping while looking
through the crowd for her friends.

Not the Duke of Arundel, of course; that would be highly
improper.

"Lord Fitzgerald!" a woman exclaimed.

Charlotte scarcely had time to brace herself before she
and William were surrounded by a selection of marriageable
young ladies and their mothers, who were all eager for their
daughters to marry a dashing young lord.

Charlotte found herself standing off to the side while
William, after giving her an eye roll that betrayed his real
feelings, greeted and flirted with an easy grace that she had
never been able to master. When one of the mothers nearly
trod on the hem of her new dress, Charlotte excused herself
and made her way over to the lemonade table.

She moved through the crowd of gossiping, giggling
young ladies and flirtatious men as though invisible, a state
that usually suited her but tonight made her feel despondent.
This was her fourth season out. If she did not secure a suitable husband this year, it would surely be her last, and she
would be doomed to spinsterhood.

Honestly, that didn't sound half bad, Charlotte admitted

to herself, if only she had a decent inheritance to live on. She loved her brother, but she had no wish to be the poor dependent spinster aunt for the rest of her days, playing old maid—and no doubt unpaid nanny—to her brother's future spouse and offspring.

At least she was not alone at the lemonade table. Her friend and fellow wallflower, Miss Felicity Doherty, had quite the same idea as her.

"Oh, Charlotte, I'm so glad you're here," Felicity whispered, hiding her words behind her fan. "Lady Wembley keeps trying to get me to take a turn on the pianoforte, and you know I hate being stared at. I'll only play everything wrong and make an utter fool of myself."

Charlotte gave her friend a sympathetic squeeze on her arm. Felicity, although possessed of a sweet nature and an even sweeter face, was terribly shy—a fact that certain overbearing ladies seemed to think could be rectified by pushing her toward center stage as often as possible.

Felicity was poorly looked after by her guardian, and so some of the older ladies in the *ton*, at various intervals, had attempted to make a project of her.

"Let's take a turn around the room, deep in conversation, and that will deter her," Charlotte suggested, trying not to think of the fact that doing so would bring her closer to the Duke of Arundel, whose dark head she had spotted across the crowd.

"Good idea. Oh, look; here comes Miranda." Felicity's dimpled face lit up as Miss Miranda Sutton strode toward them.

Miranda was tall and with striking good looks, but, as usual, she had pinned her dark hair up in a practical, serviceable style and had not bothered with rouge. Her reading glasses hung on a delicate chain around her neck, and Charlotte knew that her friend would much rather be in her library, reading the latest books on astronomy and botany, than at any ball held by any member of the *ton*.

Miranda looked relieved as she spotted them. She joined them by the stand, placing her elegant back to the rest of the room. "I simply can't bear to be cornered by the Earl of Westcott again. He is such a dreadful bore. All he talks about is horses, and I daresay he looks like one too."

Charlotte quickly turned a snort of laughter into a genteel cough.

"Miranda, honestly." Felicity blushed, although she suppressed a smile at her outspoken friend. "At least someone wants to dance with you who is under the age of fifty. I'm positive my late aunt would have had me married off to someone ancient as long as he came with an ample estate."

"All the eligible young men who aren't bores, rakes, or poor were married off last season." Miranda sighed. "Well"—she cast a sideways look at Charlotte—"apart from your brother and the Duke of Arundel, of course."

Charlotte tried not to blush fiercely at the mention of the duke. Miranda missed nothing, and Charlotte doubted that she was unaware of her infatuation with Henry. "No need to be polite. We both know William is a terrible bore. As for the duke…"

"He is coming this way," Felicity murmured, gazing over Charlotte's shoulder.

Charlotte spun around on her slipper to discover that the duke was indeed crossing the floor toward them. As she did so, his eyes met hers, and he smiled at her in a way that made her tingle from head to toe. She felt frozen to the spot, acutely aware of her friends watching her and the duke's warm smile of greeting as he walked right toward them, clearly intent on coming to engage her in conversation.

Charlotte's heart pounded. Would he ask her to dance? It wouldn't be the first time, although of course he only ever asked her out of politeness because she was William's little sister.

She didn't know whether she was relieved or disappointed when the duke's progress toward her was interrupted by the Countess of Wembley introducing him to a pretty golden-haired girl with an almost scandalously low-cut dress.

Charlotte swallowed and turned back to her friends with a smile plastered across her face. Felicity sighed in sympathy, while Miranda looked at her with a keen eye.

"I'm sure he'll ask you to dance once he escapes from the countess's clutches," Felicity said.

"Perhaps if you gave him a little more encouragement," Miranda said matter-of-factly, "then he might show you more attention. I heard Lady Knotmore say that the men were taking bets on the duke finally hunting for a wife this season."

"I…" Charlotte began to protest, then gave up. No matter how much she may try to fool herself, she could not fool her friends. There was simply no other man in the room when the duke was present—not for her, although she was absolutely certain he saw her only as the rather plain sister of his best friend.

"The duke has no romantic interest in me," she finally stated, resisting the temptation to look back over her shoulder. She wondered if he would think the golden-haired young woman was terribly pretty.

"You have never given him the chance." Miranda raised a cool eyebrow at her. "Perhaps if you were to make your interest in him clearer."

Charlotte felt hot at the thought. "I couldn't. William—"

Miranda cut her off. "If nothing changes, then nothing changes."

Felicity nodded, and Charlotte glared at her. Usually Felicity could be relied upon to support her.

"Miranda's right," Felicity said firmly, reminding Charlotte that for all her friend's shyness, she could be remarkably forthright when the occasion called for it. "Perhaps if the duke had a little indication that you see him as more than your brother's best friend, he would be more inclined to look at you as a marriage prospect. Your families are close, after all. It would be a suitable match."

"You sound like your aunt Emma," Charlotte said. "God rest her soul."

Miranda was about to speak when they heard footsteps approaching. Miranda lifted her eyebrows, and Felicity widened her eyes. A fluttering began in Charlotte's stomach as she guessed who was behind her. She turned, wearing what she hoped was an alluring half smile, and came face-to-face with the Duke of Arundel's buttons.

"Oh, excuse me," she stepped back in horror and bumped into the lemonade table with her hip. "I'm so sorry."

She winced, then heat flooded her as he reached out to steady her with a hand on her forearm.

"I do beg your pardon, Lady Charlotte," he said in that low, rich voice she knew so well. "I didn't mean to startle you. Miss Doherty, Miss Sutton." He gave them each a quick bow in turn, which thankfully allowed Charlotte a few seconds to compose herself.

"Not at all, Lord Arundel. I'm a little dizzy; it's been so warm today," she gabbled.

Why must she always be such a silly goose around him?

Of course he would never see her as anything but a little sister when she reduced herself to such foolishness. It hadn't even been particularly hot that day; certainly not for the middle of June.

She saw Miranda briefly close her eyes and Felicity almost imperceptibly bite her lip and knew that her friends were embarrassed for her.

The duke, however, looked almost disappointed. "I hope

you're not unwell? That does rather ruin my plans because I was hoping you would give me the first dance. I do believe the band is about to strike up a waltz."

"Oh! But of course, yes, I should like that very much, thank you." Aware that she was rambling, Charlotte pressed her lips together and took his outstretched hand as the music started up.

Dancing she could manage. That was certainly easier than talking to Henry, who had at some point in the past few years transformed from being William's gangly friend to the only object of her romantic affections.

They bowed to each other and began their dance. The duke's gloved hand rested lightly on her waist, but she was so aware of it that his touch seemed to burn right through the light silk of her dress, her shift, and petticoats to her very skin.

Charlotte swallowed, her mouth suddenly dry as she concentrated on keeping up with the steps. The duke was an accomplished dancer, and Charlotte was all too aware of his lean hips and long, muscled thighs in his tight breeches.

"Thank you for asking me to dance," she murmured, finding herself unable to meet his eyes. "I'm sure I would have been left in the corner otherwise."

"That's only because you and your friends insist on hiding there all night at every ball." He chuckled. "Anyone would think you were avoiding someone."

Charlotte wasn't sure what to say. She turned with the movements of the dance, glad to have a minute to gather her thoughts. The fact that he had noticed her and her habits…. It made her pulse quicken in her throat.

"Of course, that's a godsend for me," the duke went on in his easy tone. "There are far too many pushy mothers waiting for me to dance with their daughters."

Charlotte felt a crushing disappointment in her stomach. She had expected as much, but even so…. Was he always going to see her as no more than a friend? Not even that, but a friend's little sister?

"So, I'm rescuing you from their machinations?" She tried to smile, but her face felt tight.

Henry didn't seem to notice. "I'd like to think we're rescuing each other. I saw the Earl of Banbury looking at you rather intently over his glass earlier. Apparently, he was asking William how your betrothal prospects were going."

"Really?" Charlotte gaped at him, nearly losing her steps in the dance. The earl was old and a notorious fortune hunter, having gambled away most of his inheritance. Charlotte's dowry wasn't particularly impressive, but it would certainly be welcome to a man like the earl.

The dance ended too soon, and Henry bowed and held his arm out to her. "I'll escort you back to your friends."

Charlotte knew he was simply avoiding being expected to ask another young lady for the next dance, but a blush heated her cheeks as she nodded. Unfortunately, before she could take his arm, another man stepped in front of her, bowing deeply and spilling a drop of champagne on her slippers as he did so.

The Earl of Banbury.

"May I have the pleasure of this dance, Lady Charlotte?" His jowls wobbled as he smiled at her, showing his bad teeth.

Charlotte shot a horrified look at the duke, who merely shrugged as though to say, "I told you so."

The earl saw her look and frowned at the duke. "You can't be expecting to have the next dance with this fair lady as well, Your Grace? Give the rest of us a chance, won't you?" He brayed a laugh that reminded Charlotte of a donkey.

Henry inclined his head. "You're correct, of course."

He shot Charlotte a look of sympathy but then walked away, leaving her there. Charlotte looked around desperately for William but couldn't see him through the crowd. Knowing that she couldn't refuse the earl without seeming dreadfully rude and sparking gossip, she politely offered him her hand and was pleased they were both wearing gloves or else she was certain his palm would be clammy.

The music started again, a cotillion that required, to Charlotte's relief, less contact between partners than the previous waltz. Glancing down the line, she saw Felicity dancing with a young man who had a huge mustache. Miranda was nowhere to be seen.

"You dance very well," the earl told her, although he seemed to be paying rather more attention to her décolletage than her feet.

"Thank you," she said stiffly. She saw William just up ahead, dancing with the golden-haired young woman she had noticed earlier. Spotting Charlotte, he smiled with approval to see her dancing with the earl. There was to be no help from that quarter, then.

She let out a sigh of relief as the music ended, ready to escape back to her corner, but then the earl laid his gloved hand on her arm. "I would be honored to dance with you again later," he said with an air of expectation that she would, of course, be grateful to accept.

"Oh… I… that wouldn't be fair," she stammered, trying to echo his own words to the duke back at him.

He gave a surprised snort, and Charlotte hurried away before he could respond, praying he wouldn't complain about her rudeness to William—or, worse, her mother when he next saw her.

Reconvening with Felicity and Miranda back at the lemonade table, she found that Felicity looked just as uncomfortable with her own dancing experience as Charlotte had been. Miranda seemed agitated, pulling Charlotte toward them so that they created a tight ring of three.

"Have you heard about Victoria Talbot?" Miranda hissed. "I was just speaking to her sister."

Charlotte shook her head, wondering what on earth could have happened to rile Miranda so much.

"She's just gotten betrothed to the Duke of Wight!"

Felicity gasped. "That notorious old lecher! Why, he's old enough to be her grandfather."

"She could have done so much better," Charlotte protested. "Of course, the duke is rich, but…."

"He's a beast," Miranda said frankly, not mincing her words. "And his first two wives died in childbirth. She'll be the third Duchess of Wight. It doesn't bode well for her, the poor girl."

Charlotte shuddered at the thought of Victoria, a sweet girl, being married off to that terrible old man. It was awful; although, she wasn't sure why Miranda herself seemed so upset about it. Miranda was always very implacable, and Victoria had been an acquaintance rather than a friend.

Then Miranda voiced her concerns, whispering urgently to them both, and Charlotte found that she understood her friend perfectly.

"Girls, we need to start taking matters into our own hands as regards this marriage business. Because if we leave it to our families, or to chance, then poor Victoria's fate is going to be our own."

Charlotte wholeheartedly agreed.

CHAPTER 2

Henry, the fourth Duke of Arundel, needed rescuing. The Countess of Wembley had been talking to him very loudly about the charms of her young nieces for over twenty minutes now, and only a glimpse of his friend William heading toward him gave him hope of escape.

Unfortunately, however, as he turned to greet his friend, he spotted the gaggle of women behind him and realized that William had brought his own troubles along in his wake.

"Lord Arundel," William said, opening his eyes wide at Henry with a panicked expression. "Have you met Lady Huntingdon and her… er… lovely daughters?"

A quick glance at the three sullen young ladies standing behind Lady Huntingdon was enough to convince Henry that "lovely" was entirely the wrong adjective to describe them.

He bowed to Lady Huntingdon. "Charmed, I'm sure," he murmured, shooting William a scathing look that his friend pretended not to notice.

"I'm sure you gentlemen would love to dance," Lady Huntingdon boomed. She was a thickset, red-faced woman dressed top to toe in lime green, and William positively wilted at the sound of her voice.

Henry's mischievous side got the better of him. "Of course we would."

He beamed at the three young women behind their mother and offered his hand to the prettiest, leaving William to choose between the other two. William glowered at him as he followed him to the dance floor with the tallest and most sullen looking of the sisters, the other having promptly announced her need to get a drink of water.

"You were supposed to rescue me," William muttered too low for anyone else to hear as they lined up and waited for the music to begin.

"And instead, all you have done is ensnare us both," Henry responded under his breath before greeting his new partner. She was a plain girl but with a lively smile, and Henry felt a pang of sympathy for her. She didn't want to be here any more than he did, he was sure. Confound this marriage market and meddling mothers.

At the thought, he unwittingly glanced across the room to meet the eyes of his own mother, who gave him a cool nod of approval at his choice of partner. Henry bit back a sigh, regretting having allowed her to talk him and William into attending this event. She'd accepted an invitation on his behalf, and there had been no polite way to wriggle out of it.

Society had so many damn rules. He wished he were back at Oxford with William and not here in this endless round of ballrooms and dinners and afternoons at the club. It was tedious.

But his mother had her sights set on Henry being married this season and seemed deaf to his protestations. She insisted that he needed to wed. Henry, however, had determined that he never would.

Not with the dark secret of his past hanging over his head.

As the dance came to an end, Henry bowed to the young Miss Huntingdon and practically dragged William away.

"Why on earth did you bring them all over to me?" he hissed.

William shrugged helplessly. "I didn't know what else to do. I couldn't get away from her—the mother, I mean. And you're a duke, which trumps a marquess, so…."

"So you thought you would transfer her attentions to me. Capital. What a way to treat your best friend."

They both glared at each other for a moment before they simultaneously burst out laughing.

"Let's get some air on the balcony," Henry suggested. "It will give us some respite." *And get me out from under the watchful eyes of my mother*, he added silently.

On the balcony, the two young men stared out at the gardens. A lake shimmered in the moonlight, surrounded by neatly trimmed bushes. A young couple walked arm in arm among them. Newlyweds, perhaps. Otherwise, they would either be chaperoned or not walking around so boldly. Henry felt a moment's pang at the thought of his bachelorhood. He enjoyed it, of course, but did he really want to be alone forever?

Unfortunately, he had no choice.

"I saw you dancing with Charlotte earlier." William's voice cut into his thoughts.

"Yes. I saw her huddled in the corner as usual. How are her prospects this season?"

Henry liked Charlotte. She was a sweet woman, although she seemed to have suddenly grown up from the gangly, spirited girl he remembered following him and William around in the summer holidays. She was much more reserved now, but then, it wouldn't be the thing for her to be so free and easy with him now that she was out on the marriage market. They weren't children anymore.

"Not too good, unfortunately." William frowned. "The

only attention she gets is from men who are entirely unsuitable. You saw the Earl of Banbury dancing with her? I was glad to see her dancing, of course, but then she immediately ran off to her friends again."

Henry felt relieved that William wasn't considering the earl as a suitor for Charlotte. It wasn't his business, of course, but he was fond of Charlotte and didn't want her to be made unhappy by a disastrous marriage.

"She doesn't help herself by behaving like such a wallflower," William continued, his hands in his pockets as he gazed out over the garden. "She's in her fourth season. She can't afford to be so unsociable."

Henry frowned at that. He didn't find Charlotte unsociable at all; just a little shy. And he thought she looked rather pretty tonight, although he supposed she wasn't particularly noticeable in a room full of young women all vying with each other to catch the men's eyes. Personally, he thought the natural look was more attractive.

"If she just made the effort to be more fashionable or cultivate some conversational skills…." William shrugged. "She's a capital girl, of course, you know that, but I don't want to see her married off to someone who won't give her the kind of life she deserves. And our mother is determined she will marry this season."

"So is mine." Henry raked his hand through his hair, frustrated by his mother's insistence.

He wasn't in the same boat as Charlotte. As the Duke of Arundel, he was sought after. He wasn't conceited, but he was all too aware of how this game worked, and he knew that he could have his pick of most of the young women of the *ton.*

As long as his secret didn't come out.

"Henry!"

He was so deep in thought that the sound of his mother's voice startled him. She had followed him and William out onto the balcony and now stood in the doorway, her thin lips pursed with disapproval.

"Whatever are you two boys doing out here? You are here to mingle, dear, not skulk on balconies and hide in the shadows."

"Your Grace." William bowed, looking terrified. Henry's mother, the Dowager Duchess of Arundel, could reduce him to a naughty schoolboy with her sharp tongue within seconds.

"I believe I've perused tonight's share of available young ladies," Henry said, trying to inject a cool sarcasm into his tone and instead sounding merely sulky.

His mother glared at him. "Well, in that case, we may as well take our leave. Good evening, Lord Fitzgerald. Do give my regards to your mother."

Henry sent William an apologetic look as he followed his mother back into the ballroom. As she said their goodbyes to the countess, he found himself looking around for Charlotte. She was back in the corner with Misses Sutton and Doherty, their heads pressed close together, deep in conversation.

He thought back to her brother's comments about her poor marriage prospects and smiled sadly. It would be a shame if she were married off to some old lecher. Surely spinsterhood and genteel poverty would be preferable?

But, of course, not everyone was as averse to marriage as he was.

I have my reasons, he reminded himself as he gave his mother his arm and led her outside to their carriage. She maintained a pointed silence until they were well away from the manor, and he braced himself for the scolding that he knew was imminent.

"Henry," she began in a clipped voice. Her expression was unreadable inside the dark carriage. "It seems you haven't been listening to me."

"I can assure you, I have, Mother."

"Then why are you not yet betrothed? Henry, if you do not marry and secure an heir, then all of the sacrifices that myself and your father have made will have been for nothing."

Henry didn't answer her. He knew what was coming and closed his eyes against her words.

"Not every couple would raise a bastard child to be a duke, Henry. By refusing to marry, you are throwing that back in our faces. It is… ungrateful."

He sensed that if she were willing to be less ladylike, a much stronger word would have been used. But appearances were everything to her.

Hence his next objection.

"And what of the consequences for this future wife and child, Mother, if the truth were to come out? Publicly shamed, excluded from the *ton*…. Is that the life you would wish for an Arundel heir? Not to mention the innocent young woman you wish me to ensnare in such a trap."

He sensed his mother stiffen across from him and heard her sharp intake of breath. "Then we ensure that the truth does *not* come out." The finality in her tone and the way she settled back into her seat told him the conversation was over. As usual, she would have the last word.

The rest of the journey occurred in silence. When they arrived home, he helped her down from the carriage without looking at her, and as soon as he could take his leave, he marched swiftly to his own rooms.

"Your Grace, shall I get your bath and nightclothes ready?" his manservant, Grimes, asked, obviously surprised to see him home so early.

Henry shook his head. His mother's words still stung.

Bastard. Ungrateful.

He seethed with irritation, restless and unsettled, and knew there would be no early sleep tonight.

"Lay out my sporting attire, if you would, Grimes. And I

will require a carriage to take me back into town. An *unmarked* carriage."

The set of Grimes's features didn't alter. "Very good, sir."

Henry pulled on the aforementioned clothes: a simple tunic, breeches, and boots that, while of good quality, did not immediately mark him as a member of the *ton*. He untied the ribbon from his dark hair and shook the light dusting of powder from it. He glanced in the mirror at his reflection. In the candlelight, and with a grim expression on his face, he looked almost dangerous, the coiled energy just waiting to burst out.

He needed a session at the club. Snatching up his hooded black cloak, he left his rooms and took the back stairs down to the gardens where the unmarked carriage waited for him as requested. Henry rode in silence. He had no need to tell the driver his destination.

The carriage pulled up next to a side alley. Henry alighted and strode through the streets of London with purposeful steps, the crisp night air doing little to cool the irritation simmering within him. The clatter of horses and distant murmur of revelry filtered through the fog, but he paid no mind.

His destination was a modest building on a quiet street, unassuming to the casual observer but well-known among a certain echelon of society. The Plume and Feather, as it was called, catered to gentlemen seeking an escape from the polished world of balls and propriety.

By day, it was a respectable establishment, offering cigars and fine brandy to its patrons. By night, however, its back room came alive with the thud of fists on flesh and the primal roar of men relishing the physicality denied to them in their genteel lives.

Henry nodded curtly to the doorman, who stepped aside without question. He slipped inside, the warmth of the room and the pungent mix of sweat and leather enveloping him like an old coat. He passed the bar without pause and made his way straight for the back room. This was where the real action took place.

The makeshift ring was already occupied by two men circling each other with predatory intensity. Henry recognized one of them as Bramwell, an earl's wayward second son who had earned himself a reputation as both a scrapper and a rake. The other was his quarry: Malcolm Everard, the illegitimate son of the Duke of Suffolk.

Malcolm, tall and broad-shouldered, moved with a grace that belied his rough-hewn upbringing. Malcolm was a bastard, yes, but in this space, he commanded the same measure of respect that would be afforded a prince.

The bout ended with Bramwell conceding, clutching his ribs and grinning ruefully as he climbed out of the ring.

Malcolm leaned on the ropes, toweling off his sweat. His sharp eyes caught Henry's approach, and his mouth quirked into a sardonic smile. "Well, if it isn't the Duke of Arundel. Slumming it tonight?"

Henry bristled but kept his tone light. "Even a duke needs a good thrashing from time to time."

Malcolm chuckled and tossed the towel aside. "Is that so? Let's see if you've got the stomach for it."

Moments later, Henry was stripped down to his linen shirt and breeches. He stepped into the ring. The crowd murmured, intrigued by the rare sight of a duke in their midst. Malcolm approached with a pugilist's stance, his hands raised and his feet nimble.

The first few blows were exchanged with caution, both men sizing each other up. Malcolm fought like a street brawler, his movements fluid and unpredictable, while Henry relied on the technique he had honed at Oxford, where bare-knuckle bouts had been a favored pastime. The clash of styles made for an exhilarating match.

Henry landed a solid punch to Malcolm's jaw, earning a

grunt of surprise and a renewed ferocity. Malcolm retaliated with a quick jab to Henry's ribs, forcing the duke to step back and reassess. Sweat dripped from their brows as they danced around each other, and the world beyond the ring fell away.

The match ended when Malcolm feinted left and landed a devastating right hook that sent Henry sprawling onto the mat. He lay there for a moment, chest heaving, the dull ache in his jaw a welcome distraction from the torment of his thoughts. Malcolm extended a hand and pulled him to his feet.

"Not bad," Malcolm said, his tone devoid of mockery. "For a nobleman."

Henry chuckled, rubbing his sore chin. "And you're not bad for a bastard."

The words hung in the air, unintended but undeniable. Malcolm's face hardened briefly before a wry smile tugged at his lips. "We all have our crosses to bear, don't we?"

Henry said nothing, but the truth of Malcolm's words hit too close to home for comfort. Watching Malcolm collect his winnings and exchange banter with the crowd, Henry couldn't help but reflect on the contrast between their lives. For all Malcolm's swagger, his illegitimacy marked him out and relegated him to the edges of polite society. But Henry's secret, if revealed, would destroy him utterly. He wouldn't be merely ostracized; he would be condemned.

The noose or Newgate.

CHAPTER 3

Lady Charlotte set her jaw and adjusted her shawl, already dreading the discussion she was about to have. Her mother, Lady Eleanor Fitzgerald, sat at her vanity table, arranging the placement of a sapphire pin in her perfectly coiffed silver-streaked hair. Charlotte approached with caution, smoothing her dress and preparing her plea.

"Mother, I must speak with you about the recital this evening."

Lady Eleanor didn't look up from the mirror. "You'll wear the ivory muslin with the embroidered hem," she said, as though Charlotte had no say in the matter. "It's just subdued enough not to draw undue attention to yourself but elegant enough to avoid gossip."

"Actually," Charlotte began, feeling the flutter of nerves in her stomach. "I've been thinking… I don't want to play at the recital."

Lady Eleanor's hands paused mid-motion, but she still didn't meet Charlotte's eyes. "Oh?"

Charlotte rushed on before her mother could find her voice. "I'm simply not prepared. I'd embarrass the family if I were to stumble through a piece. You wouldn't want that, surely?"

Eleanor finally turned to face Charlotte, her gaze sharp. "Are you telling me you've neglected your lessons again?"

Charlotte swallowed and dropped her gaze to her hands. "I'm merely saying that I would much rather support Miss Helena Steele from the audience than risk spoiling her evening by making a spectacle of myself."

Her mother gave a long-suffering sigh, turning back to her reflection. "Very well. You're not the sort to flourish under scrutiny, I suppose. I won't have you swooning on stage simply to spare yourself embarrassment."

Charlotte blinked. That had been surprisingly easy. "Thank you, Mother."

"Yes, yes," Eleanor murmured. "But do try not to sulk all evening. It's most unbecoming in a young lady."

"Of course, Mother," Charlotte said dutifully. She paused, debating whether to broach the subject that had been occupying her thoughts since the ball. "Will the Duke of Arundel be attending tonight?"

Eleanor's sharp gaze flicked to Charlotte's reflection, her lips curving in a faint knowing smile. "I doubt it. The Steele recital is hardly the sort of event to attract him."

Disappointment settled like a stone in Charlotte's chest, but she forced a nod. "Of course not."

"Don't look so crestfallen, dear. It does you no favors," Eleanor said lightly, turning back to her preparations.

Charlotte retreated, ducking her head away to hide the blush now creeping across her face. She let her maid help her into the pale gown which her modiste had tailored to perfection, the soft fabric brushing against her skin like a whisper.

Her hair was swept up into a simple yet elegant arrangement, a few artful curls left to frame her face. It did look rather becoming, and she couldn't help a pang of disappointment that the duke wouldn't be there to see it.

They went down to their carriage together, and as it rattled over cobblestones toward the Steele residence, Charlotte stared out the window without seeing the streets as they passed.

Helena Steele was the kind of young woman whom Charlotte had always admired. She could perform before a crowded room without faltering, as though the audience didn't even exist. The Steeles were a commerce family rather than nobility but had acquired enough wealth to be invited into the edges of fashionable society.

Other girls of Helena's age and station either thrived under the gaze of that society or wilted beneath its weight. Charlotte, to her dismay, belonged firmly to the latter group in spite of having been born into the *ton*.

By the time they arrived at the Steele residence, Charlotte's nerves were somewhat calmed by the rhythmic clatter of the carriage wheels. She stepped down carefully, smoothing her skirts as her mother alighted behind her with her customary poise. They were greeted at the door by the Steele's butler, who ushered them into a reception room where the other guests mingled.

"Lady Eleanor, Lady Charlotte," Mrs. Steele greeted warmly, her birdlike features softened by her welcoming smile. "We're so delighted you could join us this evening."

"The pleasure is ours," Lady Eleanor replied smoothly, her tone as polished as her pearl necklace.

Charlotte murmured a greeting and curtsied before being swept into the room.

The chatter inside was lively, and the scent of flowers filled the air. Charlotte made her way to the refreshment table, where she fetched a glass of lemonade and drank it gracefully. She then encountered her friend, Miss Genevieve Flynn, looking pale and fidgety.

"Genevieve," Charlotte said affectionately. "You look lovely this evening."

Genevieve gave a wobbly smile. "Oh, thank you, Charlotte. I feel as though I might faint."

Charlotte arched an eyebrow. "Whatever for?"

"I'm to play the piano later," Genevieve confided, glancing nervously toward the pianoforte at the far end of the room. "I've been practicing endlessly, but my hands are trembling so much, I fear I'll make a mess of it."

"You'll do wonderfully," Charlotte reassured her. "You always play so beautifully."

Genevieve sighed. "You're lucky that your mother doesn't force you to perform at every gathering."

Charlotte hesitated. "She knows better than to make me. She would rather I sit quietly than risk embarrassing myself… and her."

Genevieve looked surprised but remained envious. "Still, it must be nice to have that kind of understanding."

Charlotte didn't reply, thinking instead of her mother's indifference. It wasn't so much understanding as disinterest. Her brother William could do no wrong, while Charlotte often felt like an afterthought. Almost immediately, she shook the uncharitable thought away, reminding herself to be fair. Her mother was simply being practical, not unkind.

The sound of a bell tinkling drew the room's attention to the pianoforte. Helena Steele had taken her seat, her serene expression betraying no hint of nerves. As her fingers glided over the keys, the room fell silent, the melody weaving a spell over the guests. Charlotte watched with admiration, marveling at Helena's talent.

Someday, she thought wistfully, *I'll find my own way to shine*. But for now, she could only observe from the shadows, where her flaws were less likely to be noticed.

Helena stood, and Mrs. Steele urged the guests to take their seats. Charlotte settled onto one of the cushioned chairs in the Steele drawing room, arranging her skirts to avoid creases. Her mother sat beside her, fanning herself idly.

Though perfectly poised as always, Charlotte could tell by the slight downturn of her lips that she was already bored.

Lady Flynn and Genevieve joined them shortly after. Lady Flynn, whose severe expression always seemed on the verge of disapproval, nodded stiffly in greeting before lowering herself into a chair with military precision. Genevieve looked flushed and tense, her gloved hands twisting in her lap. Charlotte gave her a small reassuring smile.

The room was filled with the hum of conversation and the faint tinkling of instruments being tuned. The second performer—a nervous-looking young man with a violin—took the makeshift stage.

The first strains of music filled the air, a lively jig that might have been delightful if not for the performer's obvious nerves. His bow slipped several times, producing high-pitched squeaks that made Charlotte wince. At the end of his piece, polite applause rippled through the audience, though Lady Flynn sniffed audibly.

The next performance, a harp solo by a pale and delicate debutante, was much better received. Her fingers danced expertly over the strings, producing a melody so ethereal that even Charlotte found herself caught up in it. Lady Flynn's expression softened briefly, and Genevieve leaned closer to Charlotte.

"I wish I could play like that," Genevieve whispered, her voice barely audible over the applause.

"You'll do wonderfully," Charlotte murmured back, though she could see the doubt in her friend's eyes.

A series of performances followed, ranging from competent to dreadful. A young lady's attempt at a Mozart piano sonata was marred by a wrong note that she stubbornly repeated, and a gentleman's baritone rendition of a Handel aria was woefully flat. Charlotte did her best to applaud, though she caught her mother stifling a yawn behind her fan.

Finally, Genevieve's name was announced. She blanched and clutched her mother's hand.

"Do not disgrace the family, Genevieve," Lady Flynn said in a low, clipped tone.

Charlotte touched her friend's arm lightly. "You'll be fine. Just breathe."

Genevieve gave her a grateful, tremulous smile before rising and making her way to the piano.

The room fell silent as Genevieve took her seat and began to play. The opening notes were soft but steady, and for a moment, Charlotte's heart swelled with pride for her friend. Yet as the piece progressed, Genevieve's fingers stumbled on a particularly intricate passage, and a faint tittering came from the back of the room.

Charlotte shot a glare in that direction, willing the rude observers to silence, but Genevieve soldiered on, her determination evident. By the time she finished, the applause was warm and genuine, and Charlotte clapped enthusiastically, hoping her friend would focus on the kindness of the audience rather than her mistake.

When Genevieve returned to her seat, Charlotte whispered, "You did wonderfully."

Genevieve's lips pressed together and her eyes betrayed her disappointment. Her mother's only acknowledgment was a curt nod.

The final performer was Miss Helena Steele once more. She strode to the center of the room with a natural grace, this time carrying a cello as though it were an extension of herself. Charlotte couldn't help but admire Helena's confidence... not to mention her style. Helena was short and redheaded, not the fashionable petite blonde that so many young women aspired to be now, yet she carried herself with little self-consciousness. Of course, Charlotte's mother thought her brash.

As Helena began to play, the room seemed to hold its

breath. The rich, resonant notes of the cello filled the space, creating a melody that was at once haunting and hopeful. Charlotte felt her chest tighten as the music rose and fell, sensing the emotion in each note. If only she had a talent like that; something to make the duke look at her with admiration rather than the easy familiarity that came with being his best friend's little sister.

Around the room, she noticed other guests dabbing at their eyes with handkerchiefs. Even Lady Fitzgerald appeared moved, her fan momentarily forgotten in her lap.

When Helena finished, the applause was thunderous. Charlotte clapped until her hands stung, and even Lady Flynn offered a stiff, reluctant clap.

"Too much drama for my taste," Lady Flynn muttered. "These lowborn upstarts do love to show off, don't they?"

Charlotte bit her tongue, unwilling to cause a scene, but the comment rankled her. Helena Steele might not have been born into the *ton*, but her talent and grace surpassed those of many of its members in Charlotte's opinion.

After the performances concluded, the guests rose to mingle once more. Helena was quickly surrounded by admirers, all clamoring to compliment her and ask about her music. Charlotte caught a glimpse of her glowing smile but decided against joining the throng. Instead, she gravitated toward Genevieve, who was hovering by the refreshments table with a glass of lemonade.

"You were splendid, truly," Charlotte said, hoping to lift her friend's spirits.

Genevieve gave a small shrug. "It was adequate, I suppose. Mother will say I should have practiced more."

"You did your best, and it was lovely."

Genevieve glanced around, lowering her voice as she said, "Have you heard about Victoria Talbot?"

Charlotte nodded, her expression darkening. "I have. Poor girl. It's dreadful."

Genevieve grimaced. "It's more than dreadful. It's terrifying. If I don't find a suitor soon, my mother will see me married off to the first titled man who shows interest, regardless of his age or character. Appearances are all that matter to her."

Charlotte's heart ached for her friend, who sounded so miserable. "That won't happen, I'm sure. You'll find someone suitable. Someone who makes you happy."

Genevieve gave a bitter laugh. "Happiness isn't part of the equation, Charlotte. Not for women like us. We're bargaining chips in a game we didn't choose to play."

Charlotte wanted to argue, to say that Genevieve was wrong, but the words caught in her throat. Hadn't she said the very same thing at the ball last week?

The two stood in silence for a moment, sipping their lemonade and watching the swirl of the crowd. Charlotte sensed the future looming over them, uncertain and fraught with the weight of expectations they could not escape.

Right on cue, her mother approached, accompanied by a gentleman Charlotte vaguely recognized. Sir Roger Leonard, the second son of an earl. Her mother had a resolute look on her face that Charlotte knew all too well, and she forced her face to lift with a polite expression as her mother introduced them.

Sir Roger bowed, his beady black eyes sweeping over her figure as he did so. "I must say," he began, leaning slightly closer than propriety allowed. "You're looking particularly radiant this evening, Lady Charlotte."

Charlotte grimaced. Roger Leonard was the very picture of a man who cared little for appearances—or hygiene, for that matter. His cravat was askew, his waistcoat bore a faint stain of what looked suspiciously like port, and a faint odor of stale tobacco clung to him. His ruddy complexion and the slight wobble in his stance suggested he'd had a drink or two more than was strictly appropriate.

"Thank you," she murmured, taking a small step back.

He didn't seem to notice—or care. "You know, I've always admired a lady of your... poise and refinement. Not like these other chits, fluttering about like a flock of geese." He waved a hand vaguely toward the room, sloshing the contents of his glass dangerously close to the brim.

Charlotte pressed her lips together, resisting the urge to look around for rescue. Her mother had discreetly sidled off and was talking to Lady Flynn. "That is... very kind of you to say."

"And yet," he went on, his tone turning conspiratorial, "it's a shame, isn't it? A lady of your breeding shouldn't have to endure these absurd gatherings, paraded about for the *ton* like a prize heifer. I dare say I know how you feel—these events are a dreadful bore."

Charlotte barely stifled a sigh. Leonard's words might have been marginally more tolerable if he weren't ogling her in a way that made her skin crawl.

"Indeed," she said, casting a desperate glance toward Lady Fitzgerald, who pretended not to notice.

"I was thinking," Leonard continued, oblivious to her discomfort, "that perhaps we might find a quieter corner to continue this delightful conversation. There's something about these crowds that makes it so difficult to truly connect, don't you think?"

Before Charlotte could summon a reply—or an excuse— her mother reappeared, her expression serene but her sharp eyes taking in the situation at a glance.

"Charlotte, there you are," she said, her voice smooth but firm. "Are you feeling quite well, my dear? You look a bit pale."

Charlotte seized the opportunity with a surge of relief that nearly made her dizzy. "Oh, Mama, you're right. I think the heat is getting to me." She pressed a hand to her forehead for effect. "Perhaps we should leave?"

Her mother hesitated for a moment, her gaze flickering between Charlotte and Leonard. Then she nodded. "Of course, my dear. We wouldn't want you to become unwell. Sir Roger, if you'll excuse us."

Leonard's face fell, but he rallied quickly, offering Charlotte a bow that was more a teetering dip. "Of course, Lady Fitzgerald. Lady Charlotte, I hope to see you again soon."

Charlotte offered a faint smile and murmured something noncommittal before allowing her mother to steer her away. As they made their way toward the exit, she felt a wave of relief wash over her.

Once outside, the cooler night air was a balm to her frayed nerves. The street was quieter than she'd expected, as most of the carriages were waiting farther down to avoid clogging the main thoroughfare. She took a deep breath, letting it steady her.

It was then she spotted him. Across the street, Henry—no, the Duke of Arundel—stood talking with another gentleman, his dark head bent slightly in concentration. The sight of him, so poised and assured, sent a flutter through her chest that she resolutely ignored.

On impulse, she raised a hand and waved, but the duke didn't see her. He turned slightly, his profile illuminated by the glow of a nearby streetlamp, before stepping into a waiting carriage and disappearing from view.

Charlotte let her hand drop, the disappointment settling heavily in her chest. She glanced at her mother, who was watching her with an expression that was uncharacteristically soft.

"Charlotte," Lady Fitzgerald said gently, "it's quite all right, you know."

Her throat tightened. "I don't know what you mean."

Her mother nodded, a knowing look in her eyes. "Of course you don't."

Charlotte turned away, suddenly feeling both transparent

and terribly foolish. The night air, which had felt so refreshing moments ago, now seemed far too chilly. She wrapped her shawl more tightly around her shoulders and climbed into their waiting carriage, wishing she could leave her tangled emotions behind in the dust of the London streets.

Her mother clearly knew about her preference for the duke.

How dreadfully embarrassing.

CHAPTER 4

"Ouch!" Charlotte sucked the tip of her finger where the needle had pricked it, looking over her shoulder to be sure her mother wasn't around to witness her clumsiness. Needlepoint wasn't her favorite task on the best of the days, but this morning, she was particularly distracted.

Her mother had caught her daydreaming at church earlier in the day and gave her a worried frown that made Charlotte blush, her thoughts immediately going back to the previous evening. She'd hoped her mother didn't think that she was daydreaming over the duke.

Not that thinking about the duke was unusual for her, but he wasn't the current object of her mind's wanderings. Instead, she kept thinking back to her conversation with Genevieve at the recital as well as to last week's ball and the terrible future that poor Victoria faced. It seemed all of her friends were in danger of suffering that same fate, or near enough.

There *had* to be something that they could do about it.

"Charlotte?" Lady Fitzgerald appeared in the doorway, looking pleased about something. "You have a caller, my dear."

"On a Sunday?"

"I'll tell Mary to set the table for tea," her mother replied, sweeping away down the corridor. Within minutes, Mary, the maid, arrived with the tea things and arranged them on the small wooden table near the chaise where Charlotte was sitting.

The housemaid, Sally, followed her, plumping up the cushions, checking the large piano in the corner for dust, and adjusting the ties on the curtains, which were a tasteful gold that matched the cream walls. Lady Fitzgerald, of course, was known for her impeccable taste.

"Stop fluttering, Sally." Charlotte laughed, wondering who the visitor could be that prompted such an inspection.

A sudden, wild hope flared in her. Could it be the duke?

But no. She quashed the thought as soon as it came. William was at the club, and there was no reason that the Duke of Arundel would call on *her* at a Sunday lunchtime. Yes, he had been attentive at the ball, but he had made it quite clear that was only because he was trying to escape prospective matches. He had no interest in her other than in the brotherly sense.

More's the pity.

The footman stepped into the room. "Sir Roger Leonard, ma'am."

Charlotte got to her feet, feeling dizzy as the blood drained from her face. Why on earth was Sir Roger here?

The man entered the room, followed by Lady Fitzgerald looking rather too pleased with herself, and Charlotte widened her eyes at her mother in panic. Surely, Sir Roger wasn't being considered as a prospective suitor for her hand?

Sir Roger, dressed in a garish orange waistcoat that clashed with the tasteful decor of the drawing room, bowed in front of her. Charlotte tried not to flinch as his rubbery lips met the back of her hand.

"It is a pleasure, my dear," he said, passing her a huge bouquet of flowers.

Too shocked to respond, Charlotte merely gaped at him. Her mother bustled over, shooting Charlotte a stern look.

"They are just delightful, aren't they Charlotte, dear? Sally, do go put these in water. Please sit down, Sir Roger. Will you take some tea?"

"Er, yes, they are very nice. Thank you." Charlotte sat down and then discreetly moved nearer to the other end of the chaise longue as Sir Roger sat next to her. He was wearing a heavily fragrant cologne that only blended with the odor of his sweat rather than masked it. The scent made her nose wrinkle, and she struggled to arrange her face into a polite expression as Mary poured the tea.

Her mother seated herself near the piano, chaperoning them but also making it clear that Charlotte was to entertain Sir Roger, not simply sit in the corner and allow her mother to do so.

"You're looking as delightful as ever, Lady Charlotte," Sir Roger told her, his eyes roaming her body in a way that she thought most improper.

She looked at her mother for help, but at the angle she was seated, Lady Fitzgerald couldn't see Leonard's face. Instead, she was not too subtly glaring at Charlotte, silently instructing her to make small talk. She wished, briefly, that her father was still alive. He surely wouldn't expect Charlotte to welcome the suit of a man like Sir Roger Leonard.

She swallowed and smiled politely, catching Sir Roger's eye and holding it, as if to let him know that she had caught him leering at her. But he merely winked at her.

My God, he believes I'm flirting with him! Charlotte thought, horrified. She reached for her tea, her fingers trembling around the handle of the cup.

"It's very kind of you to visit," she said, sipping her tea.

"Well, I was rather hoping you might take a turn about

the promenade with me. It's a lovely day to be outside. I took my horse out this morning, and it's quite splendid weather." He grinned at her, showing teeth that were disturbingly yellow for a man of his station who couldn't be much older than William.

"Oh, that would be wonderful, except…." Charlotte cast her mind about for a suitable excuse, ignoring her mother's glare. "I'm afraid I turned my ankle coming out of the Steeles' yesterday," she improvised quickly. "I need to rest it."

Her mother's eyebrows disappeared into her hairline. Charlotte sipped her tea again, avoiding her eyes.

Sir Roger looked crestfallen. "Well, that is a shame. I do hope it heals quickly. Some other time?"

"Of course, that would be… nice."

Sir Roger beamed, clearly not getting the hint. Instead, he moved a little closer to her, and she caught a stronger whiff of his pungent scent. Between Sir Roger's attentions and her mother's steady perusal of her, Charlotte felt trapped, and anxiety rose up in her.

"I, erm, seem to be coming down with a headache," she said, imploring her mother with her eyes, but this time Lady Fitzgerald ignored her, her stiff shoulders making it clear that she was thoroughly unimpressed with Charlotte's conduct.

There was no getting out of it, she realized. She would have to make conversation with the man. His thigh brushed up against hers in what she was sure was no mistake.

"So," she said, angling her body away from his as much as she could, "you say you were out on your horse this morning? My brother loves to ride too."

"Yes. I was hunting on my father's estate—just outside of London, you know. He has some prime deer, brought down from his estate at the New Forest. We're a hunting family, and I'm a crack shot."

Charlotte's stomach turned. She was fond of animals, and

deer were at once so graceful and majestic…. The thought of them being hunted down by this awful man was abhorrent.

"I'm not a fan of hunting, I'm afraid," she said in her primmest voice, hoping that would put him off.

Instead, he let out a great guffaw of a laugh that made even her mother jump.

"Well, I wouldn't expect you to be, my dear." He chuckled, slurping at his tea. "Young ladies are much too delicate for that sort of thing, I suppose. No, you must leave such pastimes to us men."

Sir Roger's grin was wide, revealing his unfortunate teeth once again. Charlotte allowed herself the smallest exhalation of frustration behind her teacup, hoping her annoyance was not too plain on her face. Though how the man could miss the careful control of her expression was beyond her understanding. He seemed incapable of intuiting the mood. Or her.

Her mother cleared her throat softly from the other side of the room. Charlotte felt a surge of resentment that Lady Fitzgerald was subjecting her to this discomfort. Charlotte knew that her mother was desperate to see her betrothed, but surely not to this odious little man? She couldn't imagine anyone more unsuitable.

"Indeed, Sir Roger," she said evenly, placing her teacup down on the saucer with delicate care. "I'm sure some men quite excel at those pursuits." She maintained a tone of vague disinterest, hoping he would lose enthusiasm for the conversation if he realized she was not going to simper and flutter at him.

Instead, Sir Roger leaned forward, reducing the already limited space between them even further. She caught another whiff of his sweat-laced aroma and had to stiffen her spine to keep from recoiling.

"Hunting is only one of my talents," he said. "I also know a thing or two about horseflesh. Perhaps when your ankle is recovered, I might show you my stables. My father's estate is only a short carriage ride away."

Charlotte opened her mouth, desperate to refuse, when she caught sight of her mother's narrowed gaze. The warning was clear: Do not refuse him again. Her mother's motives were transparent. If Charlotte could not charm the Duke of Arundel—or any other worthy candidate—perhaps she could be steered toward a man who, while not a duke, was at least from a noble family.

Lady Fitzgerald's priorities were never more obvious: Charlotte was to marry, and soon, and if that meant suffering through performing some distasteful courtesies, so be it.

But Charlotte had standards—surely her mother did too? For all her emphasis on station and propriety, Lady Fitzgerald was no fool. Perhaps she simply wished to see if Charlotte would stand up for herself, or gauge what she truly desired. Charlotte could hope.

"That would be… interesting," Charlotte managed, choosing each word slowly and carefully, "but I really cannot say when I'll be recovered." She gave him her most apologetic smile, praying he would accept the hint this time. "One never knows with these little twists and sprains."

He patted his knee as though they had shared a great joke. "Ah, yes. Women are more fragile in that regard. Still, I won't give up hope."

The patronizing tone made Charlotte's stomach twist. She glanced at her mother again, but Lady Fitzgerald's face was impassive.

Charlotte decided to try a more subtle deflection. "Do you enjoy attending concerts such as last night's recital?" She asked this in the mildest tone she could manage, hoping to steer the conversation toward something harmless—and perhaps boring enough that he'd run out of steam.

Sir Roger shrugged, apparently unimpressed by the topic. "I'm not much for music unless it has a good marching tempo," he said. "I find all that tinkling on pianos and scraping on violins rather tedious. Give me a good hunt, a strong horse, and a fine roast at the end of the day, and I'm satisfied."

Charlotte's heart sank. Such a man had nothing in common with her or her interests. Not that a husband and wife needed perfectly aligned passions, she imagined, but surely they must have something in common, or what would a couple talk about every day?

Although that was the least of Charlotte's objections to her would-be suitor. She eyed him surreptitiously over her teacup, taking in his bushy brows, eager expression, and air of pompous entitlement.

She glanced at the ornate clock above the piano, hoping that this would prompt Sir Roger to politely take his leave, but it seemed the man was either impervious to subtle hints or simply too self-involved to notice them. Instead of rising to depart, he remained seated, looking completely comfortable. The silence stretched, taut as a violin string, and Charlotte desperately searched for a way to break it without encouraging him to linger.

Her mother, too, appeared uncertain how to proceed. Lady Fitzgerald's fan fluttered in her hand, and the fine muscles along her jaw were tense.

"Er, how do you find London at this time of year?" Charlotte ventured, hoping a banal topic might carry them through these last excruciating moments.

Leonard's face brightened. "Ah, London," he said grandly, "a bustling hive of civilization, to be sure. Still, I find I prefer the countryside, where I can indulge in my favorite pastime without hindrance."

Charlotte tried not to sigh. He would bring up hunting again.

"Which is hunting, of course!" It was clearly his favorite subject too. He beamed, apparently oblivious to the flicker of discomfort that crossed Charlotte's face. "Nothing finer than the thrill of the chase, I say. My father's estate is full of game —deer, pheasants, even the occasional boar if one is lucky enough. Just last week, I managed to bag a fine stag. Antlers like a crown on the poor beast's head!" He laughed heartily, oblivious to how Charlotte paled at the image.

Her stomach lurched. She did not relish the idea of animals brought down for sport. A sudden image flared in her mind: A graceful creature fleeing through dappled sunlight, only to be cut down by a man's bullet. Nausea rolled through her. How could anyone boast so eagerly of such a cruel pastime?

She was beginning to feel a little like a deer in Sir Roger's sights herself. She shot a look of panic at Lady Fitzgerald, silently pleading with her mother to release her from this torture.

Her mother cleared her throat. "I'm sure country pursuits can be… invigorating," Lady Fitzgerald said evenly. "But many gentlemen of good breeding also enjoy art, museums, or even charity work in Town. Have you any such interests, Sir Roger?"

He shrugged as though this were a strange question. "I've not much patience for art or artifacts, I'm afraid. As for charity—well, that's best left to the ladies, don't you think? You have tenderer hearts for such matters."

Charlotte pressed her lips tightly together. The more he spoke, the more boorish he seemed. Based on her mother's expression, she agreed. She opened her mouth, no doubt to smooth matters over, when Sir Roger suddenly leaned toward Charlotte again.

"If your ankle continues to trouble you, my lady, I know a splendid remedy. Though I suppose a delicate lady might need something less vigorous—perhaps a sip of brandy? My father swears by it for all ailments."

Charlotte almost choked on her own frustration. "I—no,

thank you, I do not partake of spirits," she said, trying to remain polite. "I'm sure rest will suffice." She set her cup down with exaggerated care, every movement controlled. If she let her emotions slip, she might say something truly unforgivable, like begging him never to return or talk to her again.

The ensuing silence was broken only by the faint ticking of the mantel clock. After what felt like an eternity, Sir Roger seemed to realize he had exhausted his store of conversational topics. He placed his empty teacup on the table and patted his knee, as if preparing to rise.

"Well, then," he said at last, "I suppose I should not overstay my welcome. Your company has been charming, Lady Charlotte, Lady Fitzgerald." He stood and bowed low, sending a faint whiff of that cloying cologne and perspiration that Charlotte already despised. "I wish you a swift recovery, my lady," he said to Charlotte. "And I do hope to call again soon, when you are fully recovered for our walk."

Charlotte managed a thin smile and a stiff curtsy. "Thank you, Sir Roger. You are most kind."

Her mother stood as well, folding her fan neatly. "Thank you for your visit," she said smoothly. "We appreciate your thoughtfulness."

Charlotte held her breath until the footman had escorted Sir Roger out the door. The moment the latch clicked shut, she exhaled in relief and pressed a hand to her temple.

Her mother turned to her, displeasure not hidden from her voice. In fact, she looked outright angry. "I am not often left at a loss for words, Charlotte, but I fear that was one of the most blatant excuses I have ever heard. You are not injured, and there is nothing wrong with your ankle. Why create such fabrications? I was most embarrassed!"

Charlotte's cheeks heated. "Because I don't like him, Mother. I do not wish to be courted by him or have him think I am in any way interested. The very idea makes my skin crawl. I don't know why you seemed so happy for him to call on me."

Her mother raised a cool eyebrow and swept her hand toward the door of the drawing room. "Do you see anyone else calling? Anyone at all?"

That stung. Hiding her face so as not to show the sudden tears that had sprung to her eyes, Charlotte sat down again heavily.

Her mother sighed loudly. "I am sorry, dear," she said in a gentler tone. "But he is of good family, not so old as many men who seek a bride, and he has no scandal attached to his name that I'm aware of. What is it about him that so offends you? He is a good match. He has a reasonable enough fortune to keep you in a manner you are accustomed to, but not enough that he will expect a bigger dowry. This would be a very respectable match."

Charlotte's eyes widened. How could her mother not see it? Was everything about money and status? "He's coarse," she said, striving to remain calm, although inside she felt far from it. "His manners are dreadful, his hygiene questionable, his every other word a boast of killing some poor creature for sport. Did you not hear how he actually laughed at the notion that a young lady might not enjoy hunting? And he spoke of charity as though it were beneath him."

Lady Fitzgerald tilted her head slightly. "Many gentlemen hunt, my dear. It's not uncommon, and you should not hold such an aversion to it. As for his conversation…. Well, not every suitor will be a poet or philosopher. Some men are more direct. And he is not so very old—he must be what, eight-and-twenty? Barely older than your brother."

Charlotte clenched her hands in her lap. "Yes, but one can be older without being so… unrefined. He gave me no sense that he values anything I might hold dear. He seemed interested only in bragging about himself and… and staring at me as though I were a prize on display."

Her mother's gaze softened slightly. "I see. You feel he does not respect you." She paused, letting that hang in the air. "I understand such concerns, Charlotte. Truly, I do. But as I've told you before, not every courtship will begin with fireworks of admiration and understanding. Some marriages settle into comfort and tolerance rather than romance. Practicality counts for much in our world."

Charlotte shook her head. "I cannot live a lifetime with a man who sets my teeth on edge at the very first meeting. If I must marry, let it be to someone who at least tries to understand me—or at the very least does not actively repel me."

Lady Fitzgerald sighed, turning to face the window. Outside, the summer sunlight fell softly on the neat garden, where roses and jasmine bloomed in delicate profusion. "Such idealism," she murmured, almost to herself. "I only want to ensure your future is secure."

Charlotte blinked back another unexpected sting in her eyes. Lady Fitzgerald had sounded almost loving. "And I appreciate that, Mother. But how secure can a future be if every day is a trial, every conversation a torment?" She took a step forward, her voice earnest. "You said he's not old and he's from a good family—but none of that matters if I cannot respect him. Nor he me. I beg you, do not encourage him to call again."

Her mother weighed Charlotte's words for a long moment, the silence broken only by the distant murmur of voices from the servants' quarters below. At last, she folded her fan and turned back to her daughter. There was resignation, and perhaps a hint of regret, in her eyes.

"Very well," she said quietly. "If he calls again, I will not press the matter. But, Charlotte, you must understand: Your options grow fewer as the season progresses, and you cannot dismiss every man who fails to meet your high standards. I would urge you to reconsider Sir Roger... before it is too late."

Charlotte's shoulders relaxed fractionally. "I understand, Mother. But please, trust me in this. Sir Roger is not right for me."

Lady Fitzgerald shrugged, and Charlotte knew that she had not ended the matter—merely put it off for a while. "We shall see what the next weeks bring," she said, gesturing for Charlotte to follow her into the corridor. "For now, you have been spared him—but do not assume you have forever to find a better match."

Charlotte followed, grateful for the small reprieve. As she trailed behind her mother's elegant figure, she knew that she would somehow have to take matters into her own hands. She could not settle for a man who treated her like a simpleton or a trinket. There had to be some middle ground between spinsterhood and shackling herself to a man like Roger Leonard.

Charlotte inhaled, steeling herself against her nerves. She no longer had the option to bury her head in the sand or hide in corners. Yes, she might have fewer options than she desired, but she would not squander them by surrendering to despair. She *must* find a way to forge her own path—or at least reject those who would make her miserable.

After her mother left her in the corridor, Charlotte found herself lingering, staring at the intricate pattern in the wallpaper as if it could offer reassurance. The possibility that she might be coaxed—or forced—into a marriage like Victoria's had become all too real. She could almost feel the noose of duty tightening around her neck.

Quietly, she went up the stairs to the safety of her room, determined to distract herself once again with needlepoint. She took a seat and tried to concentrate, carefully placing the needle, guiding the thread, pulling it through, creating tiny, neat stitches.

But her fingers trembled slightly, her mind fixed not on the pattern but on her dim prospects. Before she knew it, she had pricked her finger once again, a small bead of red blooming on the fabric.

"Bother," she whispered, digging her fingertip into her handkerchief. Twice in one day. She wasn't accomplishing anything this way. She was too unsettled to relax, to think about anything other than escaping the future that loomed before her, bleak and terrifying.

Charlotte rose from her chair, letting the embroidery hoop rest on the table. Sitting down at her writing desk, she reached for her quill and a stack of fine writing paper. If she was going to make a change—if she wanted to avoid Victoria's fate—then she needed allies.

Her circle of friends, though varied in temperament and fortune, all shared similar concerns. Miranda, thoughtful and scholarly, was desperate to avoid a marriage that wouldn't allow her to pursue her studies. Felicity and Genevieve were like Charlotte herself: on the shy side and not beautiful enough by society's standards to have their pick of husbands.

Helena Steele was, thanks to her status on the edge of the *ton*, expected to marry to advance that status rather than for her own desires, and then there was Helena's acquaintance, Adeline, who Charlotte was sure was in much the same boat. Adeline's family were old money, but hovering close to poverty thanks to a catastrophic loss of fortune.

Together, perhaps, they could think of a solution.

Charlotte dipped her quill into the inkwell and pressed the nib lightly onto the page. In a neat, flowing script, she addressed the first letter to Miranda.

Dearest Miranda,

I am hosting a small gathering at my home tomorrow afternoon for a select group of our friends. I am aware that this is terribly short notice, but further to our conversation at last week's ball, there are matters we simply must attend to.

She paused, and then underlined must. It was important that she let her friends know that this was no simple afternoon tea but a matter of utmost urgency but without revealing anything that would alert prying eyes to her plans.

Two o'clock in the afternoon would be most suitable. I will have fresh cake and tea prepared.

After suggesting a time when she knew her mother would be out visiting acquaintances, leaving them some privacy, she repeated the process for Felicity, and then for Genevieve, Helena, and Adeline, leaving out the mention of the ball. Once finished, she sanded the ink dry and folded the letters neatly.

After sealing each with a bit of wax, she pulled the bell cord for a footman to deliver the messages and settled down to wait for replies.

CHAPTER 5

Henry had been sitting peacefully at his desk in the oak-paneled study, the late morning sunlight filtering through the tall windows and falling in bright rectangles onto the polished surface, before his mother came barging in.

He ignored her for a moment, focusing instead on the letter in his hand that he'd received earlier that week from the manager of his country estate. It was filled with details about the harvest, the current price of grain, and the projected yields for the coming season. Not the sort of reading that inspired much passion in a man of his age, but Henry found comfort in these practicalities.

Unlike the unpredictable and exhausting pressures of the marriage market, which his mother was sure to bring up any second now, the land and its cycles were reassuringly steady. He could count on seasons passing, on fields growing green and then golden, on tenants working and thriving. As long as all was handled properly.

He leaned back in his chair, pushing a strand of dark hair away from his eyes. The figures were better than expected this year—if the autumn rains held off, there would be ample wheat and a fair return. The barley, too, looked promising, and the orchard trees, newly fertilized, should yield more apples than in previous years. Such incremental improvements pleased him. They were small victories he could take pride in.

"Henry," his mother barked, clearly unimpressed that he hadn't immediately dropped his letter to address her.

"I'm rather busy, Mother," Henry said as neutrally as possible.

His mother swept farther into the room as though he had issued a warm invitation instead. She carried herself with the assured grace of someone who always knew her place—and everyone else's.

"My dear Henry," she began, gliding closer. Her slender fingers, adorned with a single emerald ring, trailed along the back of the leather armchair opposite his desk. That ring itself was worth a few orchards, Henry thought. "Whatever you are reading is not more important than what I have to say."

Henry placed the estate letter face down on his desk and folded his hands over it. He raised an eyebrow. "More important than ensuring the prosperity of our lands and the welfare of our tenants? I hope not. Without proper stewardship, the name Arundel would mean very little."

She made a small, dismissive sound. "Prosperity that ends with you will not continue, no matter how attentive you are to the barley crops, Henry." Her lips curved into a thin, knowing smile. "I am here because what I have to say concerns your future—and that of the entire line. A future that depends, my dear, on securing an heir. You cannot—you will not—keep avoiding this conversation."

Henry's face hardened, but he kept his tone calm. They had this conversation regularly, although it had grown more urgent of late. "Mother, I've told you, I'm not currently inclined to wed. I am not past my prime, nor am I without options. There is no need for alarm."

Her spine straightened, and he could see the faint lines around her eyes as she narrowed them at him. "No need for alarm? Tell that to your late father's memory. We sacrificed so much to ensure your inheritance. You are the Duke of Arundel by special arrangement, by grace and goodwill that required more than a little careful maneuvering." She lowered her voice, but it was edged with steel. "You owe it to this family's name to do your duty and produce an heir. Or shall all we have done be for nothing?"

The familiar coil of resentment and guilt wrapped around his insides. The secret of his birth weighed heavily on them both, a shadow that felt as though it clung to every corner of their lives.

"Duty," he repeated softly, picking up his quill and twirling it in his fingers. "Duty to what, Mother? To whom? I am living as a duke, managing our lands, representing our family's interests in parliament when required. I have done everything society expects of me except one thing—choose a bride. Is that not enough for now?" He winced at the note of pleading in his voice.

"No, it isn't," she said bluntly. "A dukedom must be continued. Without an heir, our line perishes in a generation. Surely you will not allow that to happen?" She took a step closer, and he could see the determination blazing in her eyes. "What is your objection? Are you holding out for some great love story? That is nonsense. Marriages of our station are not about love. They are about alliance, stability, and the future. You know this."

He pressed his lips into a thin line, putting the quill down carefully. "I know that, Mother. You needn't worry that I have rose-tinted dreams of romantic bliss." He paused, meeting her gaze. "My hesitation arises from other considerations entirely. You *know why.*"

She wasn't fazed, as he knew she wouldn't be. Instead, his mother gave him a tight smile. Then her expression softened —ever so slightly. "Henry, if you have not found a lady who suits you, it's simply because you have not tried. Have you even looked? The season is teeming with well-bred young women—granted, some are too grasping, others too dull, but there are gems among them."

His hand curled into a fist on the desk. As usual, she completely ignored his protests. "I assure you, I have looked sufficiently to know that there is no one that I have any interest in marrying."

Unbidden, an image of Charlotte Fitzgerald popped into his mind. Which was ridiculous, of course.

His mother tilted her head, considering his words. "What about the daughters of the Marquess of Hollingford? The eldest is reputed to be handsome, the younger very talented. Either would bring a fine alliance."

Henry shrugged a shoulder, dismissing the idea. "I have seen them. There is nothing in either of them that appeals to me."

"Lady Agnes Wilton, then?" his mother pressed. "She is said to be agreeable and comes with a substantial dowry."

He made a noncommittal noise and shook his head. Agnes Wilton bored him to tears, and he was fairly sure the feeling was mutual. "We would have nothing to talk about beyond the weather."

A hint of exasperation crossed her features. She tapped a finger on the armchair. "If conversation is what you seek, then you must be interested in someone with a brain, not just a pretty face. What of that Fitzgerald chit, the one who used to follow you and Lord Fitzgerald around like a puppy years ago?"

"Charlotte?" he asked, startled. Had she read his mind?

A sly smile curled her lips. "Yes, Charlotte. Isn't she out again this season? Her family is respectable, if not extraordinarily wealthy. She's well-mannered, and, from what I hear, no scandal attaches to her name. A little quiet and no great beauty, maybe, but very bright, I understand. And you already know her."

Henry went very still. He didn't like the way his mother had dismissed her appearance in favor of her mind. While she was, no doubt, bright, Henry thought she had also blossomed in other ways, and it was a damn shame she was so overlooked by society. Recalling William's concerns about her marriage prospects, he grimaced. She deserved better than some predatory old fool.

In spite of himself, his pulse quickened. Perhaps if things were different, she would make a good match. Yet the idea of tying her to him, involving her in his secret-laden existence, set his teeth on edge. Charlotte also deserved more than a marriage founded on necessity and deceit.

"Charlotte Fitzgerald is indeed a sweet young lady. However, the last thing she deserves is to be saddled with a situation like ours. I have a great respect for her and her family. I will not drag them into a tangled past."

His mother's lips parted in surprise, and for a moment, her carefully composed mask slipped. "Situation like *ours*," she repeated, her tone turning cold. "The Fitzgerald family would be honored by a match with the Arundels."

Henry's jaw tightened. He would not rise to the bait. "You know exactly what I'm talking about, Mother. Charlotte Fitzgerald deserves better than a man forced into marriage by circumstances beyond his control. She deserves a husband who can give her an honest future, free of shadows."

His mother rolled her eyes skyward, her patience wearing thin. "She isn't exactly inundated with proposals, Henry. I imagine she would be grateful for your attentions. You claim to care so much about what others deserve, yet you give no thought to your own obligations. This is not about who deserves what; it's about securing our future."

She pursed her lips. "We chose a path that allowed you to hold this title, this wealth, this position. We protected you. We shielded you from scandal. And now you hesitate to do the one thing required to ensure it was not all in vain."

He gripped the edges of the letter beneath his hands, feeling the crinkle of paper as his knuckles went white. He knew the weight of his parents' sacrifice. He felt it every day. That knowledge was what bound him so tightly, stifling his attempts to live freely.

"I am aware," he said, voice quiet, "of what you have done. But I cannot simply pick a bride like choosing a suit of clothes. Not when the consequences are so dire if any hint of the truth emerges."

She tossed her head, her voice rising a fraction. "Then keep the truth buried, as we have all these years. Stop inventing reasons to delay. You are not a boy, Henry. You are a man with responsibilities. Everyone expects you to choose a wife. If you cannot find a reason to do so for yourself, do it for the family's sake."

Henry rubbed his temples. Must she always be so relentless? He felt a headache coming on, a dull throb behind his eyes.

"Mother," he began more gently, "I am not saying I will never marry." That was a lie, of course, but he needed to placate her, or this might well continue on all day. "I'm simply saying I do not wish to do so this instant, nor under the threat of an ultimatum. I have time. I am not yet so old as to be pressed against a final deadline." He tried a small, conciliatory smile. "Surely we can agree that rushing into a disastrous match does us no favors? Better to wait a season, find someone suitable."

"Wait a season," she repeated slowly, as if tasting the words. "We have already waited. This season is half gone. Your dithering makes tongues wag. People are watching, whispering, wondering why the Duke of Arundel is so particular, or if he hides some peculiarity of his own. We can't afford more speculation. If you do not choose someone soon, I will choose for you."

Henry's eyes snapped up, his temper flaring. "You wouldn't dare," he said, his voice flat. "You cannot force me to marry."

She lifted her chin. "Do not underestimate my resolve. If I must invite suitable candidates to tea, parade them before you, and approach their fathers to strike a bargain myself. The Arundel name will not die because my son refuses to fulfill his role."

He exhaled, hands clenching under the desk. Arguing further would only deepen her determination. He knew his mother well: Once she decided on a course of action, it was nearly impossible to dissuade her. Even though she couldn't technically force him to wed, she could certainly put him into a very difficult situation.

He closed his eyes for a moment, picturing the life he wanted—freedom, security, and no risk of his secrets emerging. But that last part was impossible with marriage. A wife would be close, a partner, someone who might discover things best left buried.

Yet standing firm against his mother's demands would bring its own calamities. If she began openly meddling, who knew what messes might result? Gossip, scandal… and if the truth surfaced, it would not just ruin him, it would ruin anyone tied to him, including any unfortunate bride she foisted upon him.

The silence stretched, heavy and suffocating, and his mother watched him like a hawk. "I am not unreasonable," she said eventually, softening her tone as if to offer a small mercy. "I will give you some time to make your choice. But I mean what I say. If you cannot or will not select a suitable bride, I will do so for you. You owe that much to this family. And there are ways of changing your mind."

She was *threatening* him?

Henry nodded stiffly, knowing he had no choice but to acquiesce for now. The tension in his shoulders was almost painful. "I understand," he said coldly. "Thank you for affording me that time."

Ignoring his sarcasm, a small, satisfied smile touched her lips. "See that you use it wisely," she said, and turned to leave, her skirts whispering over the polished floor. At the door, she paused. "I do hope you'll remember your obligations when next you attend a ball or soiree. There are many eligible ladies who would make fine duchesses." Then she left, the door clicking shut with a soft finality.

Alone once more, Henry released a long, shuddering breath. The clock on the mantel ticked softly. Henry sighed and turned his attention back to the estate's affairs. He might not have a clear path forward on the matter of a wife, but at least he could control something. The earth would give its harvest, the tenants would get their fair share, and life would continue for now... but he couldn't continue to keep this storm at bay forever.

The words on the letter swam in front of his eyes, suddenly refusing to make any sense. His head was pounding, and he could no longer concentrate on considerations of corn harvests. He put the letter into the drawer and stood up. He was due to meet William at White's gentleman's club shortly and so decided to take a stroll there rather than using the carriage. Perhaps that would clear his head.

He walked down Pall Mall and soon wished he had taken the carriage after all. Couples strolled past arm in arm, young ladies with their chaperones—who were only too delighted to greet the Duke of Arundel—and a few of his peers who inevitably stopped him to inquire about his day.

Henry couldn't walk more than a few yards without stopping to make polite and boring conversation with some other member of London's fashionable set. By the time he reached White's, he was positively drained.

The club was highly exclusive. Only men of around Henry's rank or higher were admitted. It was a very different place to the club he'd boxed at just a few days before. As he entered and gave his coat to the footman, the smell of tobacco and expensive leather wafted over to him.

He walked past an imposing bust of the late King George II and made his way to his usual—and coveted—seat by the huge fireplace. William was already there, sitting at their usual table with a cigar in hand and the news sheets open in front of him.

"Reading the gossip sheets again?" Henry smiled, leaning over his friend's shoulder.

William started guiltily and quickly turned the page. "Not at all," he blustered. "That's for the women. You're early."

William waved to the waiter as Henry took his seat opposite.

"I had to get away from Mother." He groaned, rubbing his temples. The stuffy air did little to help his headache. "She's insisting I marry. Soon."

"And she's taking no notice of your protestations that you would rather remain a bachelor for the time being," William said glumly.

A statement rather than a question. Henry was well aware that his friend was in the same boat. At least, on the face of it, they were. It was Henry who held all the dark secrets.

"Lady Fitzgerald is of much the same mind, then?"

William rolled his eyes. "Absolutely *obsessed* with my duty to continue the Fitzgerald line."

"I'm well acquainted with that one." Henry stared into the glass of brandy being set down before him. Its amber-colored liquid looked all too tempting.

William handed him a cigar. "So, how did you leave

things? Does she have anyone in particular she wants you to court?"

"Oh, there were a few suggestions." Henry thought it wise not to mention that Charlotte's name had come up in the conversation. He wasn't sure what his friend would make of it, and neither did he want to examine his own feelings of fondness that had arisen for his best friend's younger sister.

Or the memory of how charming she had looked in that dress at last week's ball.

"I suppose you told her that you had no intention of marrying?" William ran his fingers around the rim of his glass thoughtfully.

"Well, what else should I say?"

"Look," William leaned in toward him, his voice dropping to a low and confidential tone. "If there's one thing I have learned recently from dealing with my own darling mother, it's that pressing your case just doesn't work. Mothers don't listen."

"So what are you suggesting?" Henry gave William a look of horror. Of course, William didn't know his deepest, darkest secrets—although he had often wished he could confide in him, if only to share the burden—but his friend had so far been firmly in the bachelor camp with him.

"Pretend to consider it. Let her believe you are at least beginning to think about it. Show a semblance of interest in a few young ladies, but don't commit. You want to be sure, after all. That way, she will think you're coming around—but what you are actually doing is stalling. That's the tactic I've adopted for the time being, and it certainly works better than having to argue my point constantly."

William grinned and knocked back a glug of brandy, pleased with his own ingenuity.

Henry couldn't help but laugh. "You're a rogue, William." He chuckled. "You were one at Oxford, and you're still one now. But maybe you're right. I could at least dance with the young ladies she points out to me, I suppose."

"That's it," William replied with a nod. "Play for time. We have years yet before we need to settle down with a bride. I don't know why they are so impatient. When the time comes, we'll choose a woman ourselves. No need for all this matchmaking."

Henry's mood darkened again. "I will never marry," he said quietly but in such a tone that William looked shocked.

"You really do mean that, don't you? It's not just that you're not ready. Why are you so against the idea? It's what awaits all of us, surely? Just not yet."

For a moment, Henry again longed to spill his secrets to William in the hope of finding relief from them for a few brief moments. But he knew that was unthinkable. William would recoil from him, and then Henry would be even more alone than he already felt. He couldn't bear to see the look on his friend's face when he realized that he didn't truly know Henry at all.

Henry swallowed back the urge to confess and forced a laugh instead, one that sounded hollow even to his own ears. William continued to watch him with open curiosity, but had the tact to let the matter drop—at least for the moment.

The hum of voices around White's, the soft clink of glasses and shuffle of newspapers, filled the silence.

A puff of cigar smoke drifted between them, and William tapped ash into a nearby tray. "You'll figure it out, I suppose," he said, finally. "I can't pretend to understand your reluctance, but I'm sure you have your reasons."

"I do," Henry said in a tone that indicated he intended to discuss it no further.

William took the hint and changed the subject.

Sort of.

"Speaking of marriage—did I mention that Sir Roger Leonard called on Charlotte yesterday?"

Henry straightened in his seat. "Roger Leonard?" He recognized the name instantly; they'd crossed paths with the man at one point or another. An earl's second son, if he recalled correctly—and a bit of an oaf, if the rumors were to be believed. "What the devil did he want with your sister?"

William gave a little shrug and lifted his glass, swirling the last of his brandy. "He wants to court her, I expect. The season is half over, and Charlotte is… well, not exactly inundated with suitors. Perhaps Sir Roger thinks she's an easy match." He pulled a face that made clear his own opinion of Sir Roger.

"An easy match," Henry repeated, his voice low. His teeth clenched unconsciously around the words. He thought about Leonard's less-than-pleasant reputation and grimaced. "Surely your mother won't encourage Charlotte to wed him."

William gave Henry a long look, one eyebrow arched. "Mother doesn't entirely approve—Leonard's habits are questionable at best. But Charlotte doesn't have many choices, does she? She's not known for her social brilliance. She's sweet, of course, and perfectly respectable, but she's not the kind to command attention in a ballroom. She doesn't flirt or dazzle the crowd."

Henry experienced a flare of defensiveness on Charlotte's behalf. "She's more than capable of sparkling when she chooses," he said quietly, though he wasn't sure if William heard him. "It's just… not her nature to compete for notice, perhaps."

William nodded, glancing at his friend as though he found Henry's mild protest interesting. "Perhaps so. But that also means fewer prospects come beating down our door. And you know how it is: If the next season arrives with no offers, talk starts turning to spinsterhood. Nobody wants that."

Henry pressed his lips together. The idea that Charlotte might feel forced into a match with someone like Roger

Leonard sat ill with him. Charlotte was a nice girl. "She deserves better."

"I agree, but unfortunately our mother doesn't. She reminds me daily that we cannot afford to let Charlotte waste away without a husband. And Charlotte herself knows that her inheritance is not so grand as to attract a wealth of suitors. Leonard, for all his faults, has at least shown an interest." William sounded frustrated. "I'd sooner see her hold out for someone pleasanter, but what can I do? She's a grown woman, and our mother wants her settled."

Henry wondered why he was so affronted. Charlotte Fitzgerald was no real concern of his. Yet, to his own surprise, he found himself blurting, "You can't seriously be considering Leonard as a brother-in-law, can you? The man is a cretin."

William winced. "Of course I'm not. He has about as much refinement as a goat. But you know how it goes: Sometimes one can't afford to be picky." He sighed and rubbed his hand across his chin. "Look here, Henry, I don't like it either. But the truth is that Charlotte's options are thin."

"Poor Charlotte," Henry murmured and then decided to say no more. He felt unnerved by his own reaction to the news.

"Poor Charlotte indeed," William echoed.

CHAPTER 6

CHARLOTTE DREW A STEADYING BREATH AS SHE SURVEYED THE drawing room for what felt like the hundredth time that morning, hoping that the maid recalled her instruction that their meeting was not to be interrupted.

The large windows let in slivers of bright spring sunlight, and the table was set with teacups, a silver pot of steaming brew, and a platter of enough fresh biscuits and cakes to feed double the amount of guests. She didn't want anyone leaving early due to hunger.

She glanced at the clock on the mantel. Almost time.

All morning she'd been anxious that her mother might discover the reason for such an impromptu meeting of young ladies, but luckily Charlotte had chosen a morning when her mother had been safely occupied with her correspondence before making her own social calls elsewhere.

She was probably arranging another awful suitor.

Finally, everything was set. The tea was steaming in its china pot, and the only thing left for her to do was to wait for the others. Every tick of the clock on the mantel tied a tighter knot in Charlotte's stomach.

She was about to pace the length of the room yet again

when the footman announced Felicity's arrival. Charlotte hurried over to greet her friend as Mary took her bonnet and shawl and Felicity thanked the maid awkwardly. Charlotte hoped Felicity would be comfortable with such a gathering; she didn't think she had ever gathered all of her friends together like this.

If Charlotte was quiet in society, then Felicity was often nearly invisible—always on the fringes, her sweet nature overshadowed by the more gregarious ladies of the *ton*. Charlotte adored her. Despite Felicity's natural timidity, her loyalty made her a dear friend. Charlotte was sure that Felicity would support her plan.

"Charlotte," Felicity said as she took her seat. "Your note sounded so urgent. Is something wrong?"

"I promise I'll explain once everyone arrives," Charlotte responded, keeping her voice calm. She gestured toward the table. "Please, do sit. Mary will pour you some tea while we wait."

Felicity nodded, looking puzzled. Charlotte glanced at the clock again, drumming her fingers on her skirts. Her nerves fizzed in her stomach.

Thankfully, she didn't have long to wait. Moments later, the butler introduced Miranda Sutton. She entered with her usual composure, her spectacles perched on her nose, her dark hair neatly pinned. Charlotte was always struck by Miranda's serene confidence, which came not from any social savvy but from her keen intellect.

"Hello, Felicity, Charlotte. This is about Victoria's betrothal, I take it? I suspect you have some sort of plan," Miranda remarked, arching an eyebrow. "You're far too deliberate a person to summon us all without good cause."

Charlotte smiled, knowing this was high praise from her friend.

Miranda then took out a notebook from her purse. "I had a few thoughts of my own," she started, clearing her throat.

Before Charlotte could respond, Helena Steele arrived. In contrast to Miranda's quiet grace, Helena walked with a bounce in her step; one that Lady Fitzgerald would have called vulgar. Helena took off her own coat and handed it to Mary, who looked quite scandalized, and then gave Charlotte a quick embrace.

"What on earth is happening? Your note was so mysterious!" Helena's red curls bobbed around her pretty face as she spoke.

"When everyone is here, I'll explain," Charlotte said, now anxiously twisting her fingers together.

"Well, whatever this is," Helena said as she took her seat, "it must be serious, to gather us together like this on such short notice."

Genevieve Flynn arrived next, looking a bit rushed, her cheeks pink from the mild exertion of hurrying up the stairs. She swept into the room, almost tripping on the edge of the rug. Felicity jumped up to steady her, and they both laughed at the close call.

"Charlotte," Genevieve said as Mary took her shawl. "I nearly spilled my tea when I read your note. It's not like you to be so insistent about a daytime rendezvous." She took in the scene—the carefully laid table, the closed door—and her eyes narrowed. "You have me all aflutter with curiosity."

"Soon, Genevieve, I promise. We're just waiting on Adeline." She glanced at the clock.

"The suspense," Helena said dramatically, "is killing me."

Miranda looked at her coolly over her glasses.

As though summoned by name, Adeline Claremont arrived last, her bright eyes shining with curiosity. Charlotte had met Adeline during her very first season, and though neither had secured a match that year—or any other—a bond had formed over the mutual disappointment and the sometimes absurd spectacles of the *ton*.

After that first season, Adeline had seemed to retire into

inevitable spinsterhood, but now, following her father's disastrous investments, her family were desperate for her to marry to secure their future. This was the very thing they all had in common: They were all lacking in the flashy looks, good breeding, impressive fortunes, or connections that made for betrothals of their choice. Instead they were all facing genteel poverty… or worse.

Charlotte thought about Roger Leonard and shuddered once more.

Adeline settled, and Charlotte took a deep breath, looking around at the five expectant faces of her friends, all of them now seated, cups of tea in hand.

"Thank you, Mary," Charlotte said, turning to the maid who was taking a suspiciously long time arranging the cakes. "That will be all. Please see that we are not disturbed."

"Yes, my lady." Mary looked disappointed but bobbed a quick curtsy and left the room. Charlotte waited until the door clicked shut behind her before stepping over to the door and opening it just a crack. The corridor was empty. Satisfied, she closed it once more and turned to face her now very impatient friends.

An uneasy stillness settled, and Charlotte braced herself. This was her idea; it fell to her to explain, but she suddenly felt terribly shy. She glanced from face to face—her friends wore expressions that ranged from polite concern to outright apprehension.

"All right," she began, pressing her hands together. "Thank you for coming. I know my note was… urgent, and I appreciate you all answering so quickly."

"Of course," Miranda said matter-of-factly, pushing her spectacles higher on her nose. "Now, do tell us what's going on, Charlotte."

"I realize you must think me quite melodramatic." A faint, nervous laugh escaped her. "But the truth is, something has happened—something that made me realize we can't simply drift through our seasons, hoping the right match will fall into our laps. Not if we want to avoid poor Victoria's fate."

Miranda made a sound of agreement, while Genevieve and Adeline's eyes went wide. Helena sat forward eagerly in her seat.

"Something has happened, hasn't it?" Felicity asked.

Charlotte nodded, her throat suddenly dry. She swallowed. "I believe Sir Roger Leonard intends to court me."

The reaction was instant: She saw five sets of eyes widen in immediate response. There was a collective gasp, followed by Miranda's soft "Oh no…." and Genevieve's perplexed "But why?"

"Roger Leonard?" Felicity looked mortified. "He's quite…" She searched for a polite descriptor. "Flamboyant."

"Flamboyant is one word," Genevieve muttered. "Odious might be another."

Helena blinked, then frowned. "Doesn't he gamble to excess? And he… smells odd?" She didn't bother disguising her distaste.

"I heard he drinks," Miranda added, "and not in moderation."

"And I've heard," Felicity said, "that he forces conversations about hunting and hounds at every opportunity."

"It's all true," Charlotte confirmed, feeling queasy as she remembered Leonard's eyes on her the day before. The thought of his hands on her…. It made her ill.

Adeline exchanged a horrified glance with Miranda, who set down her teacup so hard, it rattled in the saucer.

"Surely your mother wouldn't allow such a match," Adeline put in.

But Miranda shook her head. "She likely would. He's an earl's second son, and so the *ton* tolerates him. That said, I doubt you'd find a single woman who'd call him an ideal match." She sighed, settling back in her chair. "Poor Charlotte. Are you sure he's serious?"

"He called on me yesterday with a large bouquet," Charlotte confirmed. "I had to feign a sore ankle to avoid promenading with him. And yes, he talked about both hounds and hunting. In detail."

A collective murmur of commiseration passed through them.

Felicity reached out and patted Charlotte's hand. "That must be awful for you. Is your mother truly considering him?"

"I don't think she would outright insist upon it, no—but my options are thin. You all know that. And Roger Leonard, being an earl's second son, isn't an outlandish catch in society's eyes. Worse, he seems determined. I fear my mother—and indeed, all of our guardians—are more concerned with our financial security than our personal preference."

They all exchanged glances, hearing the honesty in these words.

"I'm not a prize in the marriage market," Charlotte continued. "With my modest dowry, I'm hardly inundated with offers. If Sir Roger proves persistent, I can't be sure how much pressure there will be. Mother wouldn't force me, but…"

"It's too easy to make it difficult to say no," Genevieve finished for her.

For a moment, there was silence.

Helena broke it by shaking her head emphatically. "He's a dreadful man. You can't possibly accept him."

"Of course I don't want to," Charlotte said firmly. "Which brings me to the real reason I asked you here." She hesitated, looking between them all. "I'm not the only one of us who's facing a grim prospect. We've each endured at least one unsuccessful season. In truth, I'm worried that if we leave everything up to luck—or our parents—we'll all end up like Victoria: Betrothed to someone who isn't right for us and forced into a marriage we despise."

There was another moment of hush as they all thought about their own pending fates. None of them could deny the truth of Charlotte's words.

"So we have to do something," Miranda announced, setting her shoulders back. "What are you thinking, Charlotte? How do you—any of us—escape this?"

Charlotte drew a breath and summoned whatever scrap of boldness she possessed. "I think we should join forces. Help each other ensure we find the right matches, or at least avoid the worst ones."

Miranda crossed her arms over her chest, clearly intrigued.

Felicity's eyes grew even wider. "But… how, exactly?"

"I don't know," Charlotte admitted. "But I refuse to continue to stand by and let my future, or any of yours, be decided by society and at our parents' convenience. I propose we take control in whatever small ways we can."

"Such as?" Adeline prompted.

Charlotte shrugged. "We have intelligence, combined social connections, and a certain cunning if we put our minds to it. Why can't we join forces and support one another? If we make a plan, an… alliance, if you will, we might just secure more suitable matches—or at least find ways to stave off unwanted suitors."

"This idea has merit." Miranda tapped a pen on her notebook as she spoke, her voice brightening with interest. "If we each gather what we hear in the ballrooms, drawing rooms, and at the promenade, we can compare notes. We can identify which men are respectable, which are rakes, which have secrets or debts. We can strategize who should dance with whom, how to encourage or discourage a suitor. In essence, we'd be turning the season into a… well, an organized campaign."

Despite the gravity of the topic, the corners of Charlotte's mouth lifted. That was exactly the sort of language she expected from Miranda, who adored structure. "Yes. Organized. We could be more effective together than alone. I know it sounds a bit mad, but it's better than waiting around for whatever fate befalls us."

Helena lifted her chin. "The idea is brilliant, but I'm not sure how I fit into it. If I'm honest, I do not seek a match at all. I fancied myself in love once but I learned from that mistake. Now, I'd prefer to focus on my music, if only my parents weren't so determined I bring our family into the *ton*."

"Then we shall do our best to help you remain unwed," Charlotte assured her.

Felicity fiddled nervously with a lace cuff. "And what of me? I'm hardly a shining star on the dance floor, or a master of drawing-room conversation. How could I help?"

Miranda reached across and patted her hand. "You have a sweet disposition, Felicity. People trust you. And you're more observant than you realize."

Genevieve cleared her throat. "Well, I can't say I'm brimming with suitors, either, but I do talk to people at these dreadful balls. My mother insists on parading me everywhere; I pick up pieces of gossip. It might be useful."

Charlotte's shoulders lost a fraction of their tension as the group reached a semblance of consensus. "So we're agreed, then?" she asked, carefully scanning each face. "We'll help one another navigate this marriage market—on our own terms?"

Adeline smirked. "And if we're lucky, we might avoid these dreadful Leonard types altogether."

"Precisely." Charlotte's smile was genuinely warm now.

"Goodness," Genevieve breathed, leaning forward. "It sounds almost… devious. I've never been devious in my life."

Miranda patted her hand, too, still holding on to Felicity's with the other. "It's more practical than devious, Genevieve.

We're merely looking out for one another in a society that often pits women against each other."

At the mention of the unspoken rule that young women were in constant competition for the most eligible suitors, a somber mood briefly settled in. Yet the notion of banding together felt both exciting and subversive. They were taught to be polite, sparkling, and grateful for any decent proposal. But here they were, talking about daring to change the rules.

"So, how do we start?" Felicity asked.

"I propose we focus on one of us at a time, and given recent events with Sir Roger"—Miranda wrinkled her nose as though at a bad smell—"we need to start with Charlotte."

Charlotte flushed slightly. This was precisely what she had wanted; but now she had to admit the most embarrassing part of all.

She had an ideal suitor in mind.

Of course, Felicity and Miranda would not be at all surprised. Indeed, Miranda gave her a knowing look.

"Charlotte," Adeline said, "Miranda's right; I think we should start with you. You have an odious suitor sniffing around, and"—she paused, exchanging a glance with the others—"there's also the matter of the Duke of Arundel."

Heat flooded Charlotte's face. Was *everyone* aware of her feelings for the duke?

"Have I been so obvious?" She groaned, raising her hands to her cheeks.

"Well," Genevieve said carefully. "I've seen how you sometimes peek in his direction at balls."

"You don't always hide it well," Helena added "Sorry."

Charlotte was mortified. "I—he's an old friend of my brother's," she murmured, fumbling for composure. "I'm sure he only sees me as William's little sister."

"Oh, I wouldn't be so certain," Miranda mused. "We've all seen him dancing with you more than once. He rarely dances at all. He's famously aloof. So perhaps there's hope."

"If we succeeded in matching you with the duke, Charlotte, think what that would mean for all of us," Genevieve chimed in, excitement edging her voice. "Having a duchess among our number would open doors to so many events and connections. We might all benefit from that influence!"

Charlotte's embarrassment grew. "You're all so kind, but I don't want us to only focus on me. This was meant to be a collective effort."

Adeline gave a wry smile. "But your situation is urgent. We can't leave you to the attentions of that awful Leonard man. And Genevieve's right; if we can encourage the Duke of Arundel to take more of an interest, then it would help us all. Plus you'd be safe from lesser suitors like Leonard. It solves two problems at once."

As they all nodded eagerly, a riot of emotions swirled in Charlotte. The truth was, she desperately did dream of catching Henry's eye. But even thinking about it felt presumptuous.

"I... I'm not sure he feels any particular way about me," she said, picking at the trim of her dress. "I'm sure I'm only a convenient dance partner when he wishes to avoid pushy mothers and their eager daughters."

Felicity piped up then, sympathy in her gaze. "That might be true," she admitted, "but I've seen the way he looks at you sometimes. There's a definite warmth there."

Charlotte's cheeks colored slightly. "You really think so?"

"There will be by the time we've finished." Helena grinned.

A gentle laugh spread through the group, and Charlotte was touched by her friends' support. The nerves fizzing inside her turned to excitement. Perhaps this could really work.

"I can't thank you all enough," she said, her voice soft. "This is more support than I ever imagined. Truly."

Miranda tilted her head. "We have to set some sort of

plan, though. The next ball is Friday at the Wentworth estate, is it not?"

Everyone murmured in affirmation. Charlotte had nearly forgotten about the invitation, although her mother had insisted they attend.

"Then let's make that our first observation post," Genevieve said. "We'll watch how the Duke and Leonard each approach you, or if they do at all. Helena can conveniently step in if Leonard becomes too forward. Adeline and I can linger near the refreshments and see what gossip we overhear about both men." She paused, a conspiratorial glint in her eyes. "I'm sure someone will be talking about who's courting whom."

Miranda nodded. "Meanwhile, Felicity and I can stay near Charlotte, ensuring she's never truly alone and that we note any signs of the duke's interest."

"You won't find it terribly tedious?" Charlotte asked.

"No more tedious than enduring a ball where everyone expects us to make small talk about the weather, the pianoforte, or the latest fashion," Miranda assured her.

A ripple of shared amusement softened the tension in the air, and Charlotte let out a breath she hadn't realized she was holding. "Thank you. I don't know how to repay you for this."

"By letting us do it," Adeline said simply. "And by being our ally in turn when it's our moment of crisis."

"Yes," Helena added. "We'll all take turns. We're in this together."

And so they huddled close while Miranda made notes on their plans. Adeline proposed they arrive in staggered intervals so as not to appear suspiciously huddled. Felicity surprised everyone by suggesting Charlotte feign a fainting spell if she needed to escape a tight spot with Sir Roger. They all laughed at the notion, but no one doubted it might be necessary.

Soon the tea service had been well used, and the plates of biscuits were reduced to crumbs. Eventually, Miranda checked her watch and murmured that she had an errand to run before teatime. One by one, the others realized they, too, had obligations.

Flushed with a newfound purpose, Charlotte stood to escort them out. "Let's gather again soon to share anything we learn after Friday," she said. "Perhaps next week, once we've had time to observe the ball's aftermath."

They rose from their seats, Adeline smoothing her skirts, Genevieve dusting off crumbs from her gloves, and Helena taking one last sip of now-cold tea. Felicity picked up her shawl, a new glint of determination in her eyes. Miranda gave Charlotte a thoughtful look.

"Remember," Miranda said quietly, "be calm at the ball. Don't appear anxious. We'll do the groundwork around you."

"I'll do my best." Acting naturally around the duke was going to be her biggest challenge.

Charlotte reached for the door just as the handle twisted on its own, and the door swung open to reveal Lady Fitzgerald.

Charlotte's heart lurched into her throat. "Mother!"

Lady Fitzgerald's gaze swept the scene as she took in the empty cups, the nearly consumed plate of biscuits, the ring of chairs. One eyebrow rose in question. "Ladies," she said smoothly. "What a lovely gathering. Charlotte, you didn't tell me you expected quite so many callers today?"

Charlotte opened and closed her mouth, at a loss for an excuse.

Helena suddenly dipped into a respectful curtsy. "We do apologize for any inconvenience, Lady Fitzgerald," she said in a cheery tone. "We promised Charlotte we would meet to rehearse a small piece for a charitable event."

Charlotte prayed her mother wouldn't pry further. She

pressed her lips together, trying not to look as guilty as she felt.

"A charitable event?" Lady Fitzgerald repeated, glancing from Helena to the others. "How generous of you, my dears."

Helena smiled, weaving her fib with surprising ease. "Yes, I thought we might combine our talents to raise funds for… oh, let's say to send blankets to orphans. I had the notion that each of us, having some skill or other, could perform something small. Charlotte's role," she continued, flashing Charlotte a meaningful look, "is to organize the refreshments and the guest list. That's why we're gathered here, to discuss some of the details in private."

Charlotte had to fight not to gape. She recognized the quick cunning in Helena's improvised excuse. Her mother, after all, was known for charitable committees and gatherings, so a philanthropic cause was less likely to arouse suspicion.

Lady Fitzgerald's expression remained politely inquisitive. "How commendable. May I ask which orphans' home you intend to support?"

Helena's eyes widened. "I…. Well, we've not finalized it yet, my lady. We were considering a few. I believe Miranda suggested a home in the west of Town."

Miranda, catching Helena's cue, nodded earnestly. "The… the St. Agnes Foundling House, I believe. I read about it in the papers. They do admirable work."

Charlotte resisted the urge to breathe a sigh of relief as her mother's suspicion seemed to waver in the face of such philanthropic zeal.

"Indeed. That is an excellent institution," Lady Fitzgerald said, inclining her head. "Very well. As long as you're not tiring yourselves out with too much excitement."

Genevieve bobbed a curtsy in turn. "We're just on our way out, Lady Fitzgerald. Thank you for allowing us to visit."

A small pause hung in the air, and Charlotte braced for

more questions. But Lady Fitzgerald stepped aside, letting the group file past into the corridor. She turned to Charlotte with a frown, though her voice remained pleasant. "You must let me know if you require any help organizing this performance. You know I do like to support our local charities."

"Of course, Mother," Charlotte managed, matching Helena's confident tone as best she could. "We will be sure to consult you if we need advice."

At least for now, Lady Fitzgerald seemed placated.

All that remained was to see if their plan would hold firm once the swirl of the ballroom engulfed them on Friday night.

It must. Charlotte's future had to hold more than Mr. Roger Leonard.

"I AM SO PLEASED YOU HAVE FINALLY COME TO YOUR SENSES, Henry."

The dowager duchess's voice had that familiar note of satisfaction as she accepted her son's hand, stepping carefully down from the carriage. The lamplights illuminated the grand facade of Lady Wentworth's town residence, where a steady stream of guests were making their way inside.

Henry forced a polite smile. "Yes, Mother, I'm sure you are."

She gave him a pointed look. "I only wish for you to meet someone suitable. It's a good thing that you are finally willing to see reason."

Henry suppressed a sigh. *Willing* wasn't the word he would have chosen. "Shall we go in?"

Once inside the polished foyer, Lady Wentworth herself welcomed them, a vision in shimmering blue silk. Henry bowed, exchanged the expected pleasantries, and his mother curtsied in turn. As soon as they were ushered beyond a set of gilded doors, Henry's mother wasted no time in drawing him close to speak more quietly.

"There are a few eligible young women I would like to

introduce to you tonight," she murmured, her eyes gleaming as they swept the room.

"Wonderful," he replied dryly, surveying the ballroom for familiar faces. A swirl of color greeted them: ladies in vibrant gowns, men in fine tailcoats, the strains of a quartet echoing from a raised dais. The scent of candles and perfume filled the air.

Henry saw William Fitzgerald standing near the far windows with Charlotte at his side. They were in conversation with another man, who had a braying laugh that drifted above the noise.

Sir Roger Leonard.

Henry narrowed his eyes. Before he could walk over to greet them—and find out what Sir Roger was about—his mother tugged his sleeve.

"Henry, pay attention," she whispered. "We must greet Mrs. Pembroke and her two daughters. They're just over there, beneath the chandelier. There, you see them?"

He nodded, giving Charlotte's distant figure one last glance. He frowned at the way Leonard leaned closer to her, practically dribbling into her bosom, but his mother was already propelling him onward. They reached a stately matron and two young women wearing interchangeable pastel gowns.

"Ah, Your Grace." Mrs. Pembroke lit up, a rehearsed smile forming on her round face. She dipped a curtsy, and her daughters followed suit. "What a delight to see you."

"I'd like to present my son," the dowager duchess said, placing a hand on Henry's arm. "The Duke of Arundel."

Mrs. Pembroke's excitement was palpable as she introduced her daughters—Miss Catherine, the older, and Miss Lucy, the younger. Both curtsied, cheeks turning rosy as they met Henry's gaze. He greeted them politely, offering a slight bow of his head. Clearly, this had been arranged by the two mothers. He swallowed his annoyance, remembering William's advice.

"It's a pleasure," Henry said, measuring his words carefully. "I trust you are enjoying the evening?"

The oldest—Catherine—clasped her hands. "Oh yes, Your Grace. The music is lovely and the company even more so."

Her sister gave a nervous laugh. "It's one of the finest balls of the season—or so everyone says."

His mother, clearly satisfied with their demure manner, pressed forward. "My son has only just arrived, but I'm sure he would be honored to dance with you both, if you haven't already promised yourselves for the evening, of course."

Mrs. Pembroke's eyes gleamed. "I'm sure my daughters would be delighted," she said, nudging them forward ever so slightly.

Feeling rather like a thoroughbred up for auction, Henry offered his arm to Miss Catherine first. As they walked onto the floor to join the forming quadrille, he caught a fleeting glimpse of Charlotte's green gown across the room. She was with William still, but Roger Leonard lingered, grinning at something Charlotte said—or perhaps leering was a better word.

Henry clenched his jaw, then forced himself to focus on his dance partner.

"You look rather thoughtful," Miss Catherine ventured as the music began. "Is the ball not to your liking?" Her voice was soft, timid.

"On the contrary," he said, guiding her through the steps, "it's quite splendid. Lady Wentworth has excelled herself." He allowed a pause before adding, "Do you attend many of these events?"

She attempted a smile. "My mother ensures we rarely miss one. She says it's important to be seen. But I do enjoy the music."

"Ah. You play, perhaps?"

She nodded shyly. "I play the pianoforte, a little."

Henry encouraged her to talk more about it, which seemed to ease her nerves. Still, through each turn and bow of the dance, he couldn't help flicking his gaze around the ballroom. Where was Charlotte now? That green gown was nowhere in sight.

When the dance ended, Catherine curtsied again. "Thank you, Your Grace. It was… an honor."

He bowed. "Likewise, Miss Pembroke."

They parted, and almost immediately, Lady Pembroke ushered the younger daughter, Lucy, forward. Another dance ensued, this time a country reel. Lucy made light conversation—chattering about her new horse, her father's country estate, the next ball. Henry responded with gentle smiles and carefully placed remarks, though his mind kept drifting toward Charlotte.

It really would be a shame if such a pleasant young woman was forced into an alliance with that buffoon Leonard.

At last, he returned Lucy to Mrs. Pembroke's side. The two sisters beamed with gratitude, and their mother looked fit to burst with pride. His own mother, standing nearby, gave Henry a subtle nod of approval.

"How lovely," she murmured, looping her arm through his. "Now, let us not dawdle, there are others to greet."

He swallowed a sigh. "Must we greet them all?"

She sent him a pointed look. "You agreed to this, my dear. Unless you have changed your mind already?"

"No, of course not," he replied hastily. "Lead on."

They strolled across the wide floor, his mother pausing here and there to exchange a word with acquaintances. A sudden hush in their vicinity made Henry glance around, and that was when he spotted Genevieve Flynn—one of Charlotte and William's family friends—standing alone near a marble pillar. She caught the dowager duchess's eye and offered a curtsy.

"Miss Flynn," his mother greeted her. "How nice to see you this evening. Are you enjoying the ball?"

"Yes, Your Grace, very much," Genevieve replied. Her gaze drifted to Henry, a flicker of nerves apparent in her expression. "Good evening, Your Grace."

Henry bowed slightly. "Miss Flynn. Have you seen Lady Charlotte Fitzgerald tonight? I believe you're friends, are you not?"

"We are," Genevieve said, her face brightening momentarily. "Charlotte is… about somewhere. I saw her a short while ago." A sly smile seemed to twitch at her lips. "Were you wishing to speak with her, Your Grace?"

His mother interrupted smoothly. "Miss Flynn, I was just about to suggest my son invite you to dance, if you're free. I recall hearing you played the pianoforte beautifully at your last recital. It's always lovely to see those with a musical ear on the floor."

A slight pink tinged Genevieve's cheeks. "I'd be delighted, of course, if His Grace has no objections."

Henry forced a polite smile. "It would be my pleasure, Miss Flynn. Shall we?"

Her face lit with joy—or was it something else? Henry had the disconcerting feeling that all the women around him seemed to be party to machinations he knew nothing about.

Genevieve put her hand on his arm, and they stepped onto the dance floor. A waltz was just beginning, a dance that Henry particularly detested—except for when he danced it with Charlotte.

Once they'd taken their positions, Genevieve cleared her throat. "You must forgive me if I'm not as graceful as some of the ladies here. I'm a little out of practice."

"Nonsense, Miss Flynn. You move quite well," he hastened to assure her.

They revolved in silence for a moment, Henry turning them to avoid colliding with another couple.

"Charlotte mentioned you might be attending tonight. She seemed rather pleased to know you might be here," she said.

"Did she indeed?"

"Oh, yes." Genevieve's skirts swished as they circled each other. "Charlotte looks lovely tonight, doesn't she? That green gown she's wearing is my absolute favorite of hers. It brings out her eyes so beautifully."

Henry blinked, momentarily taken aback by the directness of her comment. "Yes… yes, it does suit her," he said, his tone cautious. Why was Miss Flynn chattering so inanely about another woman's dress? He wondered if she was quite well.

They completed the dance with minimal further exchange, though Genevieve managed to slip in one last remark about Charlotte's "unfairly overlooked virtues." By the time the waltz ended, and they parted with a bow and a curtsy, Henry felt quite worried about Charlotte. Was her friend trying to tell him something, perhaps in an attempt to rescue her from Sir Roger?

He looked around again for Charlotte, deciding to ask her to dance. It would give them both a reprieve. But his mother swooped in the moment he stepped away from Genevieve.

"Come," she said quietly, ushering him forward. "There's someone else I wish you to meet."

She maneuvered them toward a tall woman with delicate features who stood beside her daughter. Or at least, Henry assumed it was her daughter. The young lady couldn't have looked more different from her mother, with unruly red curls and a curvy figure all but bursting out of her gown. As they approached, his mother lowered her voice.

"Helena Steele," she murmured, her tone edged with faint disapproval. "Her family isn't precisely the connection we'd desire, being New Money, but still. She is reputed to have a certain musical genius, and I hear she's closely acquainted with Lady Charlotte and her circle."

Ah, another friend of Charlotte's.

"If you are worried about… potential disgrace, the Steeles would be less likely to take offence, given their humble beginnings," she added.

Helena turned at their approach, displaying a smile that possessed a hint of mischief. Her mother, Mrs. Steele, nodded at the dowager duchess with the deference of someone who recognized the pecking order only too well.

"Your Grace," Mrs. Steele said, dipping in a curtsy. "What an unexpected pleasure."

As they made their introductions, Helena observed Henry with a discerning gaze. "The duke and I have been introduced once or twice," she said lightly, "through Charlotte Fitzgerald, in fact."

Henry nodded. "Yes, I recall." Something in Helena's expression made him feel oddly on display. There was a spark in her eyes, as though she was inwardly laughing. At him? This evening was beginning to feel quite surreal.

"Would you do me the honor of dancing?" he offered, resigned to another set.

Helena's eyes lit up. "I'd love to."

They took to the floor, and a cotillion began. Henry steeled himself for the usual pleasantries, but Helena launched straight into conversation.

"I was speaking with Charlotte Fitzgerald earlier," she said. "She looks lovely, don't you agree?"

Henry glanced at Helena, catching a faint smirk. What on earth was wrong with these women tonight? "So I've heard, more than once," he replied dryly. "She does wear that shade of green rather well."

Helena's smirk deepened. "Quite. It's nice to see her admired, especially by those who rarely attend these functions. I believe she was telling me just this afternoon how she hopes certain people might… notice her more."

Henry tried to keep his expression impassive. Was this some kind of matchmaking attempt? "Really?"

Helena shrugged. "She's modest, of course. But she deserves attention, don't you think? She's a dear girl—kind, unassuming, and overlooked far too often."

He hesitated, thrown by Helena's forthrightness. "I suppose so. Lady Charlotte is certainly very lovely. I consider her a friend of long-standing."

"Friend, yes." Helena murmured, and the dance brought them into a turn that separated them momentarily. When they came back together, she added, "I wonder if you're aware just how fond certain ladies are of you, Your Grace. Some might say it's a poorly kept secret."

His chest tightened. "I'm not sure I follow."

Helena chuckled—a musical sound with no true malice. "No matter. I suppose time will reveal the truth of it." She paused, then tilted her head, eyes dancing. "I only hope, if you find yourself drawn in a particular direction, you won't let outside pressure hinder you."

Henry frowned, uncertain how to respond. "Outside pressure is what brought me here tonight," he admitted, more candidly than he'd intended.

"Indeed." Helena's gaze flicked toward the dowager duchess, who stood across the room, observing them with hawklike intensity. "Yet sometimes, it's better to follow one's own inclination—if that inclination happens to align with… oh, certain quiet, green-gowned ladies."

He almost stumbled at the audacity of her implication. Quickly regaining his step, he forced a polite laugh. "You speak in riddles, Miss Steele."

She bobbed her head. "It's my nature, perhaps. I do love a riddle. But I love romance even more."

Henry blinked in surprise. Miss Steele was certainly more

forthright than her friends in the *ton*. But was she trying to set him up with Charlotte, or herself? He was completely baffled.

Before Henry could press her for clarification, the cotillion ended. Helena curtsied, and he bowed. "That was… a pleasure," he murmured, attempting to mask his confusion.

Helena's eyes gleamed. "Quite enjoyable, Your Grace."

With that, she sashayed off, leaving him standing alone among the milling dancers. His mother appeared almost instantly, hooking her arm through his and leading him aside.

"Well?" his mother asked. "Did you find her an acceptable partner?"

"She dances well enough," Henry murmured, replaying their conversation in his head and trying to make sense of it.

She sighed. "The Steeles are hardly the sort of family we want to marry into. But their connections could be useful in unexpected ways."

Before she could march him to another introduction, he spotted William across the floor, standing near a potted fern. Henry seized the chance.

"Mother, if you'll excuse me for a moment," he said, stepping away. "I see Lord Fitzgerald. I have urgent business to discuss with him."

He didn't wait for her approval. Slipping between clusters of guests, Henry reached William, who was sipping from a half-empty glass of champagne. His friend's posture looked tense, his eyes straying back and forth. Henry followed William's line of sight and saw Charlotte dancing with none other than Roger Leonard.

"Charlotte looks rather uncomfortable."

"She often does at these events," William replied, shrugging. "She hates the bustle, the crowd, the prying eyes. If you ever spot her alone at a ball, you'll see her with her back pressed to the wall, trying to vanish. But Leonard hasn't left her alone all night. Even those friends of hers have been trying to lead her away, but the man is like a limpet. Still, at least someone is showing an interest in her, which is a wonder considering how shy she is."

"I see." Perhaps that explained Genevieve and Helena's behavior.

"I've been dancing with a few young ladies, letting Mother think I'm coming around. Are you doing the same?"

Henry nodded. "Yes. A temporary show of compliance, as you suggested. I've danced four times already, and I daresay my mother won't be satisfied until I've circled the entire room."

One side of William's mouth hitched up wryly. "At least you have your mother's blessing to choose from a crowd. Mine keeps threatening to corner me with a wealthy widow twice my age."

They both chuckled just as the music ended, and the guests applauded politely. Charlotte and Leonard stepped apart, and from where Henry stood, he saw Leonard lean in again with a too-familiar grin. Charlotte's attempt at a polite smile looked thoroughly unconvincing.

Just then, Charlotte looked in his direction. He locked eyes with her for an instant, but then she dipped her head, wrenching her eyes away even as she made her way toward him. A hint of color suffused her cheeks, and Henry felt a surge of protectiveness.

He shoved the feeling down. Tonight was about maintaining a charade for his mother's sake, not entangling himself in the business of his friend's younger sister.

Still, he couldn't help wanting to get her away from Leonard.

With a slight shake of his head, Henry glanced around, anticipating his mother's inevitable reappearance—and another introduction, no doubt.

If he danced with Charlotte, he could rescue them both.

Charlotte reached them, looking flustered. Leonard trailed after her, a fresh glass of brandy in hand. The sight of Charlotte's discomposure twisted something inside Henry. He couldn't bear how her brow knit in distress or the tense smile she forced to her lips as Leonard reappeared at her arm. It was clear that William was going to do nothing to rescue his sister.

Henry cleared his throat. "Lady Charlotte," he said with a slight bow. "May I request the next dance?"

Charlotte blinked at him, the sudden relief apparent as her features softened. She hesitated only a moment before inclining her head. "Yes, of course. Thank you, Your Grace."

Leonard glared at him. "But I was telling Lady Charlotte about the time—"

"I'm afraid your tale must wait," Henry said smoothly, meeting Leonard's gaze without blinking. "You can continue it later, *if* Lady Charlotte wishes to hear it." He didn't bother to keep the sarcasm out of his voice.

Sir Roger's mouth clamped shut. Henry offered Charlotte his arm, and she slipped her hand into the crook of his elbow just as the musicians struck up a leisurely waltz.

Henry placed a hand at her waist, the other supporting her gloved hand in his. They began to circle the floor, moving through the steps with practiced grace. At first, neither spoke, but Henry felt Charlotte relax by small degrees—her shoulders loosened, and her exhale seemed relieved.

"Thank you," she said quietly, glancing up at him. "I... truly appreciate your intervention. Sir Roger is rather persistent."

"I could see that," he replied, guiding her deftly around another couple. "I apologize if I intruded, but you seemed uncomfortable."

Her lips curved into a faint self-conscious smile. "Uncomfortable is one word for it. It's not that he's been unkind, but… I don't quite share his enthusiasm for hunting stories. Or brandy."

"He does seem very fond of describing his exploits in gruesome detail," Henry offered.

She gave a delicate shudder. "Indeed. I'm only grateful you saved me from hearing any more of it."

They moved in silence for a moment, stepping together in time with the music. Henry found himself unusually aware of how the candlelight played over Charlotte's delicate features. Her soft perfume conjured something sweet and floral, and he felt a stab of nostalgia for the long summer days of their childhood.

As they turned again, her eyes lifted, briefly catching his. A stray curl brushed her cheek, and he fought a sudden urge to brush it aside. She really did look lovely tonight, in a natural, understated way.

He swallowed down the rush of guilt at his own thoughts. This was little Charlotte Fitzgerald, the gangly girl who used to tag along after him and William. And yet here she was, a grown woman with a quiet grace all her own.

"Thank you again," Charlotte repeated, drawing him out of his thoughts. "You've no idea how relieved I was to be rescued from that oaf."

He offered a half smile. "It was my pleasure. Truly."

Henry found himself half regretting that the waltz wasn't longer, as her guarded expression began to ease, and they moved in an easy synchronicity. But the dance ended all too soon. He led her back toward William, who was standing near a column with his arms folded.

"Your dancing has improved, sister," William said.

Charlotte rolled her eyes. "Do you remember when Mother had us both practicing our dance steps together in the drawing room? You always trod on my toes. Thankfully His Grace is more careful."

Henry let out a surprised bark of laughter. For a moment

she reminded him of the old Charlotte, before they'd all grown up and society's rules had forced their interactions to follow a particular set of guidelines.

"Your Grace."

He turned to see Lady Pembroke, although neither of her daughters were with her.

Charlotte greeted her politely, shot Henry and William a brief look, and moved off toward the refreshment table.

Lady Pembroke wasted no time. "Your Grace, I must thank you for the invitation. We would be delighted to accept."

Henry stared at her. Had all the women in the room gone mad tonight? "Invitation?"

"To your grand house party."

Henry blinked. "A house party? I haven't invited a single person to any sort of house party. I think you might've mistaken me for someone else."

Lady Pembroke looked utterly baffled. "Of course you didn't extend the invitation personally, or there would be no need for me to take the time to thank you now. I'd have done it then. Your mother invited us on your behalf, and we assure you, we will be there."

With that, Lady Pembroke offered a small dip of her head and swept away to follow Charlotte's path toward the lemonade. Henry stood frozen for an instant, blood pounding. What on earth was his mother up to now?

He turned to William, who raised both eyebrows.

"That's news to me," William said. "Did you mention anything about hosting a party?"

"Of course not," Henry ground out, his fists clenching at his sides. "Why would I do that? It's absurd. I hate these summer affairs."

William spread his hands. "Then perhaps you should find your mother before she invites the entire ton."

Henry nodded sharply. "Indeed."

He looked around the ballroom, but his mother was nowhere to be seen. With a curt apology to William, he set off in search of her, threading through clusters of chatting guests and scanning each corner of the room.

Near the far side of the ballroom, just beyond the musicians, he finally spotted her in hushed conversation with two matrons. Their eyes shone with zeal, and his mother wore an expression of smug satisfaction that he recognized all too well.

He approached, schooling his features into a mask of politeness, although he was inwardly seething. Catching sight of him, the dowager duchess dismissed the two matrons with a gracious incline of her head. They curtsied, side-eyeing him before drifting away.

"Henry," she said with mock surprise. "You seem vexed. Whatever is the matter?"

He lowered his voice. "Mother, I've just been informed of my supposed plan to host a house party. You wouldn't know anything about that, would you?"

"Why, yes," she replied smoothly, "I took the liberty of suggesting to a few friends that you might be amenable to entertaining some select families at our country estate next month."

His pulse pounded. "You did what? Mother, you can't suggest these things without my consent."

"I've done more than suggest, my dear. I've already extended preliminary invitations. And as you can imagine"—she gestured toward the room—"the idea is most welcome. You've become quite the elusive prize."

"But you never asked me."

"Would you have agreed if I had?" she countered, arching an eyebrow. "I am your mother, Henry. And I'm doing what is best for the future of this family. Of course you'll graciously host, won't you?"

He realized that backing out now would create quite a

stir. His mother had trapped him rather effectively, leaving him with no polite exit.

He clenched his jaw, knowing she was right. "I hope you realize what a predicament you've put me in."

She lifted one shoulder. "A predicament that ends with you fulfilling your duty. Now, why don't you go claim another dance? I hear Miss Lucy Pembroke is free again, and you seemed to enjoy her company."

He found no words to express the storm of outrage boiling in him. In the end, he simply turned on his heel and stalked away, heading for the refreshment table. He needed a brandy.

There would be no stopping this now. A house party it was.

CHAPTER 8

Charlotte stepped out of the hired carriage, glanced up at the nondescript townhouse, and rapped twice on the door with the brass knocker. When it swung open, she offered the butler a polite smile.

"Good morning. Miss Doherty is expecting me."

He bowed. "Yes, my lady. Do come in."

She followed him down a short corridor. Her nerves jangled the entire time, but she tried to keep her expression calm. Felicity had insisted this meeting happen at her home, and Charlotte understood why. No inquisitive mothers, no curious brothers. Just peace.

They arrived at a small sitting room where Felicity herself appeared in the doorway, hands clasped together. She dismissed the butler with a quiet word, then ushered Charlotte inside.

"I'm so relieved you're here," Felicity said, voice hushed. "I've been half afraid my invitation might have gone astray or that you'd be followed."

Charlotte chuckled. "No one follows me, Felicity. I'm hardly interesting enough for that."

"Nonsense," Felicity murmured, pressing her lips together. "Shall we go through to the drawing room? I've already prepared tea, though everyone else is wandering about the house."

Charlotte's gaze darted around. "Thank you for letting us meet here. If we'd tried this at my mother's house, I guarantee she'd hover in the next room with her ear pressed to the wall."

Felicity offered a tiny shrug. "It's no trouble. It's just me and the servants. My guardian never writes back, so I've been… living here on my own, I suppose, waiting for instructions that never come."

A crease formed between Charlotte's brows. "That must be lonely."

"It's… quiet," Felicity said softly. "Better than many young ladies' situations, I'm sure. Anyway, come in. The others are eager to see you."

Charlotte followed her into a parlor. The curtains were drawn back, letting a dim glow filter inside, revealing modest but well-kept furniture. On a small upright piano near the corner, Genevieve was plunking out a tune, her brows knit in concentration. She struck a wrong note, grimaced, and muttered to herself.

"Mother swears I'll become more accomplished if I just practice more," Genevieve said in greeting, turning on the bench when she sensed them enter. "I think her dream is that I'll dazzle some earl with a waltz I can barely play."

Felicity smiled. "It might help if you liked the instrument. There's nothing wrong with your playing."

"I like it well enough," Genevieve said with a sigh, "but there's so much else I'd rather do."

Charlotte touched her shoulder. "Well, at least you can practice here in peace. Shall we find the others?"

Genevieve abandoned the piano stool. "Lead on. Adeline's

rummaging through the library, and Miranda's lecturing your butler—sorry, I mean advising him—on how to arrange refreshments."

Charlotte laughed under her breath. "He'll survive. Miranda's always kind, just… methodical."

They made their way to a smaller sitting room at the back of the house. The instant they walked in, Adeline looked up from a half-open book, flashing a grin. Miranda was already sitting primly on a loveseat with her ankles crossed and shoulders back.

"I thought we'd never all gather," Miranda said impatiently. "We have a lot to discuss."

Adeline closed the book with a soft thud. "Charlotte, how are you? Any new developments?"

Charlotte settled into a chair, smoothing her skirts. "No, but I did learn more about the Duke's house party. William told me it was all the dowager duchess's idea, and poor Henry isn't happy at all."

"Oh?" Miranda gestured for her to go on.

Charlotte's voice wavered slightly as she continued. "He didn't even know about it until half the *ton* started congratulating him. His mother put him in a position where he couldn't refuse. Everyone believes he's hosting this gathering to find a suitable bride."

Adeline let out a low whistle. "The dowager duchess is cunning, I'll give her that."

Miranda shook her head disapprovingly. "A typical ploy. Announce it to society so he has no choice but to follow through. Then flood his estate with eligible ladies—like fish in a pond, waiting to be hooked."

Genevieve frowned. "But obviously you want to be among them, right, Charlotte?"

Charlotte's cheeks colored. "I…. Yes. I can't stand the thought of missing this opportunity. If he spends days in the countryside with some other clever young woman, I might lose what small chance I have." The thought of Henry announcing his betrothal to someone else made her feel nauseous. How would she bear it?

Felicity reached over and patted Charlotte's hand. "We understand; say no more. We just need to figure out how to ensure you're invited."

"I'm sure she will be, as William's sister," Miranda pointed out. "But we need all of us to be there so we can help Charlotte woo the duke."

"Ideally, yes," Charlotte agreed. "If I'm alone among strangers, I'll be too self-conscious to attempt anything. But with you there, we can… well, create opportunities."

Adeline snickered. "Create opportunities. That's a polite way of saying we'll meddle until he pays attention."

Miranda cleared her throat. "Subtly meddle, please. We can't be obvious, or Her Grace will sense something is wrong."

They all fell silent at the thought of raising the dowager duchess's wrath.

Then Genevieve tapped a finger on her chin. "How do we get ourselves invited, though? Charlotte's easy—her family's close with the Arundels. But what about the rest of us?"

"I have a plan," Charlotte said, shoulders straightening. "I'll ask William to suggest to Mother that we be included. That I will be too shy to bear it without my friends. It's the house party of the season, so Mother will want me to be there, and she'll want to ensure I don't embarrass her by hiding in the drawing room. She can't stand the idea of gossip."

Miranda looked thoughtful. "That might work. In the meantime, we need to consider how Charlotte should present herself while there."

"I don't know that it will make a difference how I present

myself." Charlotte slumped in her seat. "I'm sure he only dances with me at balls out of kindness."

"But he cared enough to save you from Sir Roger," Genevieve reminded her. "That's something."

"He cares about me as William's sister. I want him to see me differently." Charlotte's voice was tinged with longing.

"But this could be leverage," Miranda suggested. "Perhaps he could be persuaded to spend time with you in order to save you from the attentions of Sir Roger. But then, the more you spend time together, the more he will become attracted to you."

Charlotte was unconvinced, but Felicity nodded. "Hence the new dresses you mentioned, Charlotte. Are you still planning to visit that new modiste, Madam Baptiste?"

"Yes. Mother has been raving about her, but thankfully Adeline's coming with me. We want to keep it tasteful but step out of my usual style. Something that makes me feel confident."

"Good," Miranda stated. "Confidence is half the battle. Dress in a way that highlights your best features, and stand tall. If you act like you're worthy of notice, he might start noticing."

Charlotte gave her a weak grin. "I hope so. I'm no beauty, but maybe the right gown could help."

Miranda shook her head. "You underrate yourself. Let's not forget those big soft eyes and that perfect posture. Trust me; some gentle tailoring, maybe a color that flatters you, and the duke will think you're radiant."

Genevieve clapped her hands together. "I'm excited to see the transformation. I've heard Madam Baptiste has a knack for subtle drama."

Felicity nodded again. "Subtle drama is exactly what Charlotte needs."

Looking around at her friends' encouraging expressions, Charlotte took a breath and stood, glancing at Adeline. "Shall we head to Madam Baptiste now, before she closes for the afternoon?"

Adeline agreed readily, smoothing her skirts. "Yes, let's go. I'm curious to see her shop for myself."

Felicity rose as well and walked them to the door with Genevieve and Miranda trailing behind.

"Keep me updated," Felicity whispered. "The sooner we know you have your invitation, the calmer I'll feel."

Miranda adjusted her spectacles. "And do let us know if you want any assistance persuading William. I could offer logical arguments if it'd help."

Charlotte smiled wryly. "Thank you, but I suspect William might respond better to sentiment. I'll speak to him this evening."

They parted with warm goodbyes and stepped into Adeline's carriage.

The ride was swift, weaving through Mayfair's streets until they halted in front of a small modiste's shop. The sign read: "Madam Baptiste, Designs for the Discerning." A tasteful window display showcased a pale blue gown with delicate embroidery. It was lovely, Charlotte thought; something that she could easily imagine herself wearing.

Stepping inside, Charlotte heard the hum of hushed conversations and the rustle of fabrics. Bolts of cloth stood in tidy rows, and a couple of mannequins were positioned in the corner wearing half-finished dresses. Behind a polished wooden counter, a young woman with dark hair arranged in a sleek twist was conferring with an assistant.

She noticed Charlotte and Adeline at once, smiling as she approached. "Good afternoon. I'm Madam Baptiste. How may I be of service?"

Charlotte exchanged a glance with Adeline before speaking. "I was told you create gowns that are… fashionable. I need something tasteful but distinct; something to stand out without appearing garish."

Madam Baptiste's eyes sparkled. "You've come to the right place. May I have your name, my lady?"

"Charlotte Fitzgerald," she said, suddenly aware of the slight trembling in her fingers. She had never taken much interest in her dresses before, allowing Lady Fitzgerald to take care of their designs. "This is my friend, Miss Claremont."

Adeline dipped her head in greeting. "I'm only here for hand-holding and perhaps to order a small piece myself if I'm tempted."

Madam Baptiste gestured them toward a space where a riot of colored fabrics were neatly stacked. "I pride myself on balance: a classic silhouette, unexpected flourishes. Would you like to see some new shipments?" She produced a bolt of soft gray silk, then a second of a pale dusty blue. "Both these tones flatter fair complexions. I also have deeper colors if you wish to make more of a statement."

Charlotte studied the fabrics, running fingertips over the sheen. "I'm thinking something refined, so no gaudy prints, no heavy ruffles. But a detail or two that sets it apart. Maybe a sash or some delicate embroidery?"

"Precisely," the modiste said. "And do you prefer the Empire waist, or shall we gently lower it for a more modern line?"

A flicker of apprehension crossed Charlotte's face. "I've always worn Empire waists, but I'm willing to try something new if it isn't too daring."

Adeline put in, "We want her to feel confident—like she's stepping just beyond what's comfortable for her, but not diving off a cliff."

Madam Baptiste nodded sagely. "Then a small shift. A graceful slope, a well-fitted bodice. We can incorporate subtle embroidery along the neckline and maybe a ribbon accent at the waist."

Charlotte pointed to the dusty-blue silk. "That color is

lovely. Perhaps something in that for an evening gown. And maybe the gray for a day dress, with a hint of silver thread? Just a slight sparkle," she added quickly, feeling incredibly daring.

Madam Baptiste's lips curved in delight. "Excellent choices. Let's take your measurements. Then we'll finalize the design."

She led Charlotte behind a curtain, where a mirror stood. While Madam Baptiste measured waist, bust, and length, Charlotte asked quiet questions about possible finishing touches. The modiste sketched a few ideas on a small sketchbook, showing her how the final design might look.

Now and then, Adeline peeked around the curtain to offer her opinion. "A darker sash here," or "Perhaps more elegant sleeves."

When they'd finished, excitement fluttered in Charlotte's stomach. She pictured herself in that gorgeous dusty blue, hopefully catching Henry's eye. Maybe it would help him see her not as William's sister, but as a woman with her own quiet style. Even a potential bride.

After negotiating the timeline—Madam Baptiste promised to expedite things for a small further cost—Charlotte and Adeline thanked her warmly and departed. They climbed back into the carriage, both flushed with the satisfaction of progress.

Adeline let her head fall against the seat. "That was almost too easy. She's incredible, and you're going to look amazing."

Charlotte offered a weak laugh. "Let's hope so. I must say I'm actually looking forward to this party a little now." She stared out the window, seeing not the passersby but her own daydreams.

A short silence followed, broken only by the steady clatter of the carriage wheels. Then Adeline said, "So… when do you plan to talk to William?"

"Probably tonight," Charlotte replied. "He hates dinner-time conversations, and I don't want Mother to question me, so maybe after. I'll catch him in the library or his study."

"Fingers crossed," Adeline said, her eyes bright. "This could be an excellent opportunity for all of us."

Yes, it could well be. She only hoped she didn't botch it all up.

CHAPTER 9

HENRY PULLED ON HIS OVERCOAT, BRACING HIMSELF FOR THE early morning air, but just as he stepped into the foyer, his mother's voice sailed after him.

"Henry, dear, don't forget the guest list I left on your desk," she called, leaning over the banister. "We must finalize it soon."

He grimaced, his hand on the doorknob. "Yes, Mother. I'll look it over tonight."

"Do be thorough," she said, her tone altogether too satisfied. "We've so many interested families."

He muttered a half-hearted response and let the front door fall shut behind him. The carriage ride into town felt longer than usual, as his thoughts churned over the possibilities of how he might escape the situation he was in. *A house party forced on me by my own mother, and I can't say no without causing an uproar.* He felt rather like a fox being cornered by hounds, every path blocked.

At least he had William's company to look forward to at White's. He'd sent a hurried note earlier, pleading for a meeting. When his carriage rattled to a stop, Henry vaulted out and strode inside, relieved to find William already waiting near a corner table.

William greeted him with a wry smile. "You look like a man on the verge of running away from home."

Henry gave a tight laugh. "If only that were an option. I'd spend all of my time at the House of Lords if I thought I could get away with it." He signaled the attendant. "Two glasses of brandy, please."

They settled into their usual worn leather chairs, the hush of the private room enveloping them. The attendant returned with their drinks, placed them discreetly on the table, and vanished again.

Henry picked up his glass, his eyes fixed on the amber liquid. "My mother's done it, Will. She's told half of London I'm hosting a house party to find a bride."

William winced. "She truly didn't warn you first?"

"No. She just spread the rumor, and now I've got invitations to send, a guest list to review, and not a clue how to extricate myself." He took a quick gulp of brandy. "If I cancel, I'll look like a complete cad, and the gossip could be worse than if I just play along."

William made a thoughtful noise. "Why not just… go through with it? Keep her happy, as we said."

Henry groaned. "Why not? Because this is rather more serious than dancing at a few balls. This is my home. And, as I've told you, I don't *want* to marry."

"Which begs the question again of why?" William set his glass aside, leaning forward. "You're not that old, and I've never seen you hopelessly in love, so there's no heartbreak story. You're wealthy, titled, not exactly burdened by—"

Henry lifted a hand. "Enough." He glanced toward the door. "One moment." Rising, he crossed the room, opened the door, and waved the nearby servant away. "We'd like privacy," he said quietly, then shut them in again.

William's brows furrowed. "All right. Now I'm really curious."

Henry dropped into his chair and lowered his voice. "You know I trust you more than anyone. But there's a… complication with the dukedom. A secret. If it ever came out, it'd ruin everything. I'm not dragging a wife into that."

Silence stretched. William studied him, clearly trying to hide his surprise. "A secret. Something serious, then?"

Henry's mouth tightened. "Yes. Serious enough that I can't risk it. I don't want to saddle some poor girl with this burden."

William nodded slowly. "All right. If you say it's big, I won't pry. I'd guess your mother would do anything to keep it hidden."

"That's just it. She *has* done anything and everything, apparently including this wretched house party." Henry rubbed the back of his neck. "So how do I avoid a forced engagement? I can't flirt with ladies if I have no intention of following through."

William's expression cleared. "Simple. Never be alone with them. Have other gentlemen around. Spread the attention. If you're always in a group, no one can corner you for a private proposal or compromise."

Henry exhaled, relief flickering. "That could work, actually."

"Invite more men," William went on, his eyes brightening. "Make it a proper house party, not just a bevy of young ladies waiting to pounce. I'd be delighted to come. I'm sure Charlotte would too."

Henry forced himself not to react too strongly at the mention of Charlotte. She was on his mind far too much lately and somehow seemed to be mentioned in every conversation. "Your sister…. Yes, of course. She might enjoy the fresh air. And with you both there, I'd have more allies." He paused, swirling his drink.

William jumped in. "Adding a few of her friends wouldn't hurt either, if it pads out the numbers."

"More women." Henry shuddered.

William smirked. "I doubt many of Charlotte's friends would meet your mother's exacting standards for wealth and beauty. But Charlotte has already pleaded with me to ask you to invite them; you know how shy she gets at these things—and since Her Grace extended the invitation, our darling mama will expect her to be there. Don't worry; I'll tell her to warn them that it's not actually a bride hunt."

Henry swirled his brandy, remembering the young women he had danced with at the last ball. If they were representative of Charlotte's friends, they had been an odd bunch, chattering on about Charlotte's dress the whole time.

"We could spend time with them perfectly respectably, as I'm Charlotte's brother," William pointed out, "and therefore less time with all the other young ladies."

Henry smiled and ran a hand over his face. "Thank you, William. That isn't half a bad suggestion. Give me their names, and I will ensure Mother adds them. Thank you for your support… and discretion. Genuinely."

"Don't mention it, old chap. You're like a brother to me. Now, pass me that news sheet, will you?"

"Catching up with the gossip pages again?" Henry felt lighter for having spoken to William. Of course, if his friend knew his real secret….

They drank the last of their brandy in companionable silence. When Henry stood to open the door again, a couple of other club regulars drifted in, greeting them with boisterous calls. One of the men clapped Henry on the shoulder.

"Arundel, old man, I hear you're destined for the parson's noose soon." He barked a laugh. "Should we congratulate you now, or wait until you've selected your prey?"

Henry forced a stiff smile. "No need for condolences yet. I'm just trying to survive my mother's machinations."

The group teased him good-naturedly until they roped William and Henry into a card game. Henry played like an automaton, his mind racing over what he'd told William.

Why can't I live a normal life? Why can't I choose a bride if I wanted to, free of secrets? His thoughts ran away with him.

A stray image of Charlotte's gentle smile at the last ball flickered in his mind. He shrugged it off, blaming it on William's presence and the glass of early-morning brandy.

By the time the game ended, Henry couldn't muster more than a polite nod when the others wished him well on his "quest." He bade William goodbye and trudged out to his carriage, a strange gloom clinging to him.

If only circumstances were different. If only he could consider marriage like any ordinary man, Charlotte might be an option. After all, he knew and liked her; that was a better foundation for marriage than many had.

He shook his head sharply. *Nonsense.* She was William's sister. Beyond reach. He had real problems to deal with.

Like Mother's list on his desk.

Once he was back at home, he climbed the wide staircase to his study. On the desk lay a sheet of paper filled with neat columns of names in his mother's slanted handwriting. Daughters of earls, barons, and wealthy commoners, all presumably eager to be included in this infamous party. He sighed, dropped into the chair, and pulled the lamp closer.

All these families…. Each one hoping I'll choose their darling daughter. He scanned the names. A few seemed tolerable; most he recognized only vaguely. Then he remembered William's advice. *Invite more men. Invite Charlotte and her friends. Make it a real gathering.* Possibly the best move he had short of calling off the entire fiasco.

He dipped his quill in ink and drew neat lines through some of the ladies' names; no reason to fill the estate with hundreds of women he barely recalled. The Fitzgeralds were already there, of course. As were Genevieve and Miranda. He added in Felicity, Helena, and Adeline. They were all from reasonably respectable families, with perhaps the exception of the Steeles, but he could remind his mother of her own remarks at the ball.

He withdrew another sheet of paper and started listing eligible gentlemen he knew. A few of them were friends from the clubs, men who wouldn't mind a week in the country. He added a couple of mild-mannered fellows who might keep conversation lively without pushing Henry into a corner. The more men, the better he'd be able to avoid being singled out. A matchmaking party for the whole ton. He smiled at the thought.

Then he scrawled a note to his mother before pinning it to the revised list: *Amended. I prefer a balanced party.* He strode out to find her. When he bumped into her near the upstairs gallery, she beamed at him.

"You're back. Any thoughts on my list?"

He gave her the papers, and his mother's eyes flicked over the alterations.

"You've… removed some prominent daughters. And added the Steele girl… and several others I don't recall mentioning. Not to mention more of your gentleman friends, I see. Are you trying to turn this into a farce?" As he'd expected, she looked less than pleased. Almost angry, in fact.

"I'm the host, am I not? I want a comfortable balance. These changes might help me feel less like an exhibit. It's the matchmaking season; why not give others the chance to meet their betrotheds? It will be the house party of the season, Mother. And if more than one important match is made, people will be talking about it favorably for years."

His mother appraised him with suspicion but couldn't help the interest that flared in her eyes. Her lips twitched in delight. "Henry, are you actually involving yourself? Splendid. I'll have my secretary send the formal invitations. You'll need to sign, of course."

He nodded tersely. "I'll write some personal notes too. They will please our more influential friends."

"Excellent," she said, patting his arm. "I'm so pleased you're taking this seriously at last."

He didn't bother correcting her assumption, just retreated to his own chambers, where he instructed his butler to bring paper, ink, and wax. Sitting at a small writing desk near the window, Henry penned short, polite invitations to half a dozen eligible gentlemen he trusted; men who would join for the sporting and the dining—not for schemes to marry off their sisters.

Each letter was careful and concise: *I'd be honored if you would join me at Arundel Park for a few days of country air, good food, and conversation.* He sealed them, handed them over to the butler, and gave strict instructions. "Deliver these quietly and advise the recipients that I'd rather avoid further gossip until the official list goes out. These are my honored guests."

"Yes, Your Grace," the butler said with a respectful bow.

When he was finally alone, Henry leaned back in the chair, his eyes drifting shut. Maybe this plan could work. With enough allies around, he wouldn't be forced into any corners or compromises engineered by his mother and her cronies.

Tomorrow, the invitations would go out. He couldn't change course now. All he could do was maintain control, keep his distance, and hope that by the end of it, he wouldn't be worse off than he was already.

CHAPTER 10

 the house, letting the gentle warmth of the afternoon sun ease her worries for a moment, when quick footsteps on the gravel interrupted her solitude.

A young maid arrived, a little breathless. "My lady, I beg your pardon, but His Grace, the Duke of Arundel is here asking for you."

Charlotte stilled. She'd been tracing the outline of a fresh sprig of mint she'd plucked earlier. "The duke?" she echoed, surprised. "He isn't here for William?"

"No, my lady. Shall I let him know you're… not receiving visitors?"

Charlotte shook her head, carefully smoothing her skirts as she rose. "No, I'll see him right away. Thank you."

She left the little hideaway in the garden that had become her favorite spot, with its few rose bushes, neat gravel path, and the lone lilac that perfumed the air, and headed back inside. Her mind whirled as she wondered what on earth would bring Henry here unannounced.

In the foyer, she found him standing near the marble-topped table, absently running his gloved fingertips along its edge. At the sight of her, he straightened and offered a slight bow. Despite the tension around his rich brown eyes, he looked every bit the poised duke.

Not to mention devastatingly handsome.

"Your Grace," she said softly, curtsying. "Is everything all right? William is not here, I'm afraid." Perhaps her maid had gotten the message wrong.

"Yes, well, actually, I came to ask if you'd care to join me for a walk in Hyde Park. I, ah… need some fresh air."

Her heart did a little leap in her chest "A walk? Certainly. Let me just fetch my pelisse."

He exhaled as if relieved. "Thank you. I'll wait here."

Charlotte told a footman to let her mother know she'd be out briefly with the duke, then hurried upstairs to grab her walking shoes and a light pelisse. It was all so sudden, she half expected her mother to spring out, brimming with questions and insisting on being her chaperone, but apparently Lady Fitzgerald was occupied elsewhere. Charlotte returned in minutes, accompanied by her maid, who carried spare gloves and a bonnet.

"Shall we go?" Henry asked, a hint of uncertainty in his tone.

She offered a bright smile, trying to suppress the fizzing in her stomach. "Lead the way, Your Grace."

Outside, his carriage stood ready. A footman helped Charlotte up, and her maid slipped in quietly, taking a seat to the side so as not to intrude, although she looked as bemused as Charlotte herself felt. Henry followed, closing the door behind him. The carriage pulled away from the curb with a low rumble and the trot of hooves.

He didn't say much during the drive, and Charlotte let the silence linger, watching him from the corner of her eye. He seemed preoccupied, his gaze focused on the window and his posture stiff.

Finally, she ventured a gentle question. "You seem troubled, Your Grace. Is this about the house party?"

His shoulders lifted in a subtle shrug. "It's always about that house party these days," he admitted, then gave her a quick half smile. "We can talk once we're walking."

Soon enough, they arrived at Hyde Park, and he handed her down from the carriage. The maid followed a discreet distance behind as they set off along one of the broad paths.

A mild breeze rustled the leaves overhead. Charlotte breathed in the scent of grass and daisies, acutely aware of her arm tucked into Henry's. It felt oddly intimate, although she tried not to read too much into it.

He slowed his pace, glancing her way. "Thank you for coming. I… wanted to say I appreciate what you and your friends are doing."

She tilted her head, puzzled. "What do you mean?"

"William told me you wanted your friends to attend," Henry said, lowering his voice so it wouldn't carry. "I know you find these social gatherings difficult. He suggested that having more allies would help me navigate my mother's matchmaking efforts. I'm relieved to have some support."

When she didn't reply, Henry's eyes cut across to her. "William said you and your friends were aware of this plan?"

Her heart sank a little, but she kept her tone light. "Yes, of course. We're happy to help. Thank you for inviting them. It will make the party much more comfortable for me. If we can help spare you from some overly eager debutantes, all the better." The practical side of her was glad he acknowledged the ruse, but it also confirmed he had no personal interest in a wife at the moment.

Or in her.

In fact, he seemed to see her as an ally in his plan to not obtain a wife.

She suppressed a groan at how wrong their plans had gone.

He nodded, guiding her around a bend on the path. "I feel cornered. Mother arranged this entire thing, and now every family with a daughter is talking about it. My only defense is to invite enough people that I'm not the sole focus of their matchmaking hopes. Your willingness to help makes the prospect a bit less harrowing."

She mustered a smile. It was lovely that Henry saw her as a friend and ally, and once that would have been enough. But now, she wanted more.

She tried to speak casually. "It's good news for me, too, Your Grace. My friends can also help me dodge Sir Roger's attentions." A tiny pang struck her at how calmly they were discussing the dodging of romantic interactions. But she also knew if his mother forced him to choose a bride, he'd resent it. *Better for me to help him than to see him married to someone else.* Perhaps that was the most she could hope for.

They walked on. Dappled light fell across the path, and a few people they passed nodded respectfully at them. As they reached the trees, a young woman in a flamboyant pink dress appeared, escorted by an older lady. Her eyes lit up at the sight of the duke, and she hurried forward.

"Your Grace," she exclaimed with an overly sweet smile. "How wonderful to see you. We're looking forward to receiving your invitation soon, I trust?"

Henry tightened his jaw, returning her curtsy with a curt bow. "Good day, Miss…?"

"Brighton," she supplied, batting her eyelashes. "Mother and I have heard such delightful things about Arundel Park."

Charlotte remained silent, though the girl cast her a curious glance, her eyes narrowing.

The mother beamed, adding, "We're quite eager to join you in the country, Your Grace."

Henry's politeness was very nearly frosty. "I'm sure the invitations will go out shortly. Enjoy your walk." He then guided Charlotte past them before they could press him further. Charlotte saw the girl's disgruntled look, and she shot Charlotte an envious glare.

Once they were out of earshot, Charlotte suppressed a laugh. "She was… enthusiastic."

A weariness shadowed his features. "This is precisely what I'm dreading. Multiply that by a dozen or more, all hoping I'll propose. I'll need every ally I can get."

She tapped her free hand lightly against his arm. "We will assist as we can."

They strolled a bit farther. The shade of the trees was cool on her cheek. "I've always loved Arundel Park, you know. The gardens are so peaceful. I remember the few times that William and I visited, and you showed us that old orchard. It seemed practically magical."

His expression turned sober. "Yes, it's… a beautiful place, but it also carries problems I wish I could resolve." When she arched an eyebrow in question, he simply shook his head, his eyes shuttering. "Just family issues. I won't bore you."

She dropped the subject, sensing it touched on something he felt it inappropriate to discuss, although her interest was piqued. They fell silent, enjoying a few more minutes of calm, and Charlotte realized her nerves were entirely gone. In fact, she was quite at ease in his presence.

Eventually, Henry suggested they circle back to the carriage, and they made their return journey in a comfortable quiet.

As they approached her home, a familiar green-and-gold carriage came into view, parked at the curb outside the Fitzgerald residence.

She stiffened at once. "Oh no," she breathed, recognizing the crest. "Sir Roger."

Henry glanced at her. "You weren't expecting him?"

Panic pulsed through her, making her hands tremble. "No, although I wouldn't be surprised if Mother is. He's been… rather attentive, and I'm not in the mood to be cornered again."

Henry rapped on the carriage wall, telling the driver, "Keep going. Don't stop."

The coachman turned onto the next street, leaving the unwelcome sight of Sir Roger's carriage behind. Charlotte exhaled slowly, the adrenaline still coursing through her.

"Thank you," she murmured. "I know it's silly, fleeing my own house, but I can't bear to deal with him right now."

Henry watched her with empathy. "Is he that troublesome?"

She laced her fingers in her lap. "He's certainly persistent. My mother and William don't seem to mind him. In fact, I suspect they see him as a half-decent prospect, since I'm not exactly overrun with suitors."

A trace of frustration sparked in Henry's eyes. "It's unfair that you feel forced to avoid your own front door. If he appears at the house party, we can definitely maneuver so you're not stuck with him."

She smiled weakly. "I appreciate that. I just hope my family doesn't actively push me toward him in your home. That would be mortifying."

He frowned. "They won't have the chance—not if I can help it. You've made it clear you're uncomfortable around him. That's enough for me."

Her face warmed at his protective tone even if it was purely friendly. "Thank you. I'm sorry you have to deal with all these entanglements at your own party."

Henry shrugged ruefully. "Better to face them with allies. I'll see to it that Leonard doesn't pester you."

The tension eased from her, and she relaxed into her seat. They rolled on for a few blocks, chatting idly about nothing in particular until Charlotte had regained enough of a sense of calm to return home.

At length, she said, "I think he's likely gone now. We can head back."

Henry rapped on the carriage again, instructing the driver to circle around. Soon, they pulled up to her house. She peered out to see that Sir Roger's carriage was nowhere to be seen, thank goodness. Henry descended first, then offered his hand to help her down.

She stood on the pavement, her maid a step behind, and turned to Henry. "I'm truly grateful, Your Grace. That was a pleasant reprieve… from everything."

He inclined his head in a gesture of farewell. "I needed it as much as you did. If you require anything, especially regarding Leonard, send word, and at the house party, we'll make sure everything's in place."

She curtsied, cheeks warming. "I will, and I look forward to it. Please take care until then."

He offered a polite bow, then climbed back into his carriage. Charlotte watched it roll away, her heart conflicted but fluttering. He'd sought her out for support, a sign of trust. She only wished that trust might lead him to see her in a new light.

Preferably before she ended up wed to someone like Sir Roger.

CHAPTER 11

London
July 1813

CHARLOTTE SAT IN THE CARRIAGE, TWISTING HER GLOVES nervously in her lap. Lord Bryant's ball was supposed to be just another routine social evening. Not that she ever enjoyed them, but there would have been no reason for this one to be more anxiety inducing than any other.

Until the flowers arrived. Now here she was, staring at the florist's note in her hand, dread building in her chest.

She turned to her mother. "Must I really reserve the first dance for Sir Roger? He sent these flowers and…." Her words trailed off as she struggled to find a polite way to say she loathed the idea.

Her mother peered at her sharply. "Charlotte, the man made a kind gesture. You shouldn't snub him. One dance is all you need to grant. After that, you may do as you please."

Charlotte's stomach churned. *One dance.* It felt like an hour's confinement. But there was no appealing to her mother's sense of propriety. She nodded, hoping it wouldn't be as dreadful as she feared.

As they arrived, footmen guided them into the glittering ballroom. Music drifted through the crowd, and chandeliers sparkled overhead. Charlotte kept close to her mother during the obligatory greetings, smiling at Lord Bryant and his wife, who stood near the entrance. The polite exchange of pleasantries hummed in her ears. She couldn't shake the anxiety clawing at her.

Then, just as she was about to step aside for a moment's peace and attempt to find her friends, Sir Roger appeared at her side. He seemed to have a knack for sneaking up on her.

He bowed theatrically. "My lady," he murmured. "I trust you received my flowers?"

She forced a thin smile. "Yes, Sir Roger. They were… lovely. You have my thanks."

He beamed, clearly taking that as grand approval. "I'm delighted. And I hope you recall that we agreed upon the first dance?"

Lady Fitzgerald gave Charlotte a pointed look before drifting away, leaving her daughter to face him.

Charlotte's heart thumped. "Yes. Of course."

The music started up for a country dance. Sir Roger offered his arm, and Charlotte had little choice but to take it. Joining the forming set, she tried to calm her nerves and focus on the steps.

Yet from the moment they began, Sir Roger stood too close, gripping her hand with more force than necessary. Every time the dance required them to circle each other, he stepped in more than necessary, as though hoping to press her nearer. She edged away as politely as she could, but her discomfort soared.

"You seem out of sorts," he remarked, leaning closer. "Is something troubling you?"

She wished she could say, *"Yes, you."* Instead she merely murmured, "I'm very warm. The ballroom is quite crowded."

He flashed that smarmy grin of his. "Allow me to fetch you a refreshment afterward, perhaps?"

The dance ended at last, and Charlotte curtsied quickly, turning to escape, but he caught her elbow before she could slip off.

"I insist on ensuring your comfort, my lady," he said, guiding her away from the dance floor. His grip wasn't particularly gentle. "Come, there's a quieter spot just over here."

She tried to protest, but Sir Roger shepherded her into a small alcove behind a half-drawn curtain. She cast a worried glance across the ballroom—her mother was nowhere in sight, and William must still be talking with other guests. None of her friends had arrived, even though she was sure that at least Genevieve and Miranda would be attending.

Her pulse fluttered, and dread curled in her gut. "Sir Roger," she said quietly, "I'd prefer to return to the main room. It's most improper for us to be alone in this way."

He smiled, blocking her path. "We're only yards from the rest of the party. There's no impropriety in exchanging a few private words."

She swallowed, forcing a calm facade. "Then please, say whatever it is quickly. I don't wish to linger."

He angled himself to stand a bit too close, causing her to step back only to find herself trapped between him and a pillar. "Lady Charlotte, I've taken a keen interest in you. My intentions are quite serious."

Her throat tightened. She drew back, but he pushed forward. The alcove wasn't truly hidden from the public eye, yet it felt claustrophobic, and if anyone were to look across at them....

"Sir Roger," she said, voice trembling. "I'd rather not discuss such matters here."

He ignored her. "You're beautiful." His gaze was unsettling as it swept over her face and form. "I find myself eager to secure your hand. Don't you think we make a fine pair?"

Her heart pounded. "That's not for me to say."

She tried to push past him, but he grasped her arm.

"Why so timid, my lady?" he teased, leaning in. "Perhaps a simple kiss might seal our understanding."

She froze in horror. He was going to try to kiss her?

His brandy-tinged breath whispered over her cheek and her stomach rolled. In a burst of desperation, she shoved him backward. She wasn't sure if she'd shoved his chest or his shoulder, but it was enough to startle him. He staggered a step, his shock evident.

Then, in the same instant, a firm voice thundered behind them, "What is the meaning of this?"

Charlotte turned, relief washing through her. Henry. It was Henry. He'd save her.

He was still a few paces away, but his face was dark with fury. The tension in his shoulders told her everything she needed to know about his mood.

Sir Roger recovered his balance, plastering on a smirk. "The lady and I were merely enjoying a private conversation, Your Grace."

Henry's gaze flicked to Charlotte, who stood there shaking, hands half raised as if to ward Leonard off. She couldn't speak, her heart thudding too furiously for words to form.

"From what I can see," Henry said stonily, "this conversation is over. I believe this is my dance, Leonard. The band is about to begin again."

Sir Roger opened his mouth, but Henry stepped forward and seized Charlotte's hand, guiding her away before he could utter a protest. Her legs were weak, and she clung to his arm like a lifeline.

They merged into the dancers just as the new set started. Charlotte's pulse still hammered, the swirl of color and music seeming a long way away. Henry positioned himself across from her, one hand steady at her waist once they began the required steps.

He leaned in, speaking softly. "Are you well, Charlotte? What happened back there?"

She tried to focus on the dance moves, stumbling until he discreetly guided her. "He… forced me into that alcove," she managed, her voice quavering. "He tried to…. He said he wanted to kiss me. I pushed him away."

Henry's jaw tightened. "I see." His next words were thick with anger. "I'm sorry I wasn't there sooner."

She shook her head, still struggling for calm. "Thank you for arriving when you did."

They stepped in time to the music, though he kept a protective hold on her as though he feared she might collapse. Charlotte breathed in shallow bursts, the unpleasant memory replaying in her mind. Henry's expression was stormy, but he didn't speak again.

When the dance ended, he refused to let her step away into the crowd, instead keeping her arm hooked in his.

"Come," he murmured. "I'll take you to William. You need to go home."

She grimaced. If she asked to return home, her mother wouldn't be pleased. "I'm fine. I don't want to ruin everyone's evening."

He narrowed his eyes. "You're shaking like a leaf. I insist on escorting you safely out of here."

She relented, exhaustion setting in. Henry guided her through the throng until they found William near the refreshment table, chatting with some acquaintances. The moment William spotted Charlotte's pale face, he excused himself and strode forward.

"What's wrong?" William demanded. "Charlotte? Are you ill?"

Henry's tone was clipped. "She isn't ill. She's frightened.

Leonard cornered her and tried to… take liberties. She's shaken. You'd better see her home, William."

William's gaze flashed. "He *what?*"

He looked at Charlotte, but she could only nod, tears stinging her eyes.

Outrage twisted William's features. "I see. Thank you for intervening, Henry."

Henry released Charlotte into William's care.

She looked at him, wanting to say more, but all she managed was a faint "Thank you."

He nodded once, then melted into the crowd, tension still radiating from his posture.

William held Charlotte's elbow gently. "Come on. We'll get Mother and leave. This ball can manage without us."

Her mother was positively baffled to be dragged away so early. She fussed under her breath about missing a possible introduction to Lady Something-or-other, but William's warning look halted further protest.

After William summarized the situation, the carriage ride home passed in silence, her mother and brother both flattening their lips into matching grim lines.

Back at the house, Charlotte murmured a few vague words to her mother—she couldn't stand to rehash the details once again—before slipping away to her bedroom. She removed her cloak herself, dismissing a startled Mary when she offered to help. She needed to be alone, the memory of Leonard's attempted grab at her still making her skin crawl.

Not long after, William knocked and then, in a low voice, asked, "Charlotte? May I come in?"

She considered sending him away. Instead, she turned from the mirror where she'd been staring at her pale reflection. "Yes, do come."

He entered, shut the door quietly, and approached with a look of guilt. "I'm sorry," he said at once, his shoulders slumping. "I should've listened to you before when you said he made you uncomfortable. I brushed it off, thinking Leonard was just a bore, not a threat."

Her eyes brimmed with tears. "It's all right, William. You weren't to know this would happen."

"Still, I let you down. You're my sister. I should have made sure he didn't bother you." He hesitated, then added, "I promise I won't dismiss your concerns again."

The tightness in her chest loosened. "Thank you. I really don't want to marry him. Ever."

"You'll never have to," William said, placing a comforting hand on her arm. "I'm telling Leonard tomorrow that any suit from him will be refused, and that his behavior was unacceptable."

She let out a shaky breath, feeling relief flood through her. "He'll be angry."

"He can take it up with me," William snapped, then he seemed to remember something and gave her a measured look. "Although I suspect Henry might confront him even before I get the chance."

Her breath caught. "Why would he do that?"

William's grim expression returned. "I've known Henry for a long time. That man doesn't always show his temper, but when he's angry, it runs deep. Tonight, he looked furious. I've rarely seen him like that."

Charlotte's pulse kicked up again; she was worried for Henry now on top of her own distress. "You think he'll seek Sir Roger out? Confront him physically?" She dreaded imagining Henry in a duel or brawl over this.

William sighed. "He might. I can't say for sure. But if Leonard's still lurking at Lord Bryant's ball, Henry isn't likely to let this pass. You saw how he was."

She recalled the set of Henry's jaw, the ice in his stare. "But what if it ends in a scandal or a fight?"

"Let's hope Leonard has enough sense to back down. If

not, Henry will protect your honor; maybe more forcefully than we'd like." He gave her a reassuring squeeze on the shoulder. "Get some rest. I'll handle Leonard if Henry hasn't already. You won't have to face that man again."

She swallowed hard, tears pricking her eyes once more. The reminder of Henry's possible confrontation made her stomach clench with fresh anxiety, but William's earnest promise soothed her a little. "Thank you."

He nodded, then left her to her thoughts. She sank onto her bed, exhausted. *What if Henry truly does confront Leonard?* The notion of him risking a violent encounter on her behalf made her heart twist. She didn't want anything to happen to him.

CHAPTER 12

Essex
July 1813

CHARLOTTE CRANED HER NECK TO PEER THROUGH THE carriage window, watching as the countryside gave way to a sprawling estate. She hadn't been to the Duke of Arundel's estate since childhood, and its grandeur impressed her and intimidated her in equal measure.

Trees lined a winding drive, and in the distance stood the grand stone manor of Arundel Park. It looked imposing even through the small glass pane, its windows catching the late-afternoon sun. She clutched her reticule a little tighter, her nerves fluttering.

William, seated opposite her, noticed her discomfort. "Almost there," he said gently. "You'll be fine. Remember, you said you were excited to see the place again as an adult."

She attempted a rueful smile. "Yes, but now I'm wondering if I should have kept it a childhood memory. Henry's ancestral home always felt like a magical place, like something out of a novel. Now it seems rather imposing."

William chuckled. "Don't worry. I'm sure you'll find it perfectly welcoming."

As they drew closer, a few glimpses of a manicured garden emerged, with bright flower beds, trimmed hedges, and a fountain that sparkled in the sun. The carriage rumbled to a halt, and footmen dressed in crisp livery bustled to open the doors and take their luggage.

Charlotte was used to being attended to, but not to this level, and she smiled sympathetically at the stoic-looking footmen who must be run off their feet welcoming guests this morning.

A flush-faced butler led them inside, ushering them through the wide marble foyer with its impressive and fashionable classical columns. Charlotte felt dwarfed by the high ceilings and rich drapes. There were so many details all at once: portraits, floral arrangements, an ornate staircase curling upward. It was much grander than she was used to. However would she get Henry to notice her here, of all places?

Yet he wants me here, she reminded herself. *He asked for my help.*

A plainly clad housekeeper, her graying hair scraped back severely, greeted them politely, although she didn't look at all pleased. Charlotte suspected this impromptu house party of the dowager duchess's had come as much of a shock to the servants as it had to Henry, but she doubted the duchess would have spared a thought for them.

"Lord Fitzgerald, Lady Fitzgerald, Lady Charlotte, your rooms are prepared." She gave a low curtsey. She must be assisting the butler since so many guests were arriving at once. "If you come with me, I'll show you to them. Dinner will be served in two hours for all guests."

The mention of the other guests made Charlotte's stomach flip. She imagined a large, chattering crowd of eager ladies and gentlemen, all of them probably hoping to catch

Henry's notice and vying with each other to do so. She would be lost in the crowd.

"Come on, Charlotte, dear," her mother hissed. "Stop standing around in a daydream."

Charlotte nodded and picked up her skirts as her mother took her arm, glancing at the large grandfather clock at the foot of the huge staircase. She had just two hours to prepare herself mentally.

She followed the housekeeper down a corridor to a cozy suite with a canopy bed, cream wallpaper with a pale pink pattern, and a tall window looking onto the gardens. Her mother had the suite next door. Once inside, Charlotte released a long breath. The day's journey had been long and full of bumpy roads, restless chatter from her mother, and her own anxious thoughts.

She dropped onto the bed and closed her eyes. She just needed a moment to breathe. The gentle hush and the soft feather mattress lulled her, and before she knew it, she was drifting off.

She awoke with a startled jolt. Sitting up, she noticed the shadows had shifted. How long had she slept? There was a knock at the door. Her heart pounded as she realized dinner couldn't be far off, and she hadn't even begun to get ready.

"Yes, come in!" she called, her voice still thick with drowsiness.

The door opened a crack, revealing Adeline's face. "Charlotte?" she said in a cautious whisper.

Then Felicity peeked around her shoulder, as did Genevieve as well. All three stepped into the room before shutting the door behind them. Their expressions teetered between concern and amusement.

"You were asleep. Are you well?" Genevieve asked, taking a seat on the chair near the side of the bed.

Charlotte sat up and rubbed her eyes. "I must have dozed off. The drive here was so long. Is it nearly time for dinner?"

Adeline tossed her curls. "Let's just say, you have enough time if we hurry. We came to help you pick an ensemble. You want to stand out on the first night here."

Charlotte's pulse sped up. "Thank you. I can't believe I napped." She swung her legs off the bed, straightening her gown. "Where's Miranda?"

Felicity shrugged. "I think she's examining the library. She was most excited by the size of it. And Helena is caught up with her parents. I fear she will struggle to get away from them this week. Now, let's see about your wardrobe."

The girls rummaged through Charlotte's dresses, pulling out a few options and assessing them with appraising glances. Adeline held up a soft dove-gray gown with delicate lace trimming—one of Madam Baptiste's creations. Genevieve suggested adding a slightly bolder sash for contrast, a sunshine yellow which complemented Charlotte's coloring.

Charlotte fidgeted as they debated. "That one seems all right, but are you sure it's not too plain?"

Felicity gave her a reassuring smile. "Not with the sash. It's elegant and will look divine next to the riot of bright colors and frills the other girls will no doubt be sporting. We can pin that new brooch at your shoulder. With the sash, it'll draw just enough attention while still making sure you look like you."

Charlotte nodded, letting them bustle around while she tried to shake off any lingering sleep. "And what about everyone else? I heard Henry invited quite a few gentlemen. Are any of them interesting?"

Genevieve and Adeline exchanged a look.

"We've heard rumors about Lord Melton. He's said to be dashing," Adeline teased as Genevieve blushed. "But we won't know until we see him. He's rather reclusive when it comes to the London season, so the gossip is that he is indeed here searching for a bride."

"But we're all focused on you and the duke, of course," Genevieve said quickly.

Felicity smoothed the gown's skirt and held it up to Charlotte's face to gasps of admiration from the others. "Never mind the mysterious Lord Melton. We will have plenty of time to meet everyone, I'm sure. We have to focus on getting Charlotte's entrance right. Did you not bring your maid, Charlotte?"

"She will be joining us later," Charlotte assured them. "But it's her afternoon off, so she wanted to visit her mother, who lives nearby."

"No matter. Adeline can dress your hair."

They managed to dress Charlotte quickly, chatting about potential matches as they did so. Charlotte tried to keep her thoughts light, knowing that Henry would be busy greeting everyone during the first night. She couldn't expect to monopolize his attention.

This was just day one.

Finally ready and more than a little flustered, Charlotte joined her friends and the others heading down to dinner. Her mother and William had gone on ahead, leaving the girls to mingle amongst themselves before dinner. Although Charlotte had no doubt that should her mother catch her hiding in corners as usual, she would be swooping upon her with various young men in tow.

But Charlotte was not intending to hide in corners while she was here, at the duke's ancestral home. They had a plan. For once, she was determined to attract attention.

Stifling her nerves, she straightened her shoulders and lifted her chin, trying to look as interested and alert as possible—while not making it obvious that she was looking for Henry.

A servant directed them toward the grand dining hall, a spacious room with gleaming oak floors, boasting a long table set with silver candlesticks, and a scattering of livery-clad footmen waiting to serve. An imposing portrait of some long-dead Arundel ancestor watched them from above the fireplace, looking, Charlotte thought, rather disapproving.

Many of the guests had already assembled in the drawing room beside the dining hall, chatting over aperitifs. She spotted her mother and William standing together, but before she could take her leave of her friends and approach them, a slim young man with auburn hair stepped forward.

"Lady Charlotte, is it not? I'm Mr. Clarke, an associate of your brother's."

"Oh, I'm very pleased to meet you." Charlotte dipped a curtsey and held her hand out politely, biting back her impatience. Perhaps it would be good for Henry to see her attracting attention from others, although she had to admit, she was stunned by Mr. Clarke's forwardness.

Mr. Clarke bowed, lingering just a little too long over the back of her hand. "May I escort you to dinner, my lady?"

Charlotte had no graceful way to refuse, so she placed her hand lightly on his arm. At the table, to her disappointment, she found herself seated nowhere near Henry. Mr. Clarke sat on one side of her, her mother and William on the other. Happily, Genevieve and Felicity were seated opposite; but Henry was nowhere to be seen.

Pretending to drop her napkin, she leaned forward and scanned the length of gleaming cutlery and crystal glasses, spotting Henry right at the opposite end of the huge table. Her stomach sank. She would not be speaking to him over the first night's dinner.

He was engrossed in conversation with a small group that included two elegant young women, both of whom looked every inch the fashionable debutante. One had dark hair and bewitching eyes. She was possessed of the sort of beauty that immediately made Charlotte feel dull by comparison.

Charlotte mustered a half smile when the other woman glanced in her direction, but it went unnoticed in the buzz of conversation. She sat up, swallowing a sigh of disappointment.

"How was your journey, my lady?" Mr. Clarke asked.

"Oh, yes, very nice, if a little tiring," Charlotte answered, hoping Mr. Clarke wouldn't spend the entire meal attempting to engage her in conversation.

"Yes, it was quite the way from London, was it not?"

She answered in the affirmative, too preoccupied with wondering whether Henry would glance her way to pay Mr. Clarke much heed. A quick attempt to catch his eye by shifting in her seat failed. He seemed absorbed in whatever the dark-haired lady next to him was saying, and he was really too far away to notice her.

Does he even know I'm here yet?

She had no doubt that the dowager duchess had been in charge of this seating plan. The duchess sat near Henry and his friends and seemed delighted by every word the dark-haired beauty said.

"Charlotte, do stop staring down the table, dear. You're making it quite noticeable," her mother hissed behind a gloved hand.

Charlotte blushed and straightened herself, trying not to let her distress show on her face. Across from her, Felicity and Genevieve exchanged worried glances, clearly noticing Charlotte's slight deflation. She only grew quieter as the first two courses were served and eaten—a summer pea soup and a delicious haricot lamb.

"Have you met Lord Melton, Charlotte?" William said as they waited for dessert.

The man—as handsome as Adeline had intimated—sat opposite her brother, next to Genevieve's mother. Until that point, Lord Melton had seemed more interested in the guests to his other side—who, Charlotte had observed, were clearly close acquaintances with the set around Henry.

Charlotte nodded at him, only to be prodded under the table by Adeline's toe.

"Talk to him," her friend mouthed.

"I hear you've had a long journey, Lord Melton," Charlotte said, wincing as she heard herself repeating Mr. Clarke's drab line of conversation.

Lord Melton smiled, but she saw the boredom in his eyes, and he soon turned his attention back to his friends. Charlotte saw how his gaze kept wandering to the dark-haired woman next to Henry, and she began to wonder if this week had been a good idea at all. How were any of them, wallflowers that they were, going to compete with all these sparkling social butterflies?

Only William was given any attention by Melton and his friends, but their conversation never quite merged with Henry's end of the table, and Charlotte could only glean snippets of laughter or chatter from far off. She forced herself not to appear too crestfallen.

By the time dessert arrived, she felt thoroughly overshadowed by the more sophisticated girls giggling near Henry. They were bright, confident, and comfortable in these surroundings. She, in contrast, fought a constant swirl of nerves. She had come all this way, and it seemed like Henry hadn't so much as looked in her direction.

When the meal concluded, the ladies withdrew into the drawing room or their own rooms, leaving the men behind with their port and cigars. Charlotte and her friends reconvened in a side parlor, a space they quickly claimed as their own, while her mother joined some of the other older ladies for a game of bridge in the drawing room.

Charlotte dropped onto a small embroidered couch. "That whole dinner was absolutely awful," she muttered, trying to keep her voice low so the other women milling around the corridor couldn't hear. "Henry was so far away, I couldn't even speak to him once. Every moment I even tried to catch his eye, he was looking elsewhere. I don't believe he even knew I was there."

Adeline patted her arm sympathetically. "Take heart. It's only the first dinner. We have days ahead of us yet. I'm sure that Henry was obligated to entertain the other gentry. It would only be proper. At least Genevieve got to sit near that dashing Lord Melton."

"For all the notice he took," Genevieve said glumly, her discouragement echoing Charlotte's own.

Felicity perched on an ottoman nearby. "Yes, you're right, Adeline, but I do understand Charlotte's disappointment. We were hoping to make an impression tonight."

Genevieve crossed her arms, looking frustrated. "All these other ladies seem so well-connected. I overheard one of them bragging that her cousin is a viscount. They're already hinting at how Henry might come to *their* estate next season. It's almost predatory."

Charlotte forced a shaky laugh at the thought of the women swooping on Henry like hawks. "And all I did was fumble through conversation about travel routes with Mr. Clarke."

Her friends tried to reassure her, proposing strategies. Maybe tomorrow they could plan a walk in the gardens, or, Miranda suggested, contrive a chance for Henry to show Charlotte the library. But for now, she was thoroughly disheartened.

"Maybe we should focus on someone else?" Charlotte suggested, wishing she could sink into the floor and disappear. "There are plenty of bachelors here. Perhaps a match for you Felicity? Or we could work on Lord Melton for Genevieve?"

Miranda shook her head firmly. "We're here for you. Our priority is clear."

Felicity agreed. "Absolutely. We'll do better tomorrow.

Everyone only just arrived tonight. We can reevaluate, set up opportunities. Henry's not going anywhere."

Charlotte couldn't help but be touched and amused by her friends' stubborn insistence, although her spirits remained low. Eventually, the others drifted off to their own rooms, and she decided to return to her suite and read. Perhaps some solitude would soothe her disappointment and leave her in a better frame of mind for the next morning.

She left the parlor, thinking that she was heading in the direction of the staircase, but soon found herself lost in the unfamiliar corridors. After rounding a corner, she almost bumped into a sandy-haired gentleman who seemed equally lost. He looked to be in his thirties and smelled of port and cigar smoke.

He bowed. "Excuse me. This house is larger than I realized."

"I know exactly what you mean, sir. I'm still figuring out which wing is which." Charlotte managed a polite laugh as she made to step aside for him, but he made no attempt to keep walking. If she was seen standing alone in the corridor with an unknown man, it could cause quite the scandal. She was debating just walking around him, however rude it seemed, when he spoke again, peering at her.

"Ah, you're Lady Charlotte Fitzgerald, aren't you? I heard your name at dinner."

She inclined her head, suddenly intrigued. Heard her name from whom? Could it be Henry? She wasn't certain whether this man had been one of the crowd around him. "Yes…. I'm sorry, I don't believe we've been introduced."

He gave another small bow. "Sir Matthew Argyle. A friend of Lord Wentworth's. I was surprised to see you here, I must admit."

Charlotte raised a brow, all thoughts of escaping the man forgotten. "Surprised? Why is that, sir?"

"Well…." He hesitated, looking suddenly uncomfortable.

"Forgive me, my lady. It is most rude of me to comment on personal matters."

"Please do, sir," Charlotte said quickly. "You have piqued my curiosity."

He cleared his throat. "Well, it is only that I'd heard you were as good as betrothed to Sir Roger. The rumor around town is that you're soon to be married."

She gaped at him, her face suddenly hot, all propriety forgotten. "Soon to be married? Sir Roger has been telling people that? In those words? That is an outright lie!"

Sir Matthew's eyes widened. He coughed, flushing deeply. "That's my understanding, my lady. He's mentioned it to some acquaintances and made it sound like it was nearly settled. But perhaps I misunderstood. Forgive me, I meant no offense."

Anger flared in Charlotte's stomach, mingling with the humiliation that curled there. "It is forgiven," she reassured him. "But please put your acquaintances right. Sir Roger and I are most certainly not betrothed. Nor will we ever be."

Sir Matthew looked relieved. "Then I see I was misinformed. I do apologize for bringing it up. I've had a little too much port."

She smiled tightly. "No need to apologize, sir. It's much better that I am aware of these rumors."

He offered another small bow. "I'll let you find your way. Good evening, Lady Charlotte."

She murmured a polite farewell, her thoughts spinning.

Sir Roger's been boasting? Telling people I'm guaranteed to be his wife?

After what had happened at the ball, the very idea repulsed her.

How dare he?

And was Henry aware of these rumors? Was William?

CHAPTER 13

Henry turned the page of the report he was reading in preparation for his return to the House of Lords after the house party with deliberate slowness, listening for the faintest hint of footsteps outside the library door. He had retreated to this room as soon as breakfast ended, hoping for a quiet interval before his mother or an enthusiastic guest found him.

Alas, the sound of footfalls, quick and confident, drew nearer. Henry knew that step all too well. He looked around in mild desperation for a place to tuck himself out of sight, but it was too late. The door opened, and his mother sailed in, her skirts brushing the threshold.

"There you are," she said, tone triumphant but her eyes steely. "I have been searching for you everywhere. You can't hide in here all day. Your guests are expecting to see their host."

Henry set aside the report with a resigned sigh. "I was merely attending to my parliamentary duties, Mother. I have been entertaining guests all morning."

Indeed, Henry was beginning to get a headache from all

the chatter. It felt as though everywhere he turned, there were people hanging on his arm, and he had barely seen his actual friends, including William, the nearest person he had to a confidante.

Or Charlotte, for that matter. The supposed plan for her and her friends to act as a buffer could hardly work if they couldn't get near him.

His mother gave him a pointed look. "You have read enough for the moment. The guests have begun a game of lawn bowls before the luncheon, and you are expected to join them."

He rose slowly. "I had hoped to be excused, Mother. I'm feeling under the weather this morning."

"No excuses," she interrupted, waving off his protest without a hint of sympathy. "You are the host, and people have come from London at your invitation; many with no small amount of anticipation. Let us go."

"You mean, they came at your invitation," he grumbled.

His mother pointedly chose to ignore him as she swept out of the room. He had little choice but to follow her out through the corridors and onto the wide terrace overlooking the gardens. Beyond the fountain, a neatly mowed patch of lawn was set with wooden bowls, and he saw a cluster of guests in bright summer attire, already forming teams.

His mother scanned the gathering. "Ah, perfect. They've started splitting into pairs. You've missed your chance to partner some of the best ladies, unfortunately. I do see Lady Charlotte standing near her brother."

Ignoring his mother, Henry's heart lifted slightly at the sight of Charlotte's pale green gown and softly curled hair. She was laughing as she looked up at William, and her eyes sparkled in the sun.

He had been disappointed the previous evening to have had scarce chance to speak to her. He'd been hemmed in by his mother's most favored guests, all of whom had attempted to ingratiate themselves to him with an eagerness he had found distasteful. He had made a good show of being entertained, however, for his mother's sake. As put out as he was by this whole affair, the household had gone to no small trouble and expense to put it on.

Now, as he approached with his mother, Charlotte turned and gave him a polite smile, her cheeks flushing prettily. Really, Charlotte was underrated by her peers. Even her own family seemed to see her as a plain Jane with few prospects. It angered him that her sweetness and natural beauty were so overlooked by a society he was beginning to find more tedious with each passing day.

He nodded in greeting. "Good morning, Lady Charlotte. Do you by chance need a partner, or would I be stealing you away from your brother?"

She looked momentarily surprised, then her smile brightened. "I would be delighted, Your Grace, if William doesn't mind?"

"Not at all," William said, grinning at Henry. "I was just retiring inside for a glass of lemonade, in fact."

Henry's mother gave a satisfied little hum. "Excellent." She looked pointedly at Henry. "Have a care, my dear, and mingle a bit afterward. Everyone is eager to speak with you."

Without waiting for his reply, his mother drifted off after William, leaving him at Charlotte's side.

He mustered a quiet laugh. "She can't resist ensuring I am visible and sociable at all times."

Charlotte's eyes danced with amusement. "One might suppose that is the purpose of a house party—to socialize with your guests, no?" She smirked, making him laugh.

"You have quite the sense of humor. You really aren't given enough credit for it," he said, and Charlotte blushed pure crimson. He supposed she wasn't used to receiving such compliments, and he was oddly pleased that he had been able to bring that pretty shade of pink to her cheeks.

They stepped out onto the lawn to join the others. A footman handed Henry a pair of wooden bowls, which he offered to Charlotte so she could choose first. He glanced around, noticing a few of the visiting debutantes fluttering their eyelashes demurely his way. Coughing, he looked away and returned his attention to Charlotte.

She tested the weight of a bowl. "I used to play this with my father's guests at our country home before he passed. I do not claim mastery, but it's a sport I enjoy."

Henry smiled. "That is more experience than many young ladies can boast." He turned slightly as two giggling ladies sidled close. They began to feign confusion over the rules, casting hopeful glances at him.

"Would you be able to advise us, Your Grace?" one asked, looking innocently over at him and quite ignoring Charlotte, who he sensed bristling next to him.

He quickly said, "I am committed to assisting Lady Charlotte first, I'm afraid. I must not abandon my partner."

Charlotte's look of gratitude was accompanied by a brief flicker of something else in her eyes—something more serious. Then she gave a quick laugh. "Indeed you mustn't. I shall make good use of your expert guidance."

They practiced a few rolls, and Henry quickly discovered that Charlotte was quite adept. He did not need to correct her form at all. Nevertheless, he made a show of positioning her stance, murmuring tips and gently adjusting her elbow so onlookers could see that he was quite engaged in her success—too engaged to be interrupted further by any other eager prospective partners.

He caught a faint whiff of her perfume. It was that same fresh and floral scent she'd been wearing at a ball that brought up childhood memories of running in the Fitzgerald gardens with William, little Charlotte toddling after them.

The sensation unsettled him, but not unpleasantly; rather, it reminded him of a time when life had been easier, without all these constraining rules and expectations. He was struck by how easily he and Charlotte conversed and how pleasant it felt to stand close without any forced contrivances.

If not for the shadows of my family's past, she might be exactly the sort of wife I would wish for.

If she wasn't also his best friend's sister, of course.

Charlotte's friends had positioned themselves strategically over by a cluster of hedges, where they were intercepting other ladies whenever they drifted toward Henry with questions. He smiled to himself, grateful for their help.

The circle around him and Charlotte ensured that only one or two particularly determined young women broke through—including the most stubborn of Lady Pembroke's daughters. Most of the women didn't remain for long, but the third, elegantly dressed in cream silk, insisted that Henry come demonstrate the proper way to release the bowl. She was rather more forceful than the other two ladies had been, and she was clearly annoyed that Henry wasn't mingling as a host was expected to.

Henry glanced at Charlotte. "I am afraid my partner must come first," he said mildly. "Once she is satisfied, perhaps I shall have time to assist you."

The woman looked at Charlotte icily. Before she could protest further, one of Charlotte's friends—Genevieve Flynn, he thought—happened to trip, her drink splashing across the cream silk of the interloper's dress. In a flurry of exclamations, the lady squealed and stormed off, presumably to find a maidservant.

Henry bit the inside of his cheek to stifle a laugh. Charlotte looked half startled, half amused, shaking her head in Genevieve's direction. Miss Flynn was a picture of innocence.

Charlotte bent to retrieve her bowl, and Henry said

lightly, "I believe your defenders are in top form today. Thank you for agreeing to shield me, Charlotte. You're a good friend."

She lifted her head, and for a moment, the sunshine caught her face. Her smile vanished, replaced by a flash of discomfort before she forced it back into place. "Yes…. Thank you. And they do mean well."

Concern flickered in him. *What troubles her?* But before he could inquire, the sound of his mother's voice reached his ears. Again

"There you are, Henry," she said, stepping neatly between him and another encroaching lady. "Truly, it isn't wise to devote yourself entirely to one partner." His mother lowered her voice to add, "People shall think you have already decided." She gave Henry a meaningful look. They both knew how quickly rumor could spread.

He cast a glance at Charlotte, torn between the relief he felt in her company and dismay at his mother's interference, though he knew she was right. He didn't want their plan to compromise Charlotte's reputation in any way.

"Very well," he said at last, trying to keep the frustration from his tone. "I shall spread my attention a little more, as you advise."

His mother, apparently satisfied, moved off.

Henry turned to Charlotte. "Forgive me. It seems I am forced to leave you to your own devices for a while. I must go and mingle."

She nodded, but there was a faint line between her brows, and he sensed a sudden distance between them. "I understand. It is no trouble, Your Grace. I'm glad I was able to help this afternoon."

With a polite bow, Henry stepped away, feeling confused at the odd undercurrents in their exchange. Had he offended Charlotte somehow? Had he been too familiar with her, perhaps?

He had no time to ponder, as his mother almost immediately directed Charlotte's friend Felicity toward him, coaxing them to form a pair. He resigned himself to the new partnership, reasoning that Felicity was no doubt aware of the "arrangement."

Felicity offered a shy greeting, apologizing at once for her inexperience with bowls.

"Think nothing of it," Henry said kindly, taking a practice bowl. "At least you won't turn out to be better than I am, like Charlotte here. Shall we try a few rolls?"

Poor Felicity's coordination proved quite lacking, and after two attempts, she managed to drop the next ball directly onto Henry's foot.

"Ow!" A sharp flash of pain made him hiss through clenched teeth, nearly dropping his own bowl.

Charlotte, standing only a short distance away, turned and instinctively reached out as though to steady him. But then she froze, and her hand hovered in midair before she drew it back again.

Why the hesitation? he wondered, pressing his lips together to stem the pain.

He told Felicity he was quite all right and not to worry, even though his foot throbbed. One of the footmen hurried forward to gather the fallen bowl.

Felicity fluttered her hands, looking so contrite that she was close to tears. "I am so very sorry, Your Grace. I could not hold on properly."

He took a breath, forcing himself to ignore the insistent throbbing in his foot. "Truly, it is fine," he assured her once more. "Shall we proceed... more carefully?"

As they resumed their game—with him still valiantly ignoring the pain in his foot—he couldn't help glancing again at Charlotte. She had returned to her friends, who were chatting and watching the game unfold. She seemed subdued, and he wondered about that single moment when she had instinctively reached for him, only to draw back as though afraid.

What was she afraid of? The gossip that might ensue should she be seen to comfort him?

Or her immediate instinct to do so?

CHAPTER 14

HENRY HAD SCARCELY FINISHED GUIDING FELICITY THROUGH another clumsy attempt at bowls when a group of gentlemen hailed him from across the lawn, one of them scowling and another wearing a mischievous grin.

His gut twisted. They had been eyeing him all morning, no doubt speculating on his predicament. The moment he drew near, one of them—Sir Duncan, a jovial fellow with slightly too much brandy on his breath—clapped Henry on the shoulder in a comradely fashion.

"Arundel," Sir Duncan teased, "do you think you might spare some of the ladies for the rest of us? They're all vying for your attention, old fellow. We're getting positively overlooked."

Henry mustered a dry smile. "You are welcome to them, I assure you."

Another man, Lord Robins, raised an eyebrow. "Certainly does not seem so, Arundel, when they flutter about you like butterflies. Tell me, are we mere ornaments at your house party?"

Henry tensed, mindful that William stood close by with his arms folded, ready to jump to his friend's defense.

"Hardly. I have never encouraged such fuss. In truth, I wish you all the best in your attempts."

Lord Robins chuckled, shaking his head. "We know your mother is keen, though. She is determined you must choose someone at this party, is she not?"

Henry forced a casual shrug. "She has her aspirations, but that doesn't mean I share them. I am not yet finished with my lighthearted days of bachelorhood."

"So you say," Sir Duncan quipped. "But sooner or later, you shall have to wed. Best to resign yourself, unless you wish to be hounded by all the young women of the *ton* forever."

A third gentleman, a Mr. Redford, offered a sly grin. "There are any number of candidates to amuse yourself with. Why not give more attention to the polished ladies rather than that little wallflower?"

Henry's annoyance flared at this reference to Charlotte. He sensed William stiffen as well, though his friend held his tongue.

Henry drew a short breath. "I will assist whomever I choose, and I see no reason to dismiss Lady Charlotte so rudely."

Sir Duncan raised both hands, feigning innocence. "Peace, Arundel. No offense intended. Merely an observation."

Henry realized his temper was too near the surface. He had no wish for these men's jibes to worsen. He set his shoulders back, summoning a semblance of composure. "If you will excuse me, I have an errand to run."

He offered a curt nod and turned away, ignoring the curious stares that followed him across the lawn. William kept step with him for a moment, concern evident in his glance.

"Are you all right?" he murmured quietly.

Henry set his jaw. "As well as can be expected."

William sighed. "I know you don't like this attention, but I thank you for your defense of Charlotte."

Henry simply nodded in response, ignoring the question at the end of his friend's words. He quickened his pace toward the house, seeking refuge.

Indeed, inside the cool corridors, his tension eased a little. He needed a quieter retreat, somewhere no one would search him out with insistent demands for a stroll or conversation. The library came to mind; few guests ventured there unless they wished to appear studious, and he had discovered that many were more interested in talking of fashion, politics, or gossip than books.

Sure enough, the library was peaceful when he slipped in. Henry let out a soft sigh of relief, stepped deeper into the room, and began scanning the shelves. He was about to take down a volume on British antiquities when he heard the light rustle of skirts.

He turned to see Charlotte and Miranda examining the shelves on the opposite side of the room.

Miranda spotted him first, dipping into a stiff curtsey. "Your Grace," she said loudly, alerting Charlotte.

"Oh, Your Grace!" Charlotte looked flustered as she closed a book she had been flipping through. "We did not think anyone else would be in here at present."

He offered them a polite half smile. "Nor did I. What were you reading?"

Charlotte tapped a slim volume she held. "A bit of fiction. Something restful for the afternoon. I confess I needed a reprieve after the excitement on the lawn."

He chuckled. "I hope you didn't find the morning's entertainment too tedious."

"At least I wasn't hurt," she said tactfully. "How is your foot?"

"Better."

Miranda made a sympathetic noise. "Felicity isn't a fan of

sports. I must say I do find bowls rather dull, although there were plenty of young ladies who were suddenly *very* enthusiastic about playing."

He tried not to grimace remembering that swirl of eager faces. "They were enthusiastic, certainly. I didn't mean to neglect you, Charlotte." He hesitated, uncertain whether to confess his frustration. Instead, he cleared his throat and offered a faint bow. "I shall let you two continue your search for reading material."

Charlotte hesitated as though thinking of a response. Then she simply smiled. "Thank you, Your Grace. Enjoy your book."

The ladies departed, their skirts whispering over the polished floor. Henry watched them depart, a knot of regret tightening within him. He would like to spend more time with Charlotte, he realized. She really had grown into a most intriguing young woman. If only—

He cut off the thought and returned to scanning the shelves, eventually choosing a history text that looked promising. He retreated to one of the plush chairs by the window and attempted to read, though his mind wandered.

Only when a servant appeared to inform him that his mother had been searching for him did Henry stir from his seat. Deciding he wished to avoid her for a while longer, he tucked the book under his arm and headed out, mindful of the guests scattered about. Perhaps he could slip upstairs to his bedchamber, read there for an hour, and dodge any prying eyes.

He was halfway up the main staircase when a faint melody reached his ears. It was cello music, warm and resonant. Helena Steele, no doubt. She had mentioned hoping that her instrument could be brought along, and Henry had permitted it, believing it would provide some pleasant recitals. Miss Steele was very talented and gathering quite the reputation for her playing.

He followed the music to one of the manor's smaller salons. He pushed open the door quietly. There sat Helena by a window, absorbed in a slow, sweeping tune, her cello balanced between her knees. Henry stood quietly listening, intending to slip away before she noticed him. But an older gentleman and lady sat on a nearby chaise, and they spotted him before he could retreat.

"Your Grace," Mrs. Steele said a little too eagerly. "We had no idea you were here. Do come in."

Helena halted her bow mid-stroke, casting Henry a slightly apologetic look.

"That was lovely, Miss Steele," Henry managed, giving Helena a polite nod. "Please, do not let me interrupt."

Mrs. Steele stepped forward, beaming. "Helena is quite devoted, you know. I'm very proud of her; she's a young woman of passion and spirit. And capable of responsibility—even, I declare, that of a duchess!"

Poor Helena went crimson at her mother's boldness.

"I can see she is talented," Henry said politely. "I trust she will do well in whichever path she chooses."

Mr. Steele bowed to him. "Helena possesses many accomplishments, Your Grace. She would be an asset to any man."

Helena set aside her bow, her cheeks coloring. "Papa, please."

She was clearly mortified, but her parents pressed on regardless. For once Henry had to agree with his mother; they were vulgar.

"I have no doubt of her merits. For now, I shall not intrude." He inclined his head in Helena's direction. "Thank you for the music, Miss Steele."

Mrs. Steele pounced on that. "Perhaps we could arrange a more formal recital, Your Grace, if you so desire. Helena's playing never fails to enchant."

Helena offered him a quick, pained smile and Henry sensed her silent plea to end the discussion. "That is most generous, but I am rather busy just now. Now, if you'll excuse me, I—"

"Oh, but certainly." Mr. Steele winked. "We know you are a busy man with many decisions to make."

Henry forced a polite laugh. "Indeed." He backed toward the door, refusing to linger. "I shall leave you to your music."

He escaped the salon, tension knotted in his shoulders. The blatant suggestion that Helena might make an excellent duchess set his teeth on edge. *Do none of these people have any shame?* While Helena was a fine woman, Henry would not feel inclination toward her as a potential wife even if he had been open to the notion of marrying.

Still reeling from the encounter, he nearly stumbled into a young lady ascending the stairs. He vaguely remembered being introduced to her that morning. Catherine somebody? Fareham, maybe? She gave a start, then flashed a bright smile, slipping into an overly familiar tone.

"Oh, Your Grace! I was searching for you. I had hoped we might share a moment of conversation." She lowered her voice, glancing around the empty corridor. "Why not here? No one is about."

Henry tensed, the memory of all too many near-compromises flickering through his mind. "I beg your pardon, Miss… Farnham, is it? I fear it would not be proper for us to converse privately, unchaperoned."

She gave a light tinkling laugh. "It's Fairweather. We are only steps from the main stair. Surely that is not so improper. And what better time than now, while you are free?"

He pressed his lips together. "I must insist. We shall speak tomorrow in the drawing room or the gardens, with others present."

She pouted, clearly disappointed. "But Your Grace, I meant no offence. I only wished to say—"

He offered the faintest bow. "I bid you good evening."

Without waiting for further protest, he took the final few stairs and strode quickly down the corridor, his heart pounding. Enough of these attempts. He was not about to be cornered into marriage simply because an ambitious young woman found him alone.

Guilt prickled at him for dismissing the poor woman so abruptly, but he had no alternative. *My mother can lecture me later for my rudeness, if she must. Better that than risking a scandal.* Too many men of his acquaintance had been pushed into marriages due to being found in a compromising situation.

Upon reaching his bedchamber door, he slipped inside and locked it behind him. Only then did he release a breath of relief. He leaned against the door, allowing the tension to drain away.

He placed the book on a small table, then crossed to the sideboard where a decanter of brandy awaited. He poured himself a measure and took a fortifying sip. The warm burn eased his frayed nerves somewhat.

With care, he began to remove his coat and neckcloth, laying them over a nearby chair. By the time he unbuttoned his waistcoat, he felt both literally and mentally lighter. With any luck, he could hide in here for a while before his mother came looking for him again.

Briefly, the thought of Charlotte arose in his mind. He would welcome her calm presence now. If only he was truly free to consider his options… perhaps he could approach William for his sister's hand?

If it were only a matter of preference, he might be open to exploring a bond with her. Certainly she was the only woman who had sparked his interest. But no, he could not risk her or any woman discovering the truth.

He set his half-empty glass aside and wandered to the bed, intending to read for a time, or perhaps even doze. As he pulled back the coverlet, he noticed a folded piece of paper lying on his pillow. He froze. Had a servant left him a note from his mother? Or from William?

Frowning, he picked it up. No seal. Good god, was it some kind of love note?

Carefully, he unfolded it, then scanned the few lines that had been written in an unsteady hand. The message was brief, but each word cut like ice.

I know what you are hiding. I'll let you know what is required to ensure my mouth remains stay.

They knew his secret. Someone here *knew*.

And they intended to blackmail him.

A chill ran through him. He turned the paper in his hand, studying the penmanship. It seemed feminine, but not obviously so; it could be anyone's handwriting who had a shaky grasp, or perhaps it had been deliberately disguised.

His stomach clenched. *Who could it be?*

He thought of the unmarried miss from the corridor, of Helena's parents, or of the many cunning mothers who might rummage for leverage. Possibly someone else entirely.

His breath quickened. So many people had come to the manor, each with their own aims. Was it a guest who had put this here, or even a servant? Certainly they had more knowledge of the rooms. He tried to compare the shape of the letters to anything he had seen before, but no obvious match came to mind.

He sank onto the edge of the bed, his heart racing. Could it be real, or was it a malicious trick? If genuine, then the family's entire effort to preserve his position was in jeopardy.

What do they want?

He raked a hand through his hair, all his earlier exasperations dwarfed by this new threat. Part of him wanted to rush out and corner every soul in the house, demanding to know who had placed the note. But that would only draw suspicion to the very secret he was supposed to keep. Perhaps if he did not respond, they would approach him soon enough. Then he could discover the truth.

And find a way to silence them.

He pressed a hand to his temple, a ripple of dread coursing through him. He had managed to keep everything buried for so long. Now, it seemed he was mere steps away from potential disaster. If word spread among the guests, he would be finished, and so would the Arundel name.

His eyes drifted to the pile of pillows. He wanted nothing more than to bury himself in them and shut out the world. But the note was a silent threat that demanded attention. He took it up again and folded it neatly. He must keep it somewhere safe until he could decipher how to handle this blackmail attempt.

He rose and slipped the note into a small locked drawer of his writing desk. Then he returned to the bed and stared at the unhelpful book he had planned to read.

So much for peace, he thought hollowly. *One day into this party, and everything is unraveling.*

Never had his family's careful secrecy been so imperiled. And never had he felt so vulnerable, so alone in a house full of people.

Who knew his secrets, and what did they want with him?

CHAPTER 15

Charlotte stepped into the breakfast room and immediately caught Miranda's eye, then tilted her head meaningfully. Without exchanging a word, it was understood between them that they would take the far end of the long table, away from the prying chatter of other guests.

Charlotte moved briskly to a side table and helped herself to a cup of tea and a breakfast of honey cakes, brioche with plum jam, and some kind of cake containing caraway seeds and ginger. It smelled divine, and her stomach rumbled as she carried her tray to the secluded end of the table.

Miranda sat down beside her, bearing her own breakfast —only a black tea and single slice of brioche—and gave Charlotte a small conspiratorial smile. "I thought the duke seemed very interested in you yesterday in the library." She kept her voice low so that only Charlotte could hear.

"Do you think?" Charlotte's heart gave a little flutter.

Before Miranda could reply, Genevieve and Felicity joined them, with Adeline not far behind. In the same hushed tone, Miranda told them about bumping into the duke in the library.

"He seemed to disappear after that," Charlotte said

despondently. She had looked out all afternoon and evening for Henry, but he must have been otherwise occupied.

Helena settled into the chair opposite them. "I did see him briefly in the music room. Not that I had a chance to talk to him about Charlotte as my parents were too busy trying to matchmake." She shuddered, looking embarrassed. "It was mortifying."

Adeline patted her hand in sympathy. "Everyone wants his time, of course. I was thinking; I have a walk planned for tomorrow. Perhaps we could arrange it so that he accompanies us and you and he walk together. That will give you some proper time with him, like you had at the lawn bowls."

Miranda's eyes lit up. "A walk? Yes, that would be splendid. We must ensure he has plenty of time with Charlotte."

"And maybe we can work out some way to have you nearer to him at dinner," Helena suggested, lowering her voice further. "A change in seating, perhaps, so you won't be so far away and lost in the crowd."

Charlotte brightened at the thought, but before she could say more, a chair next to her was scraped back, and William sat down.

"What are we all discussing so keenly?" he asked. His presence silenced the murmuring conversation instantly. All eyes turned toward him.

"None of your concern, sir," Helena said, half in jest, yet with a note of challenge in her voice.

William's interest was piqued as he leaned forward. "Now I am truly curious. What secret designs are you ladies concocting this fine morning?"

A ripple of laughter died away as the table fell silent. No one knew quite where to look, except for William, who turned questioning eyes on his sister.

Charlotte cleared her throat and managed, "We were simply discussing our plans for tomorrow. A walk, perhaps."

"Then why the secrecy? Perhaps one of you has caught the attentions of a gallant young gentleman?"

William was joking, but it was too close for comfort.

Charlotte flushed, glancing quickly at her friends for support. "Nothing so daring, brother; I simply wish to have some time to talk to my friends without a throng of guests between us."

Before William could press further, a brisk voice interrupted them.

"Prepare yourselves. In an hour, the dowager duchess will have all the young ladies perform their musical talents." The voice belonged to Genevieve's mother, who had swept up to them with all the brisk authority of a lady in charge of an orchestra. "Hurry, Genevieve—you need time to practice. Which of your friends will be supporting you?"

A murmur went through the group as Genevieve's face fell. "Must I, Mother?" she whispered, silently pleading with the others to rescue her.

"Yes, you must, Genevieve. Why else do I spend all that money on a music tutor? Perhaps Charlotte will play the pianoforte also?"

Charlotte opened her mouth to find some excuse, but William answered for her. "I'm sure my sister will be delighted to play for the duchess."

Charlotte turned to him in horror as Mrs. Flynn swept away, looking satisfied.

"William…" she began.

William interjected gently. "Charlotte, you must support your friends. It isn't like you to shirk your duties."

Charlotte sighed as she saw Genevieve's pleading expression and looked around at the expectant faces. "Very well, I suppose I shall play a song on the pianoforte," she conceded. After all, her friends were doing so much for her. It would be selfish of her not to participate.

The meal continued in a subdued atmosphere as the

ladies finished their breakfast, unable to continue their plans with William in attendance. Instead, conversation ebbed and flowed between light chatter about the weather and murmurs of anticipation about the upcoming musical performance.

Charlotte, still thinking of her plans for tomorrow, cleared her throat softly as she set down her cup. "After we finish here, I'd like to take a wander in the garden, ladies," she announced. "A bit of fresh air might do us all good, no?" And it would allow them to get away from William and resume their discussion.

Her companions exchanged glances and nodded in agreement.

"Good idea, Charlotte. Let's go," said Miranda, taking the lead as usual.

Poor Genevieve took her leave and headed off to practice for the recital.

They rose, gathered their shawls, and stepped out through a side door in the drawing room and into the rose garden. With its winding gravel paths and clusters of blooming flowers, the garden provided a welcome respite from the clamor of the dining hall.

As they strolled, they encountered a group of mothers gathered around a garden table, animatedly discussing the latest social news. Sensing that this was not their hoped-for refuge, Charlotte and her friends discreetly veered off onto a quieter path lined with climbing roses artistically arranged over pretty wooden trellises.

They soon walked into a giggling group of young ladies, and Charlotte realized there would be little time before the recital to resume their chat. How unfortunate.

Before long, the soft opening strains of the musical session began to drift from a nearby hall as the players tuned their instruments, and they made their way into the recital and took their seats.

"Do you know what you're going to play?" Felicity whispered to Charlotte.

"Something by Bach," Charlotte whispered back. "Something boring but safe."

Felicity nodded. "Good choice. Keep it simple. I doubt the duke will be here."

"No," Charlotte said. "I know he detests these things."

A couple of refined singers started the program, their voices melding in perfect harmony. A talented violinist followed, eliciting appreciative murmurs from those gathered. Then, poor Genevieve stepped up.

Though her performance was marked by trembling fingers and a quavering tone, she pushed through with earnest determination.

Finally, it was Charlotte's turn. With a deep breath, she approached the pianoforte. The room was hushed with expectation, and as she sat down, she could feel eyes on her. She hated performing in public like this. Her own fingers trembled at first, but as she began to play, the notes, soft and tentative, slowly grew more confident. Thank goodness that Henry was absent, sparing her the embarrassment of her rusty skills.

When the music came to an end, Charlotte and her friends gathered in a corner to chat.

Adeline frowned, motioning toward another group of young ladies who were muttering amongst themselves and casting glances their way. "Are they talking about us?"

"Sssh," Genevieve hissed. "They're coming over."

As they turned and smiled politely, one of the more forthright young women, Miss Brighton, skewered Charlotte with a sharp look. Miss Brighton had tight blond pin curls and was wearing the season's latest bonnet in a shade of pink that clashed awfully with her complexion.

"Charlotte," the other girl began briskly, "you must stop monopolizing His Grace's attention."

"Excuse me?" Charlotte gasped, her cheeks heating.

"How rude, madam!" Miranda snapped, glaring at Miss Brighton. "Charlotte does not monopolize, she is old friends with His Grace."

Not at all intimidated by Miranda, Miss Brighton snorted in derision and addressed Charlotte again. "Old friends? You're the sister of his friend, yes, but do let the rest of us have a chance. It's not as if he'll ever actually choose you for himself."

Felicity gasped at the woman's remark, and Adeline tutted in disapproval, but Miss Brighton's companions nodded in agreement with her.

Charlotte's cheeks burned even hotter as she stammered an apology. "I'm sorry. I mean, I don't intend to monopolize him." Her voice was barely above a whisper. It was all she could do to meet their eyes.

Miss Brighton's expression was hard. "You need to remember your place, dear. Sometimes, you must let others have their moment."

The words struck Charlotte sharply, and she turned away, humiliation sweeping through her. One of the other girls laughed as though Miss Brighton's insult had been incredibly witty.

Mortified, Charlotte could only lower her face, feeling the weight of the reproach. She hurried away from the group, hot tears stinging her eyes.

CHAPTER 16

Henry had long since learned that when his mother sent for him and announced she had made plans, it was rarely for anything he wished to do. So when she summoned him to the morning room to inform him he was taking some guests on a walk into town, with a serene smile and an airy comment about his presence being required, he didn't bother attempting to argue as he had about the lawn bowls.

He arrived at the appointed place only to find himself the object of much anticipation. A small gathering of young ladies, dressed in their walking attire, turned expectant eyes upon him. Their bonnets bobbed as they murmured to one another, their hands tightening on their reticules. None of the other gentlemen were present.

He fought the urge to sigh. Clearly, his mother had orchestrated this. He was not foolish enough to believe that his presence was truly necessary for this walk, yet neither was he in a position to decline. It would be unpardonably rude to retreat now.

He managed a polite smile and adjusted his gloves. "Shall we?"

The group set off along the gravel road leading into town,

the chatter of the ladies filling the morning air. He looked around for Charlotte and her friends. He caught Miss Flynn's eye and bowed. Almost immediately, he found himself surrounded by Charlotte and her friends and breathed a sigh of relief.

He did not miss the disapproving glances some of the other women cast in their direction, but he paid them no mind. He was perfectly content with his current company and had no inclination to change it, his mother be damned. He had more on his mind today than this pretense of seeking a betrothal.

Charlotte fell into step beside him, with Felicity next to her and the other ladies behind.

"Did you enjoy your reading?" he asked after casting about for something to say. For some reason, his stomach fluttered a little. He was once again acutely aware that Charlotte was no longer just a girl, but a young woman. She looked pretty in a light blue walking dress and with tendrils of her hair escaping from its bonnet, her cheeks flushed from the summer warmth.

"Erm, yes, thank you," she said, not meeting his eyes. Was something bothering her?

"And the recital yesterday? I trust that went well? I'm sorry that I wasn't there; I had… other matters to attend to." He thought again of the threatening note, and his mood darkened. He was still none the wiser as to who could have discovered his secret, and the knowledge that one of his guests—or servants—was intent on capitalizing on this secret weighed heavily on him.

Charlotte chuckled, and just seeing the dimple in her cheek momentarily lifted his spirits. "It was… as these things usually are. I'm sure your mother enjoyed herself appraising the performers."

Henry laughed, surprised by her subtle sarcasm. Really, Charlotte was quite witty behind that shy demeanor of hers.

Before this season, he realized, they'd never truly conversed as adults without William present. It was a constant surprise how much he enjoyed her company of late. She was kind and intelligent, with a quiet humor that he found refreshing.

Perhaps this walk wouldn't be so bad after all.

The sun shone down on them, and there was a fresh breeze in the air that stopped the day from becoming uncomfortably hot. The walk into town was picturesque along a row of small thatched cottages that mostly belonged to his estate and housed those who rented the land.

He was greeted with genuine smiles as he passed the men and women going about their day, reminding him that if nothing else, he was proving to be a responsible landowner. He kept his rents reasonable and ensured there was no deprivation under his authority.

Was it wrong that he was glad Charlotte was seeing this? As though he had something to prove to her. For some reason, he wanted her to think well of him. With her in step beside him, he could almost forget about the gaggle of ladies behind them.

However, his enjoyment was short-lived. About halfway to town, a trio of ladies managed to maneuver their way to his side, effectively displacing Charlotte and her friends. He vaguely recognized some of them, including a Miss Brighton and Miss Rosalind Smythe, whose mother was a great friend of his own. No doubt the duchess would think Miss Rosalind a suitable bride, whereas Henry found her shallow and rather irritating.

"May we have a turn at your side, Your Grace?" Miss Brighton asked, casting an annoyed glance back at Charlotte and Felicity while Miss Rosalind simpered up at him, dropping him an elegant, practiced curtsey.

"Of course. Forgive my impoliteness. I find I am somewhat stretched thin trying to entertain you all." Henry kept his expression neutral, though irritation flickered through him.

Rosalind laughed as though he had told a particularly funny joke, and he felt a pang of guilt at being so irritated by her. It wasn't the young ladies' fault that he did not wish to wed them or that their own situation made it imperative that they marry soon and well, but some of them were so determined in their attention that he found it exhausting.

He did his best to remain polite, though their insistent attempts at conversation tested his patience.

The exact opposite to how he felt when he spent time with Charlotte Fitzgerald.

"Your Grace, do you find the season agreeable thus far?" Miss Rosalind asked, batting her lashes.

"I cannot say I have given it much thought," he replied evenly, avoiding her too-bold gaze.

"But surely you have attended some fine affairs?" she pressed. "I do love a good ball, I must say."

"Indeed, though I find I prefer quieter company."

"Oh, but so do I," Rosalind said quickly.

Henry sighed inwardly at her about-face on her own preferences. They were all trying so hard to be what they thought he might want. Something Charlotte never seemed to do. She was always so… Charlotte. He glanced back at her and caught her watching them, only to blush and tear her eyes away. A tingle went through him, followed by a flush of warmth.

"Are you well, Your Grace?" Rosalind said pointedly, dragging his attention back to her. "You seem distracted."

"Just a little tired," he murmured, which wasn't exactly a lie.

When they arrived in town, their first stop was the haberdashery. Relief washed over Henry when most of the ladies, including Rosalind, eagerly disappeared inside, their attention fixed on bolts of fabric and ribbons. Charlotte, however, remained outside, lingering with him.

"You do not wish to go in?" he asked, trying to hide that he was quite happy with her company.

She smiled faintly. "I do not require anything today. Besides, I much prefer the fresh air to shopping. I know the other ladies find that strange. Even Miranda likes to shop, though she generally prefers the bookshops."

"It's not strange to me. Shopping for things one needs, I understand, but most young ladies seem to have an amazing propensity to linger for hours over a piece of ribbon or a bonnet."

"You don't like bonnets?" Charlotte asked, patting her own.

Henry was about to hastily reassure her that hers was very pretty when he saw the twinkle in her eye and laughed out loud. "I do believe you're teasing me, Lady Charlotte."

"You make it too easy, Your Grace."

For a moment, their eyes met and something unspoken passed between them—something that Henry did not dare to name. Charlotte was the first to break their joined gaze, looking over the road as though the shops there were of sudden interest.

"It is a very pretty place," she said.

He could not help but agree.

Together, they stood watching the busy street, and in spite of their shared moment a minute or so before, he felt comfortable in her presence. She made a good companion. She was so incredibly easy to be around.

He found himself opening his mouth to tell her so, but just then, a figure emerged from one of the haberdashery shops across the road. He was a portly man, his face shadowed by his hat, Henry barely paid him any mind at first, but beside him, Charlotte suddenly stiffened, and he heard her quick intake of breath.

He turned to look at her and was startled to see a flicker of shock and fear cross her face. Following her gaze, he found it was fixed upon the man, who had crossed the road and was now standing just ahead of them.

Sir Roger.

Henry had never thought much of the man, but after his behavior at the ball, he positively detested him. Henry stepped slightly closer to Charlotte, his posture subtly shifting into one of protectiveness. He could hardly believe the man's audacity when he stepped toward them and bowed as though nothing at all had happened.

He should be hanging his head in disgrace.

Henry's hands curled into fists at his sides. He glared at the man, but Sir Roger's eyes never left Charlotte as he offered the customary pleasantries to them both, giving Henry a bow that Henry pointedly did not return.

Charlotte stammered a reply, stepping closer to Henry. The effect that this man clearly had on her made Henry want to deliver Sir Roger a swift punch to the jaw.

"Sir Roger. I do not believe I have seen you in this part of town before," Henry said coolly, his tone giving away none of his mounting anger.

Sir Roger smiled, though it did not reach his eyes, which were shrewd and calculating. He was up to something. It was no accident that he'd happened upon them.

"I have never had cause to visit before today, Your Grace."

Henry studied him. "And what enticed you to visit today?"

Sir Roger hesitated just long enough for the answer to seem insincere. "A simple errand."

His eyes remained fixed on Charlotte.

Henry's jaw tightened. There was an unsettling air about the man, and he did not like the way Charlotte had clenched her hands together or the way she was wringing her fingers, obviously nervous.

"I must apologize for the, ah, misunderstanding, last time

we met." Leonard gave Charlotte a deep bow. "The gin quite got to me. I assure you I meant no harm, my lady."

"Very well. Let us forget the matter," Charlotte said, but her tone was shaky.

"Provided it does not happen again," Henry snapped.

Sir Roger bowed again, the very picture of contrition. "Of course, Your Grace. I can assure you, I am most mortified by my actions."

Henry didn't reply. He saw no sincerity in the man and quite frankly did not care whether he was sorry or not. He didn't want this man anywhere near Charlotte, and neither would William when he told him of this supposedly chance meeting.

"Might I accompany you?" Sir Roger asked, his tone overly smooth. "A walk in pleasant company is always a delight. I would welcome the chance to redeem myself in your eyes, Lady Charlotte."

Charlotte looked quickly at Henry for support, and Henry did not hesitate. "We are only stopping at the bakery before returning home. There is little point in joining us."

And you will never be redeemed in my *eyes.*

A flicker of anger crossed Sir Roger's face before his expression smoothed again. "I have never seen Your Grace's country estate," he remarked casually, clearly angling for an invitation. "I hear your residence, Arundel Park, is quite something."

Henry did not extend one. Surely the man had not expected to be invited to the house party after what he'd done to Charlotte?

Instead, he turned to Charlotte, completely ignoring Leonard. "Shall we go inside the bakery while we wait for the others? There is a grand selection here, and I'm sure my mother would love a currant loaf."

He offered his arm, and she took it, practically clinging to him. A wave of anger roiled through him as he understood how much the sight of Leonard had upset her.

As they entered the bakery, Henry noted that Sir Roger did not follow but loitered nearby, his eyes never straying far from Charlotte. It was enough to set Henry's nerves on edge, and he glared at the man through the glass until Leonard had finally made his way down the road and out of sight.

They lingered in the shop for a while, Charlotte selecting a few sweet rolls while Henry purchased a loaf of fresh currant bread. They did not speak of Leonard, but he could not help but notice the tension in the way Charlotte moved. The encounter had badly shaken her.

The ladies finally completed their purchases, and they departed the shops, making their way back up the road. Henry was relieved to see no sign of Sir Roger. He hung back from the other ladies, waiting until they were a good distance away before glancing at Charlotte, who remained by his side, her eyes downcast.

"Are you all right, Charlotte?" he asked.

She hesitated. "I… I am not certain. It was quite a shock to see Sir Roger here."

Henry frowned. "What possible reason could he have to be in town? I have never heard of him having acquaintances in this area before."

Charlotte's lips pressed together. "I do not know."

Neither did Henry. But as he walked beside her, a cold unease settled in his chest. He had a dreadful suspicion that Charlotte was the very reason Sir Roger was here. Which meant he was planning something. Henry was afraid to wonder what.

CHAPTER 17

HENRY BARELY WAITED FOR THE LADIES AS HE STORMED BACK to the estate, his boots crunching against the gravel of Arundel Park's drive. The others—including Charlotte and the rest of her party—chattered as they followed at a more leisurely pace, but Henry had little energy for further conversation. His mind was a tangle of worries, one thread leading to another until he could barely make sense of them all.

William. He should tell him about Leonard's arrival and his so-called apology to Charlotte. He hesitated outside the entrance, wondering whether to go and find his friend straight away, but decided he had better clear his head first. He needed to think.

He muttered an excuse about a pressing matter that required his attention and took his leave before anyone could protest. He strode through the grand entrance and down the hall to his office, where he closed the heavy door behind him with a sigh of relief. The momentary silence felt like a balm, but it did little to calm his racing thoughts.

Sir Roger. The very name set his nerves alight. He had to

speak with William, to confide in his old friend and seek counsel on the matter, but first, he needed a moment of solitude. He poured himself a generous measure of brandy and took a sip, letting the warmth spread through him and soothe the edge of his nerves.

It was then that he saw the letter on his desk.

Unsealed. Unaddressed.

His stomach sank. Not another threat.

Frowning, he set his glass down and mentally prepared himself for whatever was inside. With trembling fingers, he unfolded the paper. The words leapt out at him:

Be at the secluded alcove of the grotto at 4:30p.m., or suffer the consequences of your secret being made public.

Henry's pulse quickened, and the room seemed to grow colder. Another note that was meant to blackmail him; no doubt a payout would be demanded in exchange for silence about the secret he guarded so closely.

One of them, anyway.

The blackmailer must be bold to leave such a note so carelessly upon his desk as if certain he would obey.

All thoughts of speaking with William vanished. Henry began to pace, the letter still in hand. He had suspected from the start that whoever was behind the first note sought to leverage his secret for financial gain or, worse, power over him.

What if the mysterious letter writer truly did know the secret of his birth?

His insides chilled at the thought. But surely that was impossible. No one could know. Unless his mother had said something she oughtn't.

But no, she would never. By doing so, she'd suffer under the weight of the scandal almost as much as he would. Perhaps he could ask for her opinion on who it might be, but if this was simply a ploy for money, he did not wish to risk distressing her unnecessarily.

He would see what the villain wanted first.

The minutes dragged until, finally, it was time. Henry donned what he hoped was a neutral expression and made his way to the gardens, keeping a careful eye on his surroundings, watching for observers who may be watching where he was going, looking for a reaction. But the house and gardens were quiet. Following afternoon tea, most of his guests had retired to their rooms or the drawing room.

The grotto where he was to meet the messenger lay at the farthest end of the grounds, secluded by hedges and old oaks. A perfect place for a clandestine meeting.

But before he could reach it, he caught sight of a young woman strolling through the flower garden, alone and unchaperoned. It was a different young lady to the one he had seen in the corridor before the appearance of the first note. His heart lurched. Could there be more than one person in on this scheme?

This did not feel like something a lady would do. Unless it was a spectacularly ruthless ploy to force him into marriage?

But then, who would want to marry into a potential scandal? Certainly not a well-bred society miss. No doubt the woman was just taking the opportunity for some private time with her thoughts—that was certainly something he could understand.

She turned at the sound of his approach, recognition dawning in her eyes. He recognized her as Miss Fairchild. He had scarcely exchanged more than pleasantries with her before today, and that only during their walk into town.

He bowed, hiding a sigh of frustration. Her unexpected presence could cause the messenger to cancel the meeting if they spotted her.

"You are quite far from the house, Miss Fairchild," he remarked, forcing a light tone. "I had assumed everyone would be taking a well-earned rest before dinner."

She offered a small laugh, tucking a loose golden curl

behind her ear and batting her eyelashes as she looked up at him. "My parents insisted I take some air. They said I looked peaked."

Henry frowned. "With no chaperone? Surely they did not suggest you wander around the grounds unaccompanied?"

"Oh!" Miss Fairchild flushed, and her eyes slid away from his.

Was she lying? Perhaps she had a rendezvous planned with one of the other gentlemen?

"Yes, I intended to bring my friend, but she is busy, and I do feel so unwell," Miss Fairchild said in a rush.

He studied her for a moment. Her skin was pink with a healthy glow, and she showed no sign of either fever or fatigue. "You appear perfectly well to me," he said bluntly, hoping his rudeness would cause her to make excuses and leave.

She giggled at that and moved a step closer. "That is kind of you to say, Your Grace."

Henry bit back another sigh. This was the last thing he needed. His every nerve was stretched taut from awaiting his unknown blackmailer, and yet here he was, trapped in idle conversation and a flirtation he most certainly did not welcome.

Charlotte would never be so brash, he thought and then chided himself for the comparison. It wasn't fair to either woman.

"Would you not be more comfortable enjoying the sun from one of the drawing rooms?" he suggested, doing his best to remain patient. "I believe the west sitting room is particularly fine at this hour."

Miss Fairchild hesitated, as if weighing his words, before fluttering her lashes once again in what she no doubt thought was a fetching manner. "But the gardens are ever so lovely at this time of day, are they not? I adore the scent of the roses."

As though to prove her point, she rose to smell a bloom on the nearby trellis, angling her decolletage at him. He quickly looked away.

Struggling to maintain his composure, Henry resisted the urge to glance over his shoulder toward the grotto. Every passing second increased his risk of missing the meeting and finding out who his blackmailer was and what they wanted. It seemed he would simply have to directly request that Miss Fairchild leave the garden. Scandalously rude, but effective. His mother would be horrified at such treatment of a guest, but what choice did he have?

Before he could do so, however, a rustling of skirts and low murmurs reached his ears. The arrival of a chaperone for Miss Fairchild, perhaps? He turned, plastering on a polite smile, accepting with a sinking of his stomach that he was not going to meet his mysterious correspondent this evening.

A group of women were approaching along the garden path leading to the grotto, obviously having decided on an early evening walk. They were mothers, mostly, though there were a few young ladies among them.

Including Charlotte.

Henry's stomach dropped as he caught the flicker of surprise and disappointment in her gaze, as she looked from him to Miss Fairchild and back again. There was a question in her eyes, and he realized what this must look like. Especially as Miss Fairchild discreetly took a step closer toward him.

He had done nothing wrong, and yet he felt inexplicably guilty under Charlotte's scrutiny. As though he had betrayed something unspoken between them.

Miss Fairchild's mother was among the group, and the moment she laid eyes upon them, she let out a sharp gasp. "Harriet!" she exclaimed, unnecessarily loudly. "What are you doing out here alone?"

"We were merely conversing, Mother," Miss Fairchild replied, a tinge of color in her cheeks.

She didn't sound at all convincing, and Henry started to wonder if the entire thing had been staged. Miss Fairchild could have seen him leaving by the side door and cut him off near the grotto.

Lady Fairchild cast a swift glance between them, her expression shifting from shock to something more calculating as her eyes rested on Henry.

"Oh, Your Grace," she gasped, a bejeweled hand flying to her ample bosom, "I do hope this is not a… compromising situation."

Henry stiffened. "Certainly not, madam. I was out for a walk and came across Miss Fairchild quite unexpectedly. She says she feels unwell. I was just advising her that it is unseemly for her to be here without a chaperone. She said it was *your* idea for her to take a walk. Alone."

Some of the other mothers exchanged knowing looks. It was clear that for Lady Fairchild, this was an opportunity rather than a true scandal. If she could claim her daughter had been alone with the duke, even for a moment, then there was a hint of impropriety. And with just a shadow of doubt, she might well push for a match. Refusing would make Henry look like the worst kind of rake.

He looked pleadingly at Charlotte, silently praying that she could see what was happening here. But she was avoiding his eyes, her complexion pale.

The other women in the group were not so easily swayed. One of the older ladies, Lady Withersby, shook her head sharply, glaring at Lady Fairchild. "I daresay nothing untoward has occurred. It *is* rather warm today. I should think Miss Fairchild merely wished to enjoy the breeze if she feels unwell. And really, Mary." Lady Withersby sniffed disapprovingly. "You should not be so remiss as to allow her to wander around willy-nilly, unaccompanied."

Lady Fairchild opened and closed her mouth like a fish. The Withersbys were above her in the social pecking order—third cousins to the royal family—and there was little she could say.

Henry silently thanked the older lady for rescuing him.

Another woman, no doubt eager to keep her own daughters in the running, nodded. "Indeed. Lady Withersby is right. Besides, His Grace has confirmed that he only just came across Miss Fairchild. They are scarcely alone with us here in attendance."

For a moment, a silent battle waged in the air, but eventually, Lady Fairchild relented. "Yes.… Yes, of course. Apologies, Your Grace. I am glad no misunderstanding has arisen."

Henry resisted the urge to sigh in relief, instead nodding curtly at the Fairchild women. "If you will excuse me, ladies," he said, inclining his head, "I have an appointment I must keep." He risked a glance at Charlotte, but she had already turned her back and was walking briskly away.

There was no choice but to try to speak to her another time. Right now he had more pressing business.

He turned and walked quickly toward the grotto, hoping desperately that he had not missed his chance. But when he reached the designated spot, there was, as he expected, no one waiting. No shadowed figure lurked in the alcove. There was no whisper of movement among the trees.

If the blackmailer had ever been here, they weren't now.

Henry cursed under his breath. Once again he had missed his chance to unravel this mystery.

His pulse hammered as he scanned the area, but it was clear that whoever had called him here was gone. Assuming they had ever intended to appear at all. He had to face the possibility that the author of the anonymous notes was simply playing with him, toying with him as a cat would a mouse.

Dread settled deep in his chest at the thought. If this was

part of some wider plan to torment him, then what would they do next?

CHAPTER 18

HENRY WAS AGAIN PACING IN HIS OAK-PANELED OFFICE, EACH measured step echoing softly on the polished floor as he tried to determine who the hell was behind the strange notes.

The room was dimly lit by the evening sun streaming through the tall windows, and the quiet was broken only by the rustle of papers and the occasional tick of the mantel clock. His mind, however, was anything but calm. He kept replaying the events of the day—the arrival of Leonard, the new note, Lady Fairchild's plan, and Charlotte's obvious distress.

Who among his guests or staff could have learned his secret?

He stopped before his desk, glancing at the note lying there. He had no need to unfold it again. Its words were still etched in his mind:

Be at the secluded alcove of the grotto at 4:30p.m., or suffer the consequences of your secret being made public.

Henry frowned and ran a hand through his dark hair as he made a mental list of the house's current residents. He did his best to recall every furtive look exchanged between certain servants and each whispered remark among guests.

For a fleeting moment, a disquieting thought crossed his mind: Might his own mother be behind this? Some kind of convoluted plan to blackmail him into a marriage? But he quickly dismissed it. The dowager duchess was as prudent as she was fierce. She would never commit to paper something that might provoke unwanted inquiry—especially not when she faced dangers of her own.

A gentle knock sounded at the door. Henry paused, but he didn't answer immediately. His mind was too absorbed, and he wanted to be alone with his thoughts. Another, more insistent knock resounded, and finally, with a reluctant sigh, he set aside his thoughts and opened the door.

There, framed in the doorway with concern etched on his face, stood William.

"Henry, you look absolutely dreadful," William said, stepping into the room and closing the door behind him. "I could see you weren't yourself at dinner. Is something disturbing you?"

Henry attempted a strained smile as he leaned against the desk. "I'm fine, Will. Merely preoccupied," he lied, though his hand automatically swept down across his face, a gesture that betrayed his distress to the man who knew him better than any other.

William said nothing but raised a knowing eyebrow.

After a moment, Henry slumped into one of the high-backed chairs. "In truth, I am far from well."

William's forehead furrowed as he pulled a chair closer and sat opposite him, leaning forward. "I thought as much. Tell me what troubles you so. I could hear you pacing the room like a caged animal as I was walking up the corridor."

Henry hesitated, then slowly retrieved a decanter and two glasses from a side table. "I received a note today," he said as he began pouring. "An anonymous letter threatening to make public a secret that, if revealed, would ruin everything." He paused, letting the gravity of his words sink in. "It demanded that I appear at a secluded alcove in the grotto at 4:30p.m."

William's eyes widened, and he sat back in his chair as the news sank in. "Blackmail, then? They wish to force you to pay up, I suspect, or at least to compel some concession. This is the secret you were referring to that day at the club, I take it?"

Henry passed one glass to William and swirled the brandy in his own as if seeking clarity in its amber depths. "Exactly so. I've been trying to think who might have known. Could it be one of our guests, a servant, or even someone from another household entirely, paying someone else?" He let out a heavy sigh and collapsed onto his chair. "I've reviewed every face, each whisper from this morning, yet I can't pinpoint the culprit. Or how they could possibly know… the things I need to keep hidden."

Although William was too much of a good friend to ask him to reveal his secret, Henry could see the naked curiosity on the other man's face.

William leaned forward, lowering his voice so that only Henry could hear, just in case any eavesdroppers potentially lurked outside. "You don't have any suspicions at all? Not a name, nor a hint?"

"Not with any certainty. It makes absolutely no sense. No one in our set, except for my mother and I, should possibly know a thing. I even considered—just for a moment—the possibility that Mother might be involved, but then I dismissed it. She would never put our family in such jeopardy."

A long silence stretched between them as they both nursed their glasses. Finally, William broke the quiet. "Henry, you once mentioned that the secret your dukedom holds is something so perilous that you'd never allow it to see the light. Assuming the messenger refers to this same secret—are the consequences of it being revealed so very catastrophic? Is it not simply a scandal you could weather with time?"

Henry's jaw tightened. "I fear not. If it were simply that, you know I would confide in you, William. No, it would be catastrophic indeed." His voice dropped to a harsh whisper. "I dare not mention it further, but you know how precarious my situation is."

William's expression grew grave as he set his glass down. "Have you any thus far unconscious inkling of who might know? Think hard. Have there been no strange looks or murmured slights? Could it be one of your own staff who has access to your private affairs, or perhaps a guest who has been watching you with unusual interest?"

Henry's eyes darkened as he considered the possibilities. "I've observed a few suspicious glances among the servants this morning. There were murmured conversations among the guests as well—discreet, but enough to set me on edge. Yet I cannot say for certain. Guests will gossip, after all. They are likely talking about no more than the usual. I have been scouring my memory for anything strange, but…. Oh."

William sat up straighter. "There is something, then?"

"I doubt it is in any way related—he doesn't have the connections to discover such intrigue—but I saw Sir Roger in town this morning. He apologized to Charlotte, who was most unsettled."

That was an understatement, he thought, recalling her distress at the sight of the man.

William frowned, and his eyes darkened with barely concealed anger. "Sir Roger in town? That is indeed strange. What business does he have here?"

Henry took a swig of his drink. "Yes, we saw him in the high street, unaccountably far from his usual haunts. None of his family hold property here, yet there he was, as if summoned. He mentioned an errand but was incredibly vague about it. It troubles me, especially since he still seems keen on getting close to Charlotte."

William bristled visibly. "After he tried to dishonor her! He's lucky I didn't challenge him to a duel, the odious little fool. You think he came here seeking her?"

Henry grimaced at the thought. "He was most keen to apologize to her—as he should. But his sincerity was a sham. He had the cheek to hint at an invitation to Arundel Park as well."

"The windbag! How dare he? You don't think he has anything to do with these messages?"

"I doubt it," Henry admitted. "He has no access to the grounds, and I doubt he is well-liked enough—or rich enough—to convince a servant to betray me or to draw another of the *ton* into an intrigue. No, I think Leonard is a separate matter."

"Still, his presence adds another layer of complication. At least for Charlotte."

Henry nodded. "I cannot fathom any other genuine reason for his presence. It appears to me that he might be maneuvering for some advantage with her. And if he intends to target Charlotte, then we must take steps to ensure she is never left alone in his path—"

Henry cut himself off as he saw that William was watching him keenly, perhaps intrigued by his display of protectiveness. He wondered what William might think if he knew that Henry harbored increasingly less than brotherly sentiments toward his friend's dear sister.

It was something he must ensure did not become obvious —not just because of William, but also because the last thing he needed was for the blackmailer to suspect that he cared more for her than his duty. He had no idea how dangerous this person may be.

A heavy silence fell, during which Henry felt increasingly agitated over the events of the day.

William, ever the steady presence, finally spoke. "Henry, we must keep our eyes and ears open. Help me protect Charlotte—she must not be left alone if Leonard remains in the vicinity—and I will watch to see if anyone is behaving suspiciously. We can assist each other."

"Thank you." Henry was grateful to have such a stalwart friend.

They drank without speaking for a time, both pondering the problems and mysteries now in front of them. Henry's head was pounding, and his shoulders were heavy with the weight of the day's cares.

"Tell me," he said as a thought struck him. "You have heard nothing untoward about me? No hint of gossip?"

William cocked his head. "I have heard nothing about you, and of course I would have told you if I had. Don't let this make you overly suspicious; jumping at shadows in every corner." His voice lowered further. "I trust you have measures in place to guard this secret and that nothing has happened that could have allowed it to come out?"

Henry shook his head and sighed heavily. "I believe I have done all that is required. And yet, I cannot shake the feeling that I've missed something." He looked at William with a pained expression. "I'm mistrustful, you're right—but only because I do not know what I will do if they succeed in exposing me."

William reached across the desk and clasped Henry's hand in a gesture of solidarity. "We will face it together, as we always have. I know you don't wish to confide in me, for reasons I do not know, but I am here to support you, nonetheless. Whatever the outcome, I will ensure you aren't left to bear the burden alone."

Henry swallowed, his throat tight. "I am grateful, William. Truly, your friendship means more to me than words can express." His eyes lingered for a moment on his friend's face before he forced himself to look away as he felt a pang of guilt. Guilt for the secrets he had kept for so long, and for his ever-complicated feelings about Charlotte.

A long, heavy silence settled in the office. The only sound was the ticking clock and the occasional sip of brandy.

Eventually, William rose from his chair. "I must take my leave now. Mother will expect me to escort her to bridge. But do keep me informed. And if you notice anything amiss—any hint that your adversaries are drawing nearer—promise me you will not delay in confiding in me. In this at least, you do not have to be alone."

Henry nodded gravely. "I promise. Again, thank you."

Left alone, Henry slumped back into his chair, the silence of the room pressing upon him like a shroud. William's words could have comforted him, but instead, all he could think of was if his secrets were exposed, he might lose the trust of his best friend.

And then there was Charlotte. He pictured her gentle smile as she walked by his side that morning and the fleeting comfort of her presence—and he felt a deep rush of emotion.

But it was an emotion he couldn't allow himself to feel. Even if William would approve a match, he could not be with her. Couldn't bring her into this turmoil.

He fell into a gloomy reverie and was unsure of how much time had passed when his mother's footsteps sounded from the corridor.

She swept into his room, oblivious to his dark mood. "Henry, you are hiding here again. Has no one caught your eye yet?" Her tone was deceptively light, but her eyes were narrow.

Henry hesitated, his mind racing. He had neither the time nor inclination for another argument with his mother, so he needed to stall. "There is potential with a few young ladies, I suppose," he answered cautiously, careful not to reveal the identity of the young lady of whom that was true. "But I would get to know my prospects better before I commit to a course of action."

He winced at his own phrasing, implying that he was sizing up his female guests as though they were a business transaction, and indeed, to most of his contemporaries, marriage was just that.

His mother looked pleased. "I'm glad. I knew you would come around to my way of thinking."

Clearly satisfied, she had turned to leave when Henry had a sudden thought. William had asked him if there were any way things that had long been kept concealed could have gotten out, and he had said no—but he was not the only one concealing them.

"Mother," he said urgently, "is there any way someone might have learned the truth of my birth?" He was surprised to find he was unable to hide the tremor in his voice.

His mother looked momentarily shocked before her face returned to its usual stern mask. "No, of course not. That is a secret best kept, and I assure you no one will discover it."

He drew in a deep breath, steeling himself to face her disapproval. "What of the man who sired me?"

She shook her head. "As far as he is concerned, there is nothing to worry about. He is gone. I promise you, this matter will not hold back your impending betrothal."

She left his room without another word.

Henry stared at the door for a moment, his stomach churning and his blood cold. His mother had spoken with conviction, but he'd seen her brief flicker of doubt. Was his biological father dead? He had no idea what else she could mean by "gone." Had something nefarious happened?

Unfortunately, since she was so certain of their safety, he strongly doubted she would tell him anything.

CHAPTER 19

SLEEP REFUSED TO COME AS CHARLOTTE LAY IN HER PINK-quilted bed, the moonlight from the small, high windows casting gentle silver patterns across the wooden floor. Her thoughts were consumed by Sir Roger.

It had been so dreadfully unexpected to see him appear that morning. His sudden presence and his arrogant air had unsettled her. Worse still was the memory of the garden encounter, when Henry had been seen with that Fairchild woman.

A sharp pain of jealousy pierced her heart. She had believed that they'd been drawing closer over the past few days. Now, she wondered if, despite his protests to the contrary, his attention had shifted elsewhere. He had been oddly distracted and she'd put it down to his discomfort of the situation they'd found themselves in, but perhaps that wasn't the case.

Unable to bear another restless minute, Charlotte swung her legs over the edge of the bed and slipped into a long, soft robe. She moved quietly through the dim light of her room and made her way to the library. She'd finished the book she had been reading the other night and now sought further distraction among the rows of leather-bound volumes.

A good library, with its rich scent of old paper and polished wood, had long been her refuge from the tumult of social expectation.

It was eerily quiet in the house as she moved through it, and the creak of the library door as she entered sounded like a scream in the silence. She perused the shelves, her fingers grazing the spines of the books, until a subtle noise from the corridor caught her attention. It was a muffled shuffle, the sound of hesitant footsteps. Had she awakened someone?

Tense, Charlotte set her book aside and crept toward the door. Peeking out, she was startled to see Henry stumbling slowly down the corridor, his usually measured gait replaced by a disordered, unsteady step. His features were slack, and a faint flush colored his cheeks.

He was drunk.

"Your Grace?" she called softly, concerned.

He paused, blinking as if emerging from a fog. "Charlotte," he managed, his tone slurred, "I fear I have had too much to drink." He hiccupped, and then put his hand over his mouth in horror.

Stifling a smile at his expression, Charlotte reached out and gently took his arm. "Come along, then. Let's get you sat down."

She guided him away from the corridor. Once inside the quiet library, she eased him into one of the overstuffed chairs by a low table and fetched him a cup of water from a nearby stand. As she helped him settle, Charlotte realized with a start that their being alone together in the library was far from proper conduct for an unmarried lady, especially as she was in her nightclothes.

She shouldn't have taken his arm and led him into a room on their own. It was not just improper but positively scandalous. Yet, when she'd seen him in the corridor, she'd cared little for such conventions. Her sole concern had been Henry's welfare.

She chastised herself silently. Unlike some of the other girls and their mothers, she had no intention of cornering him in order to force him into a marriage with her. But she couldn't bear to see him so low, stumbling like a lost child.

"Henry," she began gently, "where have you been? Has something untoward occurred this evening? Were you among the men in your office?"

No doubt there had been a raucous gathering once they were away from the women.

He rubbed his eyes with trembling fingers. "No, I remained in my office. I drank alone for the most part, lost myself in my thoughts, and then... I don't rightly remember much more than that. I was going somewhere..."

His words tumbled out in a disjointed murmur, and he began to ramble about vague threats and warnings. His voice, normally steady and controlled, now carried a tremor of disquiet that sent a shiver down Charlotte's spine.

"Tell me what's troubling you. Can I help?" She leaned forward so that he could see the concern in her eyes. Not that he was focusing very well.

He hesitated, dropping a few scattered comments that made little sense: a reference to a meeting, to an appointment, to something he could not articulate fully. His gaze drifted, and his voice grew quieter until, with a frustrated sigh, he fell silent.

Sensing that no further answer was forthcoming, Charlotte resolved that she mustn't press him any longer. Whatever was bothering him, it was something he couldn't—or shouldn't—tell her.

"Very well," she said, standing up. "You are too unsteady to remain here. Let me escort you to your bedroom, at least, so you can rest properly."

Henry nodded, obedient as a child. She had never seen

him like this, so utterly vulnerable, and it tugged at her heart strings.

He managed a weak smile as she steadied his arm, supporting him as they walked down the hushed corridor. Every step echoed in the silence of the mansion, making her wince.

Please don't let us be seen, she prayed silently, dreading the uproar that could cause.

Once they reached his chamber, Charlotte carefully helped him out of his boots and removed his jacket, though she left the rest of his clothes on, respecting both his modesty and hers. At the threshold of his bed, Henry sank down and, seemingly without conscious thought, collapsed onto the mattress.

For a moment, Charlotte hesitated. She knew she should leave him to his rest, but a pang of worry held her back. What if he grew too cold, or worse, fell deeper into his stupor? She had heard of inebriated men dying in their sleep.

Resolutely, she squared her shoulders. "I cannot leave you like this. Let me at least see to your comfort."

Gently, she draped a spare blanket over him, tucking it around his shoulders, and placed a pillow under his head. Only then, with a final, tender glance at his still-troubled features, did she leave him to rest.

On her way back to her own room, Charlotte heard footsteps coming toward her in the corridor and froze. What could she say as to why she was wandering around upstairs? She breathed a sigh of relief when she saw it was only William.

"Charlotte? What on earth are you doing up here?"

"I… couldn't sleep," she mumbled. For a brief moment, she debated not telling her brother what had transpired, but decided it was best he knew. At least then someone could check on Henry.

"Is anyone bothering you?" William narrowed his eyes.

"No, no," she assured him quickly. "But…"

"But what?" William demanded, every inch the protective older brother.

Rather more so than usual, she thought, wondering what was wrong with him. Was it related to whatever had caused Henry to get into such a state?

"William," she said patiently. "I'm fine. I really was just restless. But I found Henry in the corridor a short while ago. He seemed quite inebriated, and so I helped him back to his room. I am very worried about his state."

William's brow furrowed, but he didn't look surprised. "I shall check on him shortly. I expect he will merely wake with a headache and a world of regret come morning." His tone was worried as he asked, "Were you alone with him? In his room?"

Charlotte's heart stuttered, and she wondered how best to reply. If she admitted to being alone with him, it could cause an incredible scandal. Yes, this was just William, but the way he was looking down at her made her realize that he was not taking this lightly. They weren't children anymore.

She bit her lip before replying, "Yes, brother. And I know it looks terrible and that I should have called for a servant, but… he seemed so sorry for himself. My only thought was to get him safely to his chambers. I'm sorry."

William's eyes narrowed slightly, but then he sighed. "Charlotte, you must be cautious. You're too kindhearted for your own good. An unmarried woman should not find herself alone with a gentleman in such circumstances."

Charlotte's cheeks burned. "I did not intend any impropriety, only to help a friend in distress. It's Henry, after all—"

He cut her off with a shake of his head. "Friend or not, Henry is still unmarried. You must exercise restraint. It is your duty to be proper."

Charlotte scowled, trying not to show the prickle of hurt

she felt at the unexpected tone he was taking with her. "I understand."

Despite her outward calm, inside she seethed. Not at William, but the rules and restraints she constantly found herself under. It wasn't fair that she was restricted in so many ways.

Back in her own room, Charlotte lay on her bed for a long time, the events of the evening swirling in her mind. The image of Henry, so troubled and inebriated, mingled with the strange, tender awkwardness of being alone with him. Her thoughts also turned repeatedly to Sir Roger and how furious Henry had seemed at his appearance. Had Henry been more affected by that encounter than she realized? Did he truly care for her?

But then what was she to make of the garden incident, when he'd been alone with Harriet Fairchild? Or was Charlotte reading too much into that because her feelings for him were clouding her judgment?

As far as she could recall, he had not been particularly close to Harriet in the garden, nor had he worn that gentle smile she knew so well. Instinct told her that Henry had simply been caught unawares by a young lady vying for his attention, but the memory gnawed at her, a painful reminder that she may not have secured his affections as fully as he had hers.

CHAPTER 20

Henry sat at the breakfast table, nursing a cup of strong tea and doing his best to ignore the dull, relentless pounding in his skull.

"Are you joining us for the hunt this morning, Arundel?" Lord Eastbourne asked, cutting into a thick slice of ham.

Henry tried to focus on the other man's words, but the effects of last night's brandy lingered like a particularly irate ghost, and even the clatter of dishes and idle chatter around him set his teeth on edge.

"It should be a fine day for it," Eastbourne continued. "I believe our best riders are attending, so it should be quite the challenge."

The scent of freshly baked bread and warm butter, usually a comfort, turned Henry's stomach. He could hardly fathom how he'd feel if gunshots were to ring in his ears.

"Unfortunately, I must decline," he said smoothly, setting his cup down. "I have other matters to attend to."

Eastbourne shrugged. "As you will. Although I must say, old chap, considering this is your house party, you've been less than sociable so far."

Henry grimaced. He felt too rotten to even do the

expected thing and assure Eastbourne he meant no offense. Instead, he shrugged and grabbed his teacup again.

Luckily, Eastbourne took note of his expression and laughed instead. "Too much brandy, is it? You do have some fine liquor here, I must say."

Henry forced himself to smile. He'd been drinking too much, a consequence of his current troubles. Last night, the clear brown liquor had felt like his only escape.

As Eastbourne turned back to his companions, William, seated beside Henry, arched a brow. "Since when do you pass on an opportunity to escape the houseful of ladies?"

Henry shot him a meaningful look, remembering their agreement to ensure Charlotte wasn't left vulnerable to an unexpected encounter with Sir Roger.

"Since now," he muttered back.

William arched an eyebrow but said nothing more.

Moments later, Charlotte and Felicity entered the breakfast room late. They must have been walking outside, as their faces were bright from the fresh morning air. Charlotte's gown, a soft shade of blue that made her eyes seem almost luminous, was simple yet elegant. Her hair was pinned neatly, though a few loose tendrils had escaped to frame her face. She waved at her friends, who were seated across the room.

Even in his befuddled state, the sight of her lifted Henry's spirits, and he sat up straight as she walked in their direction. She made her way toward him, her gaze lingering on him for a beat longer than necessary before she took the seat across from him and helped herself to tea. With William next to them, he tried not to let show just how pleasant it was to have her near.

"We're going on a walk to the folly this morning," she announced, stirring sugar into her tea. "I don't suppose we'll see either of you there?"

"I'm going hunting," William announced. "But Henry here

looks as though he could use a gentle walk. You were certainly the worse for wear last night." He lowered his voice on the last sentence and looked at his sister, who blushed and avoided his eyes.

Henry groaned into his teacup, as he had a vague recollection of speaking to Charlotte the previous evening. Had he come across her last night when he had been wandering the halls, addled by brandy?

An awful thought struck him. Had he revealed anything he shouldn't?

Henry turned to Charlotte. "Actually, I believe I shall. I could use the fresh air, as William says, and I am most decidedly not in the best condition for a hunt."

Charlotte smiled at him with mischief glinting in her eyes, and for a moment, he found himself catching his breath as their gazes met. Flustered, knowing William was watching, he quickly excused himself.

"I shall see you outside the front hall after everyone has changed into their walking clothes, my lady," he said, bowing politely to Charlotte and then to Felicity before walking away.

Midmorning, he joined the ladies where they were gathered outside, having prepared for their walk. The morning sun cast long, golden streaks across the manicured gardens, the scent of roses and freshly turned earth filling the air. The grounds made such a pretty picture that Henry could almost forget his current cares.

Almost.

His stomach sank as he saw the ladies gathered close to Felicity and Charlotte, including their friends and a few others, and realized that he was unlikely to get Charlotte on her own—at least not in a way that would go unnoticed— during this walk.

As the women curtsied and simpered at him, he fancied that he could feel the weight of their expectations pressing down on him. Their eyes tracked his every movement, eager and assessing. For a moment, he wished he had braved the hunt.

He quickly fell in beside Charlotte and Felicity, who, to his amusement, was casting sharp glances at another pair of ladies. They set off down the path, the folly visible in the distance, a small, elegant ruin atop a gentle slope. The morning sun was mellow, the breeze mild, and Henry was just beginning to relax when Charlotte stumbled beside him.

With a sharp gasp, she fell forward. Henry caught her before she hit the ground, steadying her with both hands.

"Are you all right, my lady?" he asked, concern furrowing his brow. "That was quite a tumble."

She winced as she tested her foot, yelping as soon as she tried to put any weight on it. "I—I think I rolled my ankle."

Immediately, the other women crowded in, expressions ranging from concern to irritation.

Felicity stepped in their way, tilting her head up at Henry. "She should rest and get that looked at. Could you escort her back to the house, Your Grace? I'm sure the other ladies will join me on my walk."

Henry shot Felicity a look of gratitude and seized the opportunity before the other women could contradict her. "Excellent idea. As your host, I must indeed insist that I shall escort her back. We wouldn't want her further injuring herself." He met Charlotte's gaze and held out his arm. "Shall we?"

Charlotte hesitated only briefly before nodding. Henry placed her arm over his, supporting her as they turned away from the group.

"Wait!" Miss Harriet Fairchild protested. "What of a chaperone?"

Henry stopped cold. That was a very valid point. One he had not considered in his eagerness to spend time with Charlotte away from the others.

Miranda stepped forward. "I will accompany them back. I have been reading the most fascinating treatise on local orchid varietals and will gladly return to it early."

Henry smiled at her. "That would be most welcome, Miss Sutton."

The disgruntled stares of the other young ladies burned into his back as the three of them split off from the group, but he hardly cared, although he did feel faintly guilty that he was able to take the opportunity to accompany Charlotte only because she had injured herself.

As they made their slow way toward the house, Miranda immediately dropped behind them, as if she were a maid performing chaperone duties. It was slightly unusual but Henry was grateful for the privacy. He cleared his throat, wondering how to broach the subject of his drunken evening.

"Charlotte, about last night..." he murmured, too softly for Miranda to hear.

She peered up at him, her lips twisting slightly in amusement, although he could also see concern flickering in her eyes. If only he could remember what he'd said to her.

"Yes?"

"I wanted to apologize. I hope I wasn't in any way inappropriate."

Her brows knitted together. "So, you recall seeing me?"

"Not entirely," he admitted, shamefaced. "I remember... shadows of it. Talking to you in the corridor near my room." He stopped as he recalled that he couldn't remember getting into bed or taking off his boots—which had been neatly placed near the bed when he awoke that morning. "You helped me to my room, didn't you?" He pressed his hand over his eyes, utterly embarrassed.

She nodded, shifting her weight slightly against him. "Yes. I did. You were... rather inebriated, and I couldn't leave you for one of your other guests to find. But you said—and did—

nothing inappropriate, Your Grace. You can rest assured of that."

Relief curled in his stomach. "Then I owe you my thanks as well as my apologies. I received some unpleasant news yesterday, and I fear I didn't handle it well."

She hesitated. "May I ask what news?"

He exhaled, unwilling to burden her as he had William, in spite of the fact that he instinctively knew that he could trust Charlotte just as much as he could her brother. "Nothing that need concern you. I was simply… preoccupied."

Her frown deepened, but she didn't press him further. Instead, she limped a little more heavily, and he carefully tightened his grip on her waist to keep her steady.

"Oh, my!" Miranda exclaimed from behind them. "This is a green-winged orchid."

They turned to face her.

She adjusted her spectacles and straightened from where she was bent over a delicate purple flower. "Would you mind overly if we were to delay for a few minutes while I examine the orchid? I was reading about this particular species only this morning."

"Of course, you must," Henry insisted. A thought struck him. "There is a bench by the lake only a couple of hundred yards away. Do you see it?"

Both women looked around, shielding their eyes against the sun.

"I see it," Miranda confirmed.

"Charlotte could use a rest. We shall retire to the bench to rest until you are finished." He glanced at Charlotte. "If that's acceptable to you?"

She nodded. "That would be nice, Your Grace."

He escorted her to the bench, taking as much of her weight as he could. Once they arrived, he helped her sit down and then settled beside her. He found himself stealing glances of her more than he ought to, noting the way the sunlight danced on her hair and her lashes fluttered against her cheeks as she looked out at the water. It was unsettling, this growing consciousness of her, an acute awareness of every detail of the way she looked, the way she moved.

She turned her head and caught him looking at her, her eyes wide and innocent. He couldn't help himself; his gaze dropped to those full, pink lips.

"Your Grace?" Something like hope flared in her eyes.

He wanted to kiss her. So very badly.

She looked back at him, her eyes soft, her breath uneven. Her cheeks were flushed and her pink lips softly parted.

Her mouth was barely inches from his.

A deep, dangerous hunger surged within him, sweeping away all of his usual iron self-control. Before he could think better of it, he brushed his fingers along her jaw, tilting her chin just slightly so that he raised her face to his. She was holding her breath, staring up at him in wide-eyed wonder. He hesitated, giving her the chance to pull away, but she didn't.

Instead, her eyes fluttered closed as she tipped her face farther up to his. Her lips parted a little more in anticipation, and he could hold back no longer.

He kissed her, crushing his mouth against hers, feeling a wild desire rise up in him to have her, to make her his. But he forced himself to slow down, to be gentle with her. Charlotte melted into him, gripping his coat tightly.

It was a slow, lingering kiss, filled with something unspoken that had been simmering beneath the surface for far longer than Henry had ever allowed himself to be conscious of. But now it all came bursting into awareness.

God, he *needed* this woman. The world shrank to just this —the scent of her, the softness of her lips, the warmth of her body against his. Time seemed to stand still, and everything else was forgotten. There was just him, and Charlotte.

Then a sharp voice from behind him shattered the moment, ringing through the soft summer air.

"What the hell do you think you're doing?"

William stood a short distance away, a rifle over his shoulder, and his expression thunderous.

CHARLOTTE TOOK A DEEP, SHAKY BREATH, HER HEART pounding in her chest as her gaze darted from Henry to William and back again. She could still feel the press of Henry's lips against hers, the warmth of his touch, the way time had slowed in that perfect, breathtaking moment.

He had kissed her. *Henry had kissed her.* And then...

This.

William stood rigid on the bank, glaring at both of them, his mouth hanging open in shock. His rifle was still slung over his shoulder, and his grip on it looked dangerously tight. His focus narrowed on Henry, sharp and furious. Charlotte swallowed hard as Henry leapt to his feet and stepped slightly in front of her as though to shield her should William decide to use that gun.

But she knew it would never be *her* that her brother shot at.

"What on earth is going on?" Miranda called from farther back. "William? What is the matter?"

Charlotte briefly closed her eyes. Darling Miranda must have been so distracted by the plant life that she hadn't noticed the kiss. When Miranda drew near, Charlotte held up her hand to stay her and slowly got to her feet.

"Put the gun down, William," she said, forcing her voice to remain steady even as her whole body trembled.

"I don't think I will," William replied, his voice clipped. "I'm still deciding whether I want to use it." He didn't look at Charlotte as he spoke. His eyes were still boring into Henry.

Charlotte's stomach twisted. She had seen William angry before and knew he could be quick-tempered when provoked, but this was different. This was a cold, sharp, deliberate fury. It terrified her, especially with him gripping that rifle.

Henry took a step toward William, raising his hands as though to placate him. "This isn't what it looks like, I assure you."

The words hit her with the force of a slap. Charlotte stared at Henry's profile, but he wouldn't look back at her.

It wasn't what it looked like?

Then what was it?

A mistake? A lapse in judgment?

For her, that kiss had been something she'd dreamed of for longer than she cared to admit, but for Henry it apparently hadn't meant much at all. She looked from him to William, and fury scorched through her veins. She met Miranda's eyes and noted the confusion there but now wasn't the time to explain.

William's eyes darkened at Henry's words. "Is that so?" His voice dripped with skepticism. "Because to me, Your *Grace*, it looks an awful lot like you had your hands all over my sister."

Miranda's eyes widened. Charlotte's cheeks burned, and she tried to calm herself, to remember that she didn't actually want to smack her brother or Henry.

Miranda started forward but Charlotte motioned for her

to stop. She didn't want her friend to be at risk while William was so clearly furious.

"William," she began, stepping forward to intervene.

"Do not try to defend him, Charlotte," he interrupted. "How long has this been going on? How long has this rake been taking advantage of you and how far have you allowed him to go?"

Her jaw dropped. Did he honestly believe that they'd been sneaking around behind his back? If so, how could she make him see that nothing had been going on before this? That until today, she hadn't even dared to believe Henry saw her as anything more than William's little sister?

But of course he would react this way. If anyone else were to find out what had happened between them today, she would be utterly ruined. Even that cretin Sir Roger would consider her beneath him.

Before she could figure out what on earth to say, another horrible thought occurred to her. "Where are the other gentlemen?" If William was here, then surely the rest of the hunting party were close behind. "Is the hunt coming this way?"

William's gaze flicked to her, his jaw still tight and the pulse at his temple throbbing. "Lord Fairweather was feeling ill and decided to return to the house for lunch," he said. "I rode back with him and then walked this way to catch up to both of you and the other ladies. And thank the heavens I did, or how much more damage would you have done to my sister's reputation?"

Charlotte exhaled roughly. At least the rest of their houseguests were not here to witness this altercation. Things weren't quite *that* bad.

"Miranda was present," she said stiffly. "Nothing would have progressed further."

William snorted. "Miranda was paying more attention to the flowers than the world around her, as usual."

Miranda flinched, and Charlotte narrowed her eyes at her brother's unkind words.

"I meant Charlotte no harm," Henry said finally, drawing William's attention back to him. "I would never seek to disgrace her. She turned her ankle. I was escorting her back, accompanied by Miss Sutton. Charlotte needed rest so we sat and… I never intended harm, you must believe me."

William made a scoffing noise. "Please, Henry. I saw you kissing her. Do me the courtesy of not lying so brazenly to my face."

Henry sighed and gave a curt nod. "I went too far. We shared a moment, and I could not help myself. The fault is mine, not Charlotte's."

Charlotte stiffened. *A moment.* That was all. As if it had been some fleeting, inconsequential thing. As if it hadn't set her entire world spinning.

William let out a short, humorless laugh. "A moment? That won't do. You cannot expect me to forget about this."

He took a step closer to them both, still gripping his gun. "So, I assume if you're willing to go around kissing unmarried ladies where anyone could see, then that means you've resolved whatever your 'problems' concerning matrimony were."

Henry's brow creased. "What do you mean?"

"You must be ready to offer Charlotte marriage. Surely you are not such a cad as to think otherwise."

Charlotte's breath caught. Marriage? Everything had happened so quickly that she hadn't fully processed the implications of what had happened. Of course marriage would be the reasonable expectation after being caught in such a way.

But Henry didn't want to marry—and according to William, there was a deeper reason for this. She looked over at Henry, her confusion rising like a tide.

What problems?

What had actually been keeping him from marriage? And why had William spoken as though he knew something she didn't?

"No," Henry said, his face pale.

Any hope she had that Henry might say yes—that he might look at her and see a future—vanished in an instant.

"I haven't resolved anything. And I cannot—*will* not—marry Charlotte. I'm sorry."

He looked horrified at the very thought. As though the idea repulsed him.

Charlotte covered her mouth, tears burning her eyes. So much for his claim to care for her. He would rather see her ruined than marry her.

Something inside her cracked. She had feared rejection before, feared that Henry might not return her feelings. But this was even worse.

He wouldn't marry her. Not just couldn't.

Wouldn't.

What was so wrong with her that it was so utterly impossible? That he could kiss her, but then refuse to marry her when the stakes—for her, at least—were so high?

Any chance of a future began to crumble to dust before her eyes. Before, she had been terrified of being married to someone she disliked. Now, that would be a haven compared to the societal rejection that would follow. William had no intention of keeping this quiet, that was clear.

And Henry…

Henry didn't want her.

Her throat tightened, and she forced herself to drag in a breath. Then she lifted her chin, determined not to let them see how much this hurt. Miranda darted around William and strode to Charlotte. As soon as she reached her side, she looped their arms together, and Charlotte drew comfort from her friend's silent support.

"You're sorry?" William demanded. "What the hell good is

that? You kiss my sister, but she isn't enough for you? You've treated her as though she's no better than a woman from the taverns! Is that how you see us? Are we so far beneath you?"

Charlotte shrank into Miranda, the accusation stinging bitterly, but he was right. William was right.

Henry's lips thinned. His expression had become opaque, and Charlotte had no idea what he was thinking. "You know it's not that."

"Then what is it?" Charlotte asked before her brother could respond, finding her voice at last. "Because I must confess that I'm at a loss to understand this treatment from you." She straightened her shoulders and stood her ground in spite of her distress, staring directly at him, forcing him to meet her eyes.

Henry ran a hand through his hair, looking suddenly exhausted. "It isn't you, Charlotte. It's me. There are things about me that you don't know. Things I can't explain."

She swallowed hard. "Try."

He hesitated and looked away, but that was answer enough.

She laughed, but it was humorless. "Right. Of course. Because I'm just William's little sister, aren't I? No need to explain anything to me. I don't matter. I was just, what, a dalliance for the *moment*?" She flung his words back at him.

Henry took a step toward her. "Charlotte, please...."

"Don't, Your Grace." She held up a hand, blinking back the sting of her tears. "You've made yourself perfectly clear."

Henry's jaw clenched. "I'm trying to protect you. There are reasons..."

"But you won't share them?" she demanded. "You won't explain?"

"I can't."

William, who had been staring at them with a grim expression throughout their exchange, exhaled sharply. "Unbelievable," he muttered, shaking his head. He turned to

Charlotte and held out his hand. "Come, Charlotte. I will escort you back to the house while I decide what must be done about this."

She nodded, not trusting herself to speak. Her heart was in pieces, her stomach twisted into knots. How had everything gone so wrong so quickly?

She pivoted away from Henry, unable to even look at him lest he see her despair. She allowed William to take her other arm, wincing at the renewed throbbing in her ankle.

William turned back to Henry. Before leading Charlotte away, he said curtly, "You will never speak to Charlotte again. You will stay away from her, or you will have me to answer to. You… utter *cad.*"

At the insult, and the contempt in William's voice, Henry's hands curled into fists at his sides. "I'm sorry. I didn't mean for this to happen."

"But it did," William snapped. "If you won't marry Charlotte and save her from this scandal, then you have no need to be in her company again. You're going to ruin her."

Charlotte inhaled sharply, praying Henry would make a stand or perhaps take back everything he'd just said because surely he didn't mean it, but Henry didn't argue with William's words. Didn't fight for her. Didn't say a damn thing.

And that silence and resignation hurt more than anything else. Even more than his spoken refusal to be wed.

William was seething, his face a shade redder than usual, and Charlotte could feel his fury radiating from him in almost tangible waves. She tried to urge him away, but he let his temper get the better of him, brushing her arm away and spinning back around.

"You should never have been alone with her," he bit out, his voice low and controlled but brimming with anger. "How could you do this to my sister, of all people? You have practically been part of our family. We grew up together!"

Charlotte saw a flicker of hurt in Henry's eyes. *So, this upsets him, but not the rest. He really doesn't care about me, only my brother.*

"William, I—" Henry stepped forward, his hand stretched out toward William.

"No," William snapped, smacking Henry's hand away. "I trusted you. I trusted you to look after my sister. And you let me down."

Charlotte's gut clenched at his words, not just with hurt now but guilt. Perhaps if she and her friends had never started scheming, this wouldn't have happened. But at the same time, she was angry. Because as much as she hated being at the center of their argument, being spoken about as though she had no say in the matter at all was even worse.

But even more than that, she hated the look on Henry's face. The sheer horror at the thought of being forced into marriage with her.

"I expect you to either stay away from her," William continued, his voice like steel, "or resolve your damned problem and do right by her."

Again, this mention of a mysterious problem. She wondered if it was the same issue that Henry had referred to when drunk the night before. She dared a glance at Miranda, hoping her friend might have insight that Charlotte did not, but Miranda was wide-eyed and tightlipped, obviously afraid to speak and draw attention to herself.

But what did it matter now anyway? The point was clear: Henry wanted nothing to do with her. She had been foolish to ever believe it could be otherwise.

But if that was the case, then she was done with being ordered around by either of them.

She took a breath, willing herself to keep her voice steady. "Miranda will take me back to the house. We can't have poor Henry being tempted and trapped by my presence, can we?"

Henry flinched at her words, and William looked shocked

at her impropriety, but she didn't give either of them a chance to respond.

Looking now at William, she tilted her chin defiantly. "And you don't get to dictate my life. I may be your sister, but I know my own mind and will make my own choices."

She turned on her heel—an action she immediately regretted as pain shot up her ankle. But she didn't stop. She refused to stop.

With as much dignity as she could muster, she leaned on Miranda, unhooked her arm from William's, and hobbled away, ignoring William calling after her, ignoring the ache in her chest, ignoring even the overwhelming urge to break down and cry.

Henry had made his choice, and she refused to stand there and watch him regret his actions. And if he didn't regret them? She *really* didn't want to see that.

Fortunately, Miranda didn't speak during the walk back except to murmur an apology, repeated several times over. Charlotte assured her she had done nothing wrong, but even still she barely managed to hold herself together as she climbed the front steps of Arundel Park, her ankle protesting with every step.

The humiliation, the hurt, the overwhelming frustration —everything pressed against her chest like a weight she couldn't shake.

She needed to leave right now, before news of this scandal broke and she had to face either Henry or her brother again. She didn't even want to see her friends. She just wanted to go home.

She shook Miranda off, limped up the stairs, ignoring the offers of help from the servants, and made her way to her mother's room. She found Lady Fitzgerald sitting at a window, a cup of tea in hand, looking utterly at ease. Of course, Lady Fitzgerald hadn't gone traipsing through the countryside with the younger women.

Charlotte took a steadying breath, then walked straight into the room. "Mother, I want to leave," she announced without preamble. "Right away."

Lady Fitzgerald lifted a brow and set down her teacup carefully, trying to hide her surprise. Charlotte stifled an impatient cry of frustration. Must her mother insist on behaving properly even when there was no one else to see them?

"Leave, my dear? Whatever for?"

"I've had enough of this house party," Charlotte said, her voice sharp with frustration. "I've hurt my ankle, I do not like the company, and I want to go home."

Her mother studied her, still cool and composed. "What's happened?"

"Nothing," Charlotte replied, all too quickly.

Lady Fitzgerald sighed, folding her hands in her lap. "Charlotte, don't be ridiculous. You're clearly distressed about something. What is it?"

Charlotte turned away from her mother, pressing her lips together. "I simply don't wish to stay."

Her mother watched her in silence for a long moment. "We are committed to staying until the end of the week," she said finally. "Leaving halfway through will cause unnecessary gossip."

Charlotte whirled to face her, barely able to contain her frustration. "So what if it does? What does it matter?"

There will be plenty of gossip soon enough.

She would deal with *that* when she had to.

Lady Fitzgerald's expression barely wavered. "It matters because we do not invite speculation where it isn't needed. A sudden departure would be noted. Questions would be asked."

Of course. Of course it was about appearances. It always was. For women, anyway. As Henry had just illustrated, men could escape such traps to some degree. It was not Henry's reputation that was about to be ruined.

"Perhaps you should rest," her mother continued, her tone placating. "Take a nap, calm yourself, and we can discuss this later. You're clearly overwrought."

Charlotte let out a hollow laugh. She was tiptoeing on the edge of utter hysteria, but she no longer cared. Why would no one *listen* to her and what she wanted? "I don't need a nap, Mother. I need to leave."

Lady Fitzgerald's eyes narrowed slightly. "You're being irrational."

"No," Charlotte said, trembling with emotion. "I'm being treated like my feelings don't matter. *Again.*"

Her mother sighed as though Charlotte were a petulant, spoiled child rather than a grown woman with cares and desires of her own.

Charlotte drew in a breath, forcing herself to keep her emotions in check. A wave of despair washed over her, numbing her fury. "I'd hoped, just for once, for someone to care about what I want," she said more quietly now. "For you to listen to me instead of forcing me to do things I don't want to do. But as usual, my happiness is the last thing anyone is concerned about."

Charlotte turned on her heel before her mother could respond, her ankle throbbing as she strode from the room.

She couldn't leave.

She couldn't even control that.

CHAPTER 22

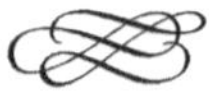

HENRY TOOK AN URGENT STEP IN THE DIRECTION CHARLOTTE had fled, his heart hammering wildly as her words rang in his ears, but William's firm grip landed on his shoulder, halting him in place.

"Let her go," William growled. "She needs to be alone right now. Forcing her to speak of her feelings will only push her further away. I've learnt this about my sister over the years… and you seem to know her well enough that you should realize this."

Henry cursed sharply under his breath at both William's words and the implication in them. He ran a hand roughly through his thick, dark hair, frustration gnawing at him as he paced restlessly across the manicured lawn.

"Damn it, William, I never intended any of this," he rasped, though his anger was directed at himself rather than his friend.

What had he been thinking?

He should never have kissed Charlotte, knowing he couldn't marry her. No matter how much he might want to.

William's piercing eyes narrowed, his jaw clenching visibly, anger emanating from every rigid line of his posture.

"Perhaps," he began icily, "you shouldn't have been kissing her, then. You are hardly short of female attention. Do you need to turn your attentions to my sister? You've known her since she was a child."

Henry stopped pacing and spun sharply to face his friend, his dark eyes blazing. "But Charlotte is no longer a child. She is a woman—a grown woman who deserves to be respected and treated as such."

William's expression darkened further, a sardonic edge curving his lips. It bothered Henry to see the sudden contempt on his friend's face. "Oh, I am well aware of how grown she is. But you, Henry—you've been treating her far too much like a grown woman already and certainly not in a manner befitting an unmarried lady."

Henry's gut twisted, the guilt making it difficult to breathe. "I didn't mean to. I just didn't think."

William set down the gun and shoved him. "Perhaps that's the problem. You should have *thought*."

Henry staggered backward before catching himself.

There was a pause as the two men glared at each other, then, just like he had when they were scrapping as boys, William charged Henry, grabbing him around the waist and grappling him to the ground. Henry was still stronger than William though, and he caught him in a headlock, but William kicked out, causing Henry to bellow with pain as his boot caught Henry's shin.

"Is this really necessary?" Henry panted.

William elbowed him in the ribs, but Henry grabbed him again until they were tussling on the ground.

"You ruined my sister!" William shouted, rolling him onto his back. William's rifle lay discarded on the ground next to them, but neither man made any attempt to reach for it as they tumbled across the grass.

"I didn't mean to!" Henry yelled as he hooked the other man to the ground when he tried to stand.

"I'm getting sick of hearing that," William snarled, twisting Henry's ear.

They fought for a while longer, neither doing serious damage to the other. Eventually, they sprawled side by side on the damp ground, breathing raggedly.

It was Henry who spoke first, breaking the heavy silence that settled between them. His voice was softer now, tinged with genuine remorse. "I'm sorry, William. Truly." Henry's eyes fixed on the cloud-filled sky above. He hated that they'd fallen so far. "I swear on my honor, I never intended to compromise Charlotte. I honestly just intended to walk her back to the house after she was injured. But I can't deny what I feel for her. It was never meant to happen this way, but the kiss—I couldn't help it. I love her."

William was silent for a long moment, catching his breath. He rolled over to study Henry's face and slowly his expression softened. "You do, don't you?"

Henry nodded, surprised by the admission. Now he'd said it out loud, he knew it wasn't just undeniably true but had been for some time. "More deeply than you could possibly imagine. And were it not for the secrets I carry and my obligations toward my family name—these cursed obligations and dark truths—I would ask for Charlotte's hand without hesitation. She deserves nothing less from me, but I can't give her that, which is why I am deeply sorry I kissed her as I did. I should have had more self-control."

"Can your secret be so important that you would break my sister's heart?" William asked.

Henry shook his head wretchedly. "She wouldn't wish to marry me if she knew."

William pushed himself into a sitting position, brushing grass and dirt absently from his clothing, a thoughtful expression settling across his features. "Have you considered that it may be finally time to face this secret that holds you back? It cannot be anything so bad. I know you. Whatever it is, it can't be any wrong that you've done. Why don't you be honest with her and see what she wants? Give her the option, at least? You owe that much to her and to yourself."

Henry sat up beside him, fatigue weighing heavy on his soul. "I cannot subject Charlotte to that. She would ruin herself out of love for me."

William shook his head, his disappointment plain. "Then you must keep away from her. At all times. I will keep quiet about what has happened here today, but you must leave her be if you would not hurt her further."

Henry nodded even as the thought of never seeing Charlotte again threatened to tear him in two.

William laid a hand on his shoulder. "Can you not confide in me? It may not be so bad as you fear. Perhaps together we can find a way around it. Or I can help you bear your burden at least."

Henry rubbed a hand over his face and exhaled roughly. He should never have let things come to this. "Perhaps. Let me think on it for this evening. Certainly, I could do with an ally while I still have this unknown blackmailer to deal with." He met William's eyes. "Thank you. I don't deserve your friendship after what I've done."

William reached out a hand and helped him to his feet. "Forgive me too. I should never have insinuated anything further had occurred between you and Charlotte. It's only—" He hesitated, choosing his words carefully. "If you truly have no intention of marrying, you must keep your distance, as I've said. Her heart is tender enough without you inadvertently encouraging feelings that will only cause her deeper pain. If you cannot own this secret to her, you must go away for a while so she can heal."

Heaviness settled in Henry's chest, along with a sinking sensation he could not shake, for he knew William was right. "You speak the truth."

Perhaps some time on the Continent was needed, away

from the situation he had created. Maybe that would rid him of this blackmailer. But could he actually physically leave the woman he loved? Was he capable of making himself do so?

As they began the slow walk back toward the house, William glanced sideways. "Will you never tell me what is it exactly that holds you back?"

Henry paused, considering his reply. "Give me time."

William stopped briefly, turning fully to face his friend. "Henry, you have always been my closest friend, more akin to a brother. You know any secret you entrust to me would never be betrayed."

"I do know," Henry admitted, his throat tight. "But the habit of secrecy runs deep, drilled into me since boyhood. It's not easily undone."

William offered an understanding nod, pressing the matter no further. In silence, they continued toward the house, the large stone façade soon coming into view, imposing yet familiar. He could lose all of this if his true origins came out, but for once, he didn't care. He was tired of bearing such a grave responsibility.

As they reached the drive, Lady Fitzgerald appeared at the entrance, concern etched deeply into her features. "William, do you have any idea what's wrong with Charlotte? She is demanding to leave and acting most unlike herself. I have never heard such defiance from her. She is quite over-wrought. Do you think she is ill?"

Henry's stomach twisted painfully, guilt and fear entwining. The thought of Charlotte departing before he had the chance to speak with her again sent panic surging through him even as he knew he should keep his distance. He just... hated the thought that he had driven her away.

William gave his mother a reassuring smile, though Henry recognized the worry behind it. "I'm sure it's nothing serious, Mother. According to Henry, she turned her ankle and is perhaps in some pain, but I'm assured it was a tumble, nothing more. I think this is all just too overwhelming for her. You know what she's like. Perhaps it would be best to take her home."

Lady Fitzgerald's brow remained furrowed, her eyes narrowing slightly as she studied her son, her skepticism evident. "Very well, but I must see that Charlotte is not having some kind of turn. She was terribly upset, and I would not like to offend Her Grace by leaving early."

Henry bowed to her, which gave him the opportunity to hide his face. He felt sure that Charlotte's mother would read his guilt written all over it. "Not at all, my lady. I will speak to my mother. There will be no offence if Charlotte wishes to leave. Indeed," he said as he straightened. "I am becoming quite tired of the whole affair myself."

He left William to deal with his now bewildered mother and took the stairs to his rooms, reflecting on his last words to Lady Fitzgerald. He really had had enough. This whole affair was draining him and setting his teeth on edge. He wanted his guests to go so he could deal with whatever conflict awaited and plan his trip abroad.

As well as nurse his broken heart.

He went to his mother's room, where he found her perusing her gowns, no doubt deciding what to wear for tonight's dinner.

"Henry! Why are you not with the ladies at the folly? You must make yourself agreeable, or all my efforts will have been for nothing."

Anger flared within him, hot and unexpected. "Your efforts? Your efforts are precisely why I'm in this impossible position. If not for your choices, I could have had a chance at happiness without endangering someone I care about!"

She stiffened, her eyes narrowing in shock and displeasure. "How dare you speak to me in this manner—"

"I dare because it is the truth," he interrupted fiercely.

"Understand this: I have no intention of marrying any of those women."

"Henry!"

"No, Mother," he said, his tone firm. "I am done with this charade. No matter how much you beg and plead, I will not marry. I will not carry this secret on any further for another generation to deal with. I will hear no more on the matter."

Before she could reply, he turned abruptly and walked out of her room.

CHAPTER 23

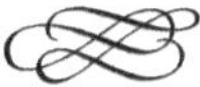

"MAKE SURE THE FIRST NOTE GOES TO LORD ARUNDEL AND the second to my brother, Lord Fitzgerald," Charlotte whispered, pressing the notes and two coins into her maid's hand.

Mary bobbed and hurried off down the corridor.

Charlotte breathed a sigh of relief that she had not been overheard or observed. She shut the door and leaned back on it. What a wretched day.

She could still feel the press of Henry's lips on hers and remembered his delicious spicy scent as he'd pulled her into his arms… but she *must* stop thinking of it. He had made it clear that he didn't want her, that she was only a dalliance.

A knock came at the other side of the door, and she jumped, her hand flying to her chest. Was it Mary? Had someone apprehended her and discovered the notes?

Heart pounding, Charlotte opened the door to see Helena, Felicity, Adeline, Genevieve, and Miranda crowding together in the doorframe, their faces both eager and concerned.

"What happened earlier, after you left with Henry?" Felicity asked, searching Charlotte's face. "Miranda will not tell us anything but she's most distraught."

"I'm not distraught," Miranda said briskly, although she was certainly paler than usual. "I am being discreet and respecting my friend's privacy."

Helena scoffed. "You are being no help at all."

Adeline ignored them. Her brow creased with concern. "You look pale. Is your ankle so painful? Did something awful happen?"

Charlotte burst into tears.

Felicity's eyes widened. "Oh, my dear! What is it?"

Miranda hustled Charlotte into the room and got her to sit down near the window. Adeline poured her a glass of water while Helena shut the door and pushed a chair in front of it so no one could come in. Genevieve thrust her handkerchief into Charlotte's hand.

"It was awful." Charlotte sobbed, her tears coming thick and fast as the presence of her friends caused all her emotions to well up at once. "William caught us, and then Henry said he never could, and then I told Mother I wanted to go home, and I'm so sick of all of them, and…."

She stopped and blew her nose. Her friends exchanged glances at her garbled rush of words.

"Slow down," Genevieve said, rubbing soothing circles on her back. "And start at the beginning. Miranda said you turned your ankle and Henry escorted you and her back to the house, is that right?"

Charlotte nodded and took a breath. Her voice steadier now, she told them, with flaming cheeks, about kissing while Miranda was distracted by her flower. Felicity gasped, Adeline tutted, and Helena grinned in delight as she recounted how she had melted in Henry's arms.

"I am a terrible friend," Miranda bemoaned, but no one paid her any attention.

They all listened, rapt, as she told them how William had come across them, and Henry had called the kiss nothing but a moment of foolishness.

"He insisted he would never marry me," she whispered, her eyes burning with shame as she stared at the floor. "Even when William said he had ruined my honor and reputation."

"Not if no one hears of it," Adeline said flatly. "I'm sure your brother won't want it to be known. It's his reputation too, and Miranda has already proven to be steadfast."

Charlotte reached for Miranda's hand and squeezed it. "Thank you, my friend."

Miranda squeezed back in an unusual display of affection. "I should have done better in the first place."

"William may be concerned for his own reputation, but men are never affected by such things as women are," Felicity muttered to Adeline.

"Hopefully, in this, he is discreet," Adeline replied.

Miranda's expression grew thoughtful. "While I witnessed most of these events myself, I must admit that this behavior does not seem typical of the duke, from what we've seen and all you've told us of him. Didn't he imply there is some kind of secret that prevents him from marrying?"

Charlotte wiped her eyes, remembering Henry's odd words. "That's true."

"Which may explain his reluctance to marry at all," Genevieve chimed in.

Miranda nodded. "Yes," she said, drumming the fingers of her free hand on her thigh. "That might explain things. I've always thought that the duke is uncommonly fond of you, Charlotte, and the kiss does not surprise me… although I do wish I'd played the role of chaperone more effectively. The duke's reaction to William though… it's not characteristic of him."

"Perhaps he is just an absolute cad, like all men," Adeline said glumly.

Helena hissed at her to shush, but Charlotte shook her head bitterly. She didn't need her friends to spare her feelings. She could not possibly be crushed any further than she already had been by Henry's words.

But Miranda, always the practical one, thought otherwise. "No; it makes too little sense. I would suggest that this mention of a secret means there is a good reason why Henry insisted that he cannot marry you. So it may not be that he doesn't wish to, but rather that he feels he can't. We must get to the bottom of whatever this secret is."

As the other girls nodded, hope flickered in Charlotte's breast, but she quickly suppressed it. She couldn't allow herself to be disappointed again. Henry's words had seemed so final. He would never marry her.

She rested her hands on her lap, willing herself not to hope, not to believe that there could be any explanation that might change Henry's stance. "It doesn't matter what the secret is. The only thing that matters is that he refuses to marry me. He sees no future with me."

Helena huffed. "Oh, nonsense. Men are stubborn creatures, and Arundel is one of the worst of them. He could be making excuses."

"He didn't look as though he was making an excuse," Charlotte murmured, replaying the scene once more. "He looked... wretched."

"That's what makes this all so strange," Miranda said, leaning forward. "If he didn't care, he would not have looked so wretched. And that is why we must find out what, exactly, is holding him back."

Charlotte lifted her gaze to Miranda's, her stomach a tangle of knots. "And if it's something insurmountable that truly prevents him from marrying me?"

"Then at least you will have answers," Miranda said simply. "At least you will know whether to fight for him or let him go."

Charlotte bit her lip, clenching the folds of her gown. The idea of letting Henry go sent an aching pang through her chest, but the thought of fighting for him, only to lose in the end, was equally unbearable.

"I've already written to him," she confessed. "I sent notes to both him and my brother."

Her friends exchanged wary glances, and Genevieve's voice was gentler than usual when she spoke. "What did you write in your note to the duke?"

Charlotte hesitated. "I asked them both to meet me," she admitted. "In the library after tea. Although I'm devastated he won't marry me, neither do I want him to be forced into it by my brother."

Felicity looked confused. "But I thought we wanted him to marry you?"

"Not under coercion!" Charlotte swallowed her pain. "I will not be like that woman who sought to trap him in the garden. If we are to wed, it must be because he wants to."

Helena squeezed her hand. "I think it's brave," she said, "to release him from any obligation even though there may be consequences for you. But even so, you deserve an explanation for his behavior. Miranda may be right. Perhaps he wants to but can't."

"I doubt he will even come," Charlotte said, letting out a humorless laugh. "He was desperate to be rid of me earlier."

Helena scoffed. "If he doesn't come, we'll make him regret it."

Miranda raised an eyebrow. "Helena—"

"Oh, don't look at me like that, Miranda. It infuriates me how we women are treated. Charlotte deserves better than this."

They all nodded, but Charlotte sank into a gloomy silence that continued as she got ready for luncheon with the other women. She eyed her mother warily as they escorted each other downstairs, but Lady Fitzgerald said nothing about her earlier outburst.

The luncheon itself was a blur.

Charlotte sat through it, hearing conversations but not truly listening, her thoughts circling endlessly around Henry, the afternoon's humiliation, and the note she had sent to him. She moved food around on her plate, barely eating, and when she spoke, it was only when directly addressed, her responses short and polite.

No one seemed to notice her distraction save for her mother, who shot her a couple of searching looks and once mentioned that she was unusually quiet, even for her. Charlotte only smiled thinly and assured her that she was well.

After luncheon, the ladies remained gathered in the drawing room for polite conversation. The voices around her blending into meaningless chatter as Charlotte sat among them, but her mind was elsewhere, though she tried to hide how closely she was paying attention to the ticking of the grandfather clock in the corner of the room. When the time came and the opportunity arose, she excused herself under the pretense of fetching a book from the library.

Her heart pounded as she walked through the dimly lit corridors. When she reached the library, she hesitated for only a second before stepping inside, holding her breath at the thought of seeing Henry again.

Henry and William were already there. They stood by the hearth, engaged in low conversation, but both turned when she entered. William's face was inscrutable, but Henry looked as though he had been waiting for her. His gaze met hers, filled with something unreadable that sent her pulse skittering.

She felt another flare of hope. Could Miranda have been right?

She looked away from him, not wanting to betray her emotions.

Instead, she shut the door behind her and took a steadying breath. She had come here with a purpose, after all.

"I won't be coerced into marriage," she said, lifting her chin and turning to face her brother first. "And I certainly won't have Henry forced into it either. He has made his feelings against marrying me entirely clear, and I don't wish to be married to a man who doesn't love me and will only end up resenting our marriage."

William's brows rose slightly, but he said nothing. Henry's expression didn't change, but his hands clenched at his sides, and his jaw pulsed.

Charlotte faced him head-on and steeled herself to say what she needed to.

"I care for you, Henry," she continued, her voice steady despite the pounding of her heart. "I had hoped…. I had hoped you might feel the same. But I refuse to spend my life bound to someone who doesn't want me. Despite what happened earlier, I will not let my brother and mother force you to marry me."

She let the words settle between them and the truth of them hang in the air.

Henry took a sharp breath and stepped toward her, reaching for her, but she pulled back before he could touch her, more out of surprise than anything else. Henry's face fell. He looked suddenly vulnerable, even boyish. The rush of affection she felt for him couldn't be suppressed.

"Charlotte," His voice was rough and low, almost pleading. "It isn't that I don't want you."

Her heart twisted, and she sank her teeth into her lip, reminding herself not to get her hopes up. "Then what is it? Why do you keep pushing me away?"

He said nothing, the pulse still throbbing in his jaw. She had never seen him so obviously conflicted. Although she did not wish to push him when he was distraught, she also needed answers, and she knew this might be her only chance to get them. Her hands tensed in the folds of her dress.

"Why can't you marry me, Henry?"

Still, he didn't speak. Charlotte's gaze flicked to William, who had been uncharacteristically silent until now, watching their exchange keenly. He clearly knew something she didn't, and that made her angry.

"Do you know?" she demanded.

William shook his head. "No. I know that Henry would marry you if he could and that there is a reason he cannot, but he hasn't told me what secret he is protecting."

Charlotte's stomach clenched. "Then tell us now," she said, turning back to Henry. "Tell us so we can understand. If you don't, Henry—if you refuse to give me a reason, then I will have no choice but to believe that you simply don't care about me—about either of us."

Henry's shoulders slumped, his entire posture shifting as though the weight of the world had settled upon him. "I will tell you both," he said hoarsely, refusing to meet their eyes. "But I do not expect you will understand." He gestured toward the seating area near the fireplace. "Sit down. You must promise me that what I'm about to confess will not leave this room."

Charlotte glanced at William, whose face was now lined with concern. Then she turned back to Henry and nodded, her throat tightening. "You do not need to ask that," she assured him as she and William took a seat. "Tell us, please."

Henry angled himself toward the window so that his profile was half in shadow. He stared out at the grounds as though looking anywhere else would shatter his resolve. Charlotte and William sat across from him, waiting. The silence stretched, thick and heavy, until at last, Henry let out a breath and spoke.

"Very well." He closed his eyes, his voice becoming matter of fact and distant. "I was ten years old when I found out. I overheard my parents arguing. My father—" He paused, shaking his head as though banishing the word. "The duke. He was furious about something I'd done. I can't remember what. My mother kept telling him to lower his voice, but he didn't care. He was shouting about how they shouldn't have expected more from me. How breeding would always win out, and I was no son of his."

Charlotte sucked in a sharp breath. Beside her, William stiffened.

"What are you saying?" William asked carefully. "What did he mean?"

Henry glanced at them, his expression unreadable. "I am not the true heir to the Arundel title. My mother and father couldn't conceive, so they… found another way."

Charlotte's stomach heaved. "You mean—"

"My mother had an affair," Henry confirmed. "And then they passed me off as the duke's son. He knew, of course. From the very beginning. They planned it together. He could not let his name die. They knew no one would ever question them because they were the Duke and Duchess of Arundel." A bitter smile curled his lips. "But it was a lie."

Charlotte's mind reeled. She could scarcely comprehend what he was saying. "You were raised as his son," she said slowly. "You inherited his title. That makes you the duke. Your father accepted you and took you on as his heir."

His jaw clenched. "It makes me a fraud. And my father scarcely tolerated me. He never formally adopted me because it was all so secret and because of that, the title should legally belong to my cousin's husband. Which is what my father wished to prevent. He hated that side of the family and did not want his paternal name and line to die out. In short, I am a criminal."

William swore under his breath and raked a hand through his hair. "Christ, Henry."

Charlotte stared at him, at a loss as to what to say.

"I have spent my entire life knowing that my title, my status, everything I am is built on a lie," Henry continued, his voice tight. "If the truth ever came out, everything my mother and father worked for would be destroyed. Something she reminds me of daily."

Henry paused then and looked at Charlotte, and there was such naked emotion in his eyes that she almost gasped out loud. "If it were just myself, I would not care, believe me. I am tired of the trappings of high society, and weary of the secrecy. But my mother—"

"She would face ruin," Charlotte whispered.

"Yes. If anyone ever found out, she would be cast out of society entirely, without a penny to live on, and possibly face prison too. It would destroy her utterly. And I…." He exhaled sharply. "I would lose everything. Which means, so would any wife of mine. I can offer you nothing but a life of living a lie, under the threat of poverty and disgrace. I could not do that to any woman… least of all you, my darling."

Her pulse pounded in her ears. Even with this horrific news, her heart leaped to hear him call her darling. "But how could anyone possibly find out, if the only people who knew were your parents?"

"That's what I thought," Henry murmured. "But someone here—at this very house party—knows."

William frowned. "The notes."

Charlotte looked from one man to another, now thoroughly confused. "Notes?"

Henry nodded. "I have been receiving anonymous letters. The first note warned me that my secret wasn't safe. Then the second one demanded that I meet them, but no one ever showed up. Someone is playing a game with me, and I don't know what they want. If they make this public knowledge, I will be finished. And my mother…." He shook his head. "She will be disgraced."

Charlotte's throat constricted. She had come here expecting an argument of some kind, probably another rejection. She'd suspected he was keeping a secret but she had not foreseen this.

William leaned forward, his expression grim. "And you think that if you were to marry, the risk of this coming out increases?"

Henry made a sound in the affirmative. "Marriage means heirs. If I have a son, and my lineage is ever called into question, it could destroy not just me but him as well. I can't, in good conscience, subject someone else to this. I can't subject *Charlotte* to this, or any children we may have."

Charlotte sat very still, her hands curled into the fabric of her gown. Her mind spun as she tried to process the seriousness of what Henry had been carrying all these years. She understood, now, why he'd pushed her away, but all she could feel was deep hurt for the way he had been suffering and outrage that someone would dare to threaten him so callously.

Still… something didn't sit right.

"Henry," she said carefully, "what of your true sire? Could he be involved?"

Henry grimaced. "I asked Mother and she assured me that I need not concern myself with him."

William's eyes widened. "Is he no longer for this world?"

"I cannot be certain, but she gave that impression."

"Surely he could have told someone earlier in his life?" Charlotte prompted.

"It's a possibility," Henry allowed. "I will ask Mother for more information. But it is also possible that I'm not the only one who overheard my parents arguing about my parentage. Members of the staff may well have become aware over the years."

Charlotte inclined her head, acknowledging the truth of

this. "If someone at this house party knows, then they must have a reason for waiting. They haven't revealed anything yet. That means they want something from you. And surely that is something more than money, otherwise why not make the demand quickly and be off with the fruits of their scheme?"

Henry chuckled humorlessly. "Yes, that's what worries me."

William leaned back, scowling. "So, what now? You just wait for them to make their next move?"

"What choice do I have?" Henry asked. "If I go looking, I could tip them off and force their hand. And if I try to bring whoever it is to justice by alerting a Bow Street Runner to the blackmail, I will also be exposing myself. As you can see, they have me in quite the bind."

Charlotte's insides flipped over as she looked at him. He was clearly exhausted. Defeated and alone.

At least, he had been.

He wasn't alone anymore.

"We'll figure this out," she said softly. "Together."

Henry's gaze flicked to hers. "Charlotte—"

"I mean it," she said firmly. "You are not the only one who has something to lose here. Whoever this is, they are trying to manipulate you. But they don't get to decide how this ends."

William nodded. "I can't believe I'm saying this, but Charlotte's right. Whoever is behind this has made a mistake. They think they have the upper hand, but they don't. You have us. I will not have the happiness of my sister and best friend destroyed by some schemer, nor by the mistakes of your parents. None of this should be on your shoulders."

For a moment, Henry said nothing. He searched their faces, his jaw tight. Then, finally, his shoulders dropped, just slightly. For a moment, he looked almost as though he might cry. "Thank you," he whispered, his eyes shining. "Both of you."

There was a moment's silence, and then Charlotte swallowed. "So, tell me, Henry," she said quietly but firmly, setting her shoulders back with resolve. "As we are now all in this together. What do we do now?"

CHAPTER 24

Charlotte's heart pounded as she steeled herself to ask yet another important question. She knew that what she was about to do would be considered scandalous by many, but she didn't care. Her feelings for Henry were unchanged by this news, however unwelcome it might be.

"Henry," she said carefully, watching him. "Is this truly the only reason you refuse to marry me? Your illegitimacy?"

Henry's gaze flickered to hers. His shoulders tensed as though bracing for something. "Yes," he admitted. "It is the only reason. I care for you deeply, Charlotte." He glanced at William as though to check whether his friend would be angered by his declaration.

Charlotte fought to contain her smile. Now was not the time for it, no matter how long she'd waited to hear those words. "So if not for this… if there was no risk…" She hesitated, her pulse thrumming in her ears. "We would be married?"

William let out a strangled noise beside her. "Don't mind me. I'm only her brother. Why, I adore listening to you two fawn over each other."

Charlotte's mouth twisted in amusement, but she ignored him. Her focus was entirely on Henry.

He nodded, his eyes burning into hers. "I adore you. More than I should. More than is safe." He swallowed. "You are intelligent, kind, far too good for me, and the most beautiful woman I have ever known. If not for this cursed situation, I would marry you in a heartbeat." His voice dropped lower, rough with emotion. "I would be proud to call you my duchess."

Charlotte's breath hitched. For one perfect, stolen moment, she allowed herself to revel in his words. And then she straightened her spine and raised her chin.

"Then that settles it," she said firmly. "I will take the risk."

"What?" William and Henry both asked at once.

She met Henry's stunned expression with unwavering determination. "I love you. I am not afraid of this. If you will have me, I will marry you."

William shot to his feet. "Absolutely not. Have you lost your mind? This isn't some reckless adventure. This is your life. You can't throw yourself into possible disgrace like this."

She narrowed her eyes at her brother. "It is *my* life, indeed. Not yours. Not anyone else's to control. I choose this. I choose Henry."

Henry looked stunned. "I would not have you suffer because of my family's wrongdoing."

"And I say once again, it is my life and my choice." Charlotte met each of their gazes in turn, her expression calm. She had never felt so sure of anything in her entire life. "I am prepared to take the risk."

"The risk is too high!" William protested. "If this gets out, you'll be ruined, both of you! I don't wish to lose either of you over this madness."

Charlotte glared at her brother. Must he still insist on controlling her future, even now? "It is my risk to take."

William ran a hand down his face, visibly torn. "You need my approval to marry."

Charlotte pursed her lips. "We could elope."

Both Henry and William gaped at her. Henry looked utterly shocked but also oddly proud, while her brother was simply horrified.

"You wouldn't," William hissed.

Charlotte crossed her arms. "I highly doubt Henry would, given that you're his best friend. But if I must, I will find a way."

"You will not," William insisted, looking to be at the end of his tether now.

Charlotte glared at him, refusing to back down.

Henry stepped between them, a hand raised for peace. "Enough," he said firmly. His entire body was tense. "Charlotte, you can't take this risk. I won't allow it."

Her heart clenched at his words. "You said you wished to marry me."

"Yes," he agreed, his voice quieter now. "But I cannot put you in danger. I would never forgive myself if anything happened to you because of me."

Her throat burned, and she fought with everything she had to stand strong. "Nothing has happened to you so far. This secret has stayed buried for decades."

Henry grimaced. "And yet, someone else here knows. Someone who could destroy us."

William jerked his chin up. "Which means we cannot simply ignore the blackmailer and hope that they go away. They could destroy you."

Charlotte took a deep breath. "Then the answer is simple," she said, looking between them. "We find out who they are and make them stop."

Henry and William both looked at her as though she'd suggested they sprout wings and fly.

"Stop?" William repeated dryly. "What will make them do that? Do you think we should just ask them nicely?"

Charlotte ignored his barb, looking to the duke instead. "What do they want, Henry? Money?"

Henry let out a long breath. "I assume so. Although, as they have not simply said so, I fear there may be more at stake."

Charlotte thought for a minute. "Then we offer them money. Whatever other game they are playing, surely a generous enough offer will entice them to give it up. The dukedom has the funds, doesn't it?"

Henry's jaw worked as if he wanted to argue, but after a beat, he sighed. "The dukedom can afford to pay."

William still looked incredulous. "And if they don't take the money?"

Charlotte hesitated, glancing at Henry. "Then we find out what else they want. An offer of money could draw them out."

Henry gave her a long, searching look. "This is dangerous."

Charlotte raised her eyebrows. "So is living a life of regret."

A heavy silence settled over the room. Henry dragged a hand through his hair, exhaling sharply.

William looked like he wanted to shake them both. "Please do not let her do this."

Henry made one more attempt to dissuade her. "Even if you are willing to take the risk, and we find the blackmailer and pay them, are you also willing to risk any children we may have? Because they would be burdened with the same danger. It's unlikely that the truth would come out, but if it did, they could lose everything. Their place in society, their security, their future."

Charlotte didn't even blink. Her voice was calm, steady. "Obviously, we wouldn't have children until the blackmailer is identified and dealt with. Then, we would give it time and wait to see if they went away before moving forward. It would be a risk, but a relatively slim one, and eventually, anyone who knows the truth will die. Secrets don't last forever, but neither do the people who keep them. When they're gone, there will be no one left to tell."

He stared at her as though seeing her for the first time. He shook his head slightly, as if trying to clear it. "I can't believe you're willing to do this... to make this sacrifice. For me."

"Neither can I," William said sharply before Charlotte could respond. His arms were folded across his chest, and his expression was thunderous. "You can't seriously be encouraging this madness, Henry. You're gambling with your futures. I won't stand for it."

"You don't have to stand for it," Charlotte replied, her tone clipped. "Once again, it's not your decision to make."

William's jaw tightened. "I'm your brother. I am legally responsible for approving any marriage you make, and *once again,* I will not approve this. It's too dangerous."

Her cheeks flushed. "And what would you have me do? Marry Sir Leonard? Shrink into a quiet corner of society as a spinster, or wait to be foisted upon some ancient peer with gout and three dead wives? If you won't approve my marriage to the man I love, I shall simply run away. I have some small means."

Henry's head came up at that, eyes wide. "Charlotte."

"Don't worry," she said, forcing a brittle smile. "I couldn't really run off. I know my family wouldn't let me. But neither will I dance to anyone else's tune for any longer."

Charlotte felt as though a dam had burst within her, setting free all of the feelings and frustrations she had repressed over the years. However precarious her situation, for once she knew she possessed the inner strength to deal with it. This crisis had leant her a resolve that she had never experienced before. She and her friends had decided to steer their own futures and she wouldn't waver now.

Henry began to pace, agitation rolling off him in waves. "I don't want anything to happen to you," he said at last, stopping in front of her. "You don't understand what this secret means. I've kept it buried for years. We thought we were safe. Now that we aren't, we can't just... pretend there's no danger."

"I'm not pretending anything," she said softly. "But you're frightened because of a 'maybe.' A 'what if.' And I refuse to let fear make every decision for me. What I'm suggesting is not recklessness. It's a calculated risk. And from where I'm standing, the risk is no greater than continuing to do nothing and hoping the blackmailer loses interest."

Henry exhaled, long and slow.

William looked between them and then shook his head. "This is insane. You can't be serious." But he sounded less angry now. Charlotte knew her brother, and he was weakening.

"I am completely serious," she said. "But no one needs to decide anything tonight. Henry, I know this is a lot for you to decide. I'm not asking for an immediate answer. Just that you consider it. And that we all start strategizing how to find out who this blackmailer is."

There was a long silence.

Then, Henry gave a tight nod. "I'll consider it."

They both looked at William.

"I can't believe I'm saying this to either of you," he grumbled. "But yes, I'll think about it."

Charlotte stood up, sensing the edge of her courage had been reached. Any more, and she might begin to cry again. "Good night, William. Henry."

She felt their eyes on her as she walked sedately to the door. She slipped out of the library and walked as calmly as she could through the corridor until she reached Felicity's room.

When she knocked, it opened almost immediately to reveal all five of her friends already gathered inside as though they had been expecting her. She had no doubt that they were on tenterhooks for her news.

"Well?" Adeline asked, not even giving her a chance to enter. She tugged her in and shut the door before hurrying back to her seat.

"Tell us everything," Genevieve said, leaning toward her.

Five pairs of eyes stared at her in anticipation.

Charlotte shook her head. "Not everything, I'm afraid. I gave my word to the duke that I wouldn't speak of certain things."

That sobered them slightly, and they gave her a moment to sit down and compose herself. Felicity passed her a glass of water and Miranda sat beside her.

"Will he marry you?" Helena asked, as ever the most forward of the bunch.

Charlotte looked down at her hands. "I don't yet know. He tried to say he couldn't… but also said that he wants to and that he cares deeply for me." She felt herself flushing. "He said he would like nothing more than to make me his duchess."

A collective gasp went around the room.

"I knew it," Miranda said smugly. "It was the only logical conclusion to be drawn."

Felicity rolled her eyes at her scientifically minded friend, but in a way that showed her fondness.

"Then what's stopping him?" Helena asked. "This secret? What is it?"

Charlotte gave her a look. "Well, that's obviously one of the things I can't talk to you all about."

They all groaned, but none of them pressed for details.

They were good friends. It was one of the reasons Charlotte loved them.

"Is the secret… one that prevents your marriage?" Felicity asked tactfully.

Charlotte sighed. "I don't believe it should, no. But my brother and Henry himself do not agree. In truth… it could cause problems, even societal disgrace. I can say no more."

"Yet you still want to marry him?" Felicity asked quietly. "In spite of… whatever it is?"

Charlotte smiled as she remembered Henry's declaration of love for her. *Love.* "Yes."

"Then we'll just have to make it happen," Helena said firmly.

All present nodded, their expressions determined. Charlotte's smile grew. It helped, being with them. It always did. She knew she would have their unwavering support… even if the Arundel secret came to life.

She returned to her bedchamber early, having decided to forego dinner. She was exhausted and needed time to be alone and process the events of the day. Her maid helped her undress in silence.

Once her hair had been brushed, Charlotte climbed into bed with a sigh. She didn't even reach for a book. A deep night's sleep was needed before she had to face Henry's decision in the morning.

Then she saw it. A single folded note resting on her pillow. Her stomach twisted as she picked it up.

The handwriting was unfamiliar, and the message was short. Charlotte sat frozen, the note trembling in her hands as she stared at the words written there.

If you value your future, stay away from Lord Arundel.

CHAPTER 25

Henry peeled himself out of bed before the sun had fully risen, the pale morning light seeping in through the heavy curtains. He had slept little if at all. Charlotte's voice still echoed in his head, soft but resolute, declaring her willingness to risk everything for him.

For a future with him.

He'd tossed and turned, torn between logic and longing, between the life he had carefully protected and the one Charlotte had dared to offer him.

And then when he did drift off to sleep, there were dreams where he replayed kissing her by the lake, but this time there was no William to interrupt them. This time, Henry continued kissing her and buried his hands in her hair, unpinning it so its lush weight fell around her face and shoulders. He'd released her mouth and trailed kisses down her neck and brushed his lips over her decolletage…

He splashed water onto his face, hoping the chill might shock some clarity into his thoughts. It didn't.

He dried off, dressed quickly in his walking coat and boots, and made his way out to the gardens, craving solitude before the house began to stir. The quiet morning air was preferable to the noise in his head.

The gravel crunched beneath his feet as he strolled past the wisteria-clad trellises and the dew-speckled lawns. The morning mist was still heavy over the grass, curling around the hedges and hanging low among the roses like a secret waiting to be whispered.

The sky was soft and muted, the kind of gray-blue that whispered of a quiet but warm day. He followed the winding path toward the rose garden, hands in his pockets, his thoughts circling.

He'd told himself years ago that a solitary life was the price of his inheritance. He'd known that he'd never marry, never have children, never expose another soul to the danger that followed the truth of his birth. But now...

Now, there was Charlotte.

Her laughter. Her fire. Her bravery. Her kiss.

The thought of a life with her felt more real than any dream he'd dared let himself consider, and that terrified him. The idea of a future with Charlotte had once seemed an impossible fantasy. Now, it hovered just out of reach, both tantalizing and terrifying. She would risk everything for him. Could he let her?

That was the question he had to answer now.

He reached the edge of the rose garden, only to pause as he spotted movement ahead. A small figure was standing among the flowers, her pale shawl gathered around her shoulders. It was Miss Felicity Doherty, Charlotte's closest friend, with a maid lingering nearby.

She turned at the sound of his footsteps. "Lord Arundel," she said, blinking at him with wide, sleepy eyes. "You're up early."

He bowed politely. "As are you. It's not often that one finds company in the garden before breakfast."

She brushed a stray curl behind her ear. "I never sleep well in unfamiliar beds."

He nodded, understanding that all too well. "I rarely sleep soundly myself these days, and it's such a beautiful morning that I thought the fresh air might clear my head. And you? You are also out for a morning walk?"

He wondered for a moment if she was meeting a lover, but from what he knew of Charlotte's friend, he doubted it. She seemed even shyer than he had once thought Charlotte to be.

"Yes, I was just stretching my legs." After a pause, she added, "I am glad I ran into you."

"Oh?"

"Yes, I…." Felicity looked a little flustered now and unable to meet his eyes. "I mean, I suppose we are all worried about the situation. With Charlotte, I mean."

Henry stopped walking. He looked at her, his brow furrowing. "She told you?"

Surely after their conversation last night, Charlotte would not have revealed his family's shame to her friends?

"Only that she made you an offer," Felicity said quickly. "She didn't tell us anything you'd shared in confidence. She would never do that. She just said that she wanted to find a way forward. With the… betrothal." Felicity blushed, obviously aware that she'd said more than was seemly.

Henry looked away. The roses were blooming brilliantly this season, their petals heavy with morning dew, but he gazed at them without seeing them, his mind preoccupied. "Then she will have told you of her suggestion. It's more tempting than it should be."

Felicity said nothing, just gestured for him to walk with her. They moved slowly between the beds of white and blush-pink blooms, their steps quiet on the stone path, and he glanced over his shoulder to check that the maid followed.

"If I may be so bold as to ask, Your Grace, what is your

hesitation? Whatever it is that you must keep to yourself, well, if Charlotte is not put off by it, and you both wish to be wed, then why let it stop you?"

He was silent for a beat. "She's risking everything," he said finally. "If the truth comes out—about me—it won't just be a scandal. It could cost her her place in society. Not to mention her security and her peace." He kept his eyes trained ahead, watching the sun catch on a bloom just beginning to open. "She's offering to risk too much. I couldn't live with myself if she regretted it."

Felicity's mouth dropped into an O, and Henry guessed that Charlotte had not revealed just how much trouble his secrets could cause.

"So you see," he continued, "she might think she understands the risks, but—"

"But you think she doesn't?" Felicity interrupted him rather more sternly than he would have expected from her.

He blinked in surprise. "No. I just worry for her." He stopped, frowning. "She will regret it. One day."

Felicity studied him carefully. "Do you think that Charlotte is silly? Or naive?"

That took Henry aback. "Of course not. I think she's one of the most intelligent women I've ever met."

Felicity smiled. "Then why," she asked gently, "don't you trust her to make her own assessment of the situation?"

Henry stopped walking, turning to look at her fully as he processed her words.

Felicity continued, "You say you're worried she'll regret it. That she doesn't know what she's agreeing to. But if you believe her to be as intelligent as you say, why wouldn't you trust her to come to her own conclusions? To make her own decisions?"

Henry opened his mouth, then closed it again. He looked down at Felicity. She wasn't accusing him—there was no heat in her voice—but the certainty of her words struck him.

"You're trying to make the choice for her," she went on. "I know it comes from a place of love. But it's not entirely fair, is it?"

He exhaled, the breath catching in his chest. "No," he admitted. "I suppose it isn't, when you phrase it like that. But—"

"Respect," Felicity cut in, "isn't just about admiring someone. It's about allowing them the autonomy to choose their own way even if their choice frightens you."

The words landed like a stone in his gut. Heavy. Unignorable.

Felicity touched his arm briefly. "She loves you, Henry. That much is obvious to all of us. Let her decide. I know you care for her. Anyone with eyes can see that. But if you love her—even a little—then you must let her make her own decisions. Don't protect her by dismissing her."

Henry let out a breath and looked down at the gravel beneath his feet. The morning air was cool against his skin, but his thoughts burned hot. He didn't speak again for a long moment. When he did, his tone was quieter. More humbled.

"Thank you, Miss Doherty. I needed to hear that. You are right."

She gave a polite curtsy. "I'll leave you to your walk, then."

With that, she disappeared down the path with the maid, leaving Henry alone with the roses and with the weight of the truth she'd just handed him. If one of the things he loved so much about Charlotte was her quiet strength, he could hardly seek to take that away from her.

Sighing, he made his way back through the gardens. When he returned to the house, the halls were just beginning to stir. As he moved toward the breakfast room, he spotted Charlotte coming down the corridor. She looked tired, as though she too had wrestled with her dreams all night, but she was lovely, nonetheless.

"Lady Charlotte," he said, stepping toward her. "Might I speak with you in my office?"

She looked surprised but nodded. "Of course, Your Grace."

She followed him down the corridor, and he held the large oak door for her as she slipped inside. The office was quiet and still. Morning light filtered in through the high windows, turning strands of her chestnut hair to gold. For a moment he just watched her, drinking her in before closing the door behind them.

"Charlotte. How do you feel about everything this morning?" It was always possible that she had changed her mind during the night.

She tilted her head, thinking about his question before she responded. "I feel as though I understand you more now than I did before. Why you acted the way you did yesterday. I can't imagine what it's been like, carrying that secret for so long. But I haven't changed my mind."

The relief that flooded him was proof enough of what his own decision was. He reached for her hand and took it gently between his own. "There is nothing I want more than to marry you. To have a life with you. If I thought there was no danger..."

She squeezed his fingers. "But there is, I know. Henry, I...." She shook her head. "Never mind."

Her eyes were shaded, and he realized with a pang of remorse that she was preparing herself for another rejection.

"There is. There's no denying that. But we can fight it. Together. I would like to speak with William and your mother. To announce our engagement. But I must make it clear that I won't continue with the wedding itself until I'm sure the danger has passed."

She smiled radiantly. "Then I'll wait. I'll wait for you."

He pressed her hand to his lips. "We've already waited too

long for each other. Let's go and find William and your mother."

They encountered Lady Fitzgerald first, in the morning room, thankfully alone and sipping her tea. Charlotte approached her, with Henry alongside.

"Mama," she said. "There's something you should know."

Lady Fitzgerald looked up.

"We are to marry," Charlotte declared, raising her chin, rather proud of herself.

Lady Fitzgerald blinked once and then broke into delighted laughter and clapped her hands

"Oh, my darling girl! Of course. I've hoped for this for weeks, but had quite given up expecting it to ever happen. How marvelous."

Henry flushed. "I must caution you, my lady, that our marriage will not take place until we've addressed some... circumstances." He looked over at Charlotte, who gave a brief shake of her head. There was no need to scandalize Lady Fitzgerald with the truth unless it became absolutely necessary.

"Nonsense," she said, waving a hand. "You'll work it out. You're young and clever. I'm simply thrilled. We must have a betrothal party."

"We're not making it public knowledge just yet," Charlotte warned her, but Henry could tell his fiancée's mother was already planning her conversation with the modiste about dresses.

He grinned at Charlotte, and they left to find her brother.

William, unsurprisingly, was less enthused.

They located him in the parlor, reading the paper. When they told him, he set it down slowly.

"You've persuaded him, then," he said flatly. "Have the two of you quite taken leave of your senses?" There was no hostility in his voice, just a weary resignation.

"Possibly," Charlotte replied. "But I'm certain of this."

"As am I," Henry interjected.

William looked at him appraisingly. "You promise to protect her, Henry? Whatever the outcome of this?"

Henry inclined his head. "With my life."

William sighed but then nodded. "Then I suppose I'll try to be happy about it. For you both. But if anything happens to her—"

"It won't," Henry said firmly. "And I have heeded your advice. We will—with your blessing—be betrothed, but I won't be going ahead with the wedding itself until this issue with my mysterious letter writer is solved."

William looked thoughtful. "Perhaps the betrothal will draw them out. We should think about how best to announce it publicly—and mark who is there. It will need to be carefully planned."

Relieved to have William on their side, Henry nodded. Then William grinned suddenly, grabbed his hand, and pulled him into a tight embrace.

"You goddamn scoundrel! Now we really will be brothers." They were both less than dry-eyed as they pulled away from each other, although they quickly wiped at their faces to disguise that fact. Henry saw Charlotte smile to herself and roll her own eyes.

"We should tell my mother before we plan anything further," Henry said. "She will be going into breakfast. I'll ask her to come outside, and we can tell her quietly."

However, as they entered the breakfast room together, his mother caught sight of them walking together, and her eyebrows flew up into her hairline, especially when she saw William alongside them. Before Henry could say anything, she hurried over to them and grabbed his arm.

"Something has happened," she exclaimed. "What is it?"

"Nothing, Mother." Henry winced as heads started to turn their way. "We have something to tell you. If you have a moment."

"Oh my goodness!" The dowager duchess pressed her hand to her mouth as she looked at the three of them in turn. "Are you two…?"

"Mother, keep your voice down!" Henry hissed, rather louder than he had intended. "I hardly wanted to tell you here, but yes, Charlotte and I are betrothed."

Her eyes widened. Henry could hardly blame her. It was only yesterday that he had threatened to call a halt to her entire engagement scheme. She looked from him to Charlotte, and then her eyes softened.

"I'm very pleased," she said, smiling at them both.

"We aren't making it public knowledge yet," Henry told her.

Unfortunately, at that moment, Miss Brighton, seated not far off, gasped dramatically. "Goodness! Did I just hear that His Grace is engaged? "

Every gaze in the room turned to them.

CHAPTER 26

HENRY MENTALLY CURSED HIMSELF FOR NOT ASKING HIS mother to leave the breakfast room before he had broken the news. Of course someone would overhear, of course the entire table would fall silent, and of course it would be Miss Brighton who all but shouted the news like a crier in the square.

His mother bit back a smile, her eyebrows rising with delight. She slipped her hand around his arm. "Is it really true and not some jest, Henry?" she asked, barely concealing her glee. She spoke loudly enough that anyone who might have failed to hear Miss Brighton's proclamation couldn't possibly miss it.

He nodded stiffly. "Yes. Charlotte and I are betrothed."

The gasps that followed from various corners of the room might have been more fitting if he'd just announced an elopement or a scandal.

Someone, likely one of the younger misses, piped up, "But where's the ring?"

Charlotte sent him a panicked look.

"It hasn't been arranged yet," William smoothly cut in. "The decision was made only this morning."

A louder voice, shrill with indignation, broke through the murmurs of excitement now filling the room. "Well, what on earth are the rest of us going to do for the remainder of the week? This is most discourteous, I must say."

All heads turned toward the speaker, a Mrs. Darrow, Henry thought, whose daughter—he couldn't remember the girl's name—had taken every opportunity to flutter her eyelashes in his direction for the past four days.

Henry bowed to her and managed a polite smile, though his patience was wearing thin. "There are still other gentlemen present who may be in search of a wife, Mrs. Darrow. The ball tomorrow night will go ahead as planned. I see no reason why anyone should feel their time here has been wasted."

That earned him a few reluctant nods, though none from Mrs. Darrow herself.

Breakfast was finally served, though the atmosphere in the room had shifted. He could feel eyes on his back and hear whispers exchanged behind napkins. Charlotte took her place at the table, composed but pale, and he noticed the way she kept her gaze fixed on her plate. He knew all of this attention and gossiping would be painful for her.

His mother sat beside him and leaned in. "Why didn't you tell me sooner? I would've liked a private word before you told the entire county."

"It wasn't exactly planned this way," Henry muttered, hoping she didn't probe any further and suspect something was amiss.

"Well, I'm pleased," she said. "More than pleased. I'll speak to Lady Fitzgerald today. We must begin planning the engagement dinner."

Henry made a vague noise of agreement, but his eyes were elsewhere. Across the table, two of the unmarried women were watching Charlotte with unmistakable disdain, gossiping to each other behind their gloved fingers. Charlotte, to her credit, ignored them. He was proud of her for that.

Still, a protective instinct rose in his chest, and he had to remind himself that there was little he could do in the middle of breakfast. If anyone dared say anything cruel to her, however, he was more than happy to put them straight. Now he no longer had to hide his feelings for her or appease the others.

When the meal finally ended, he checked in with Charlotte to ensure she was well, then stood and made his way toward his study, craving a moment's quiet before the inevitable questions and congratulations the day would now bring.

He didn't get it.

William caught up with him just before he reached the door.

"Well," William said as they stepped inside the room. "That was quite the breakfast announcement."

Henry shut the door behind them. "Don't start."

"I'm not starting anything," William said, dropping into a chair like he owned the place. "I'm merely expressing sympathy. You've quite set the cat among the pigeons at this party, and all before luncheon."

Henry gave him a flat look, though his irritation was beginning to ease. "It wasn't supposed to happen like that."

"I gathered. But it's done now. You may as well enjoy the show."

At least William seemed to have thoroughly accepted the situation. Henry was relieved not to have lost his friend over this. There had been a few horrible moments during the past days when he had thought he would.

He poured himself a glass of water and leaned against the sideboard. "I'll enjoy it once we've figured out who's threatening to upend my entire life."

William sobered. "Right. That."

Henry ran a hand through his hair. "It's not that I regret it. I don't. But that wasn't how I wanted everyone to find out."

William smirked faintly. "No, I imagine you had something slightly more dignified in mind."

Henry sighed. "Just a little."

There was a beat of silence before William said, more seriously, "We'll sort this out. The blackmailer. The chaos. All of it. Just hold steady."

Henry nodded slowly. "I hope so. Because for once, I'd really like to have something that's mine. Something that isn't tangled up in secrets."

William didn't smile. He was staring at the carpet by the door. "What is that? We missed it coming in." The tone of William's voice told Henry exactly what his friend had seen before he even looked and confirmed that another message had been pushed under the door.

He frowned and stooped, plucking up the envelope. There was no seal, no name on the front. Just a hurriedly folded note inside.

William peered over his shoulder, his mouth a grim line. "Another anonymous letter?"

Henry didn't answer. He unfolded the note and scanned the lines. His stomach dropped like a stone.

Break off your engagement to Lady Charlotte immediately. If you don't, your secret will be made public knowledge.

"It's the blackmailer again," Henry said tightly. "They're obviously unhappy about the engagement."

"Well?" William prompted. "What does it say?"

Henry handed it to him silently.

William read it twice and tossed the note onto the desk with a look of disgust. "Bloody hell. No name. No signature," he said. "Same handwriting, I take it?"

Henry gave a short nod. "Definitely the same hurried scrawl."

William folded his arms. "They must have slipped it under while we were still at breakfast."

Henry sank into the chair behind his desk, rubbing at his forehead. "So they were there. In the room. Watching."

"Or heard about it shortly after. We can't be sure they were in the room at the moment the announcement was made."

Henry swore under his breath. "But the timing…. It had to have been soon after. Too soon to be a coincidence."

William made a sound of agreement. "So let's think. Who was there? Who reacted? Did anyone leave during the meal?"

Henry stared at the far wall, mentally replaying the scene. "Lady Wilmington was near my mother. She looked as though she'd bitten into a lemon."

"Her daughter is one of the hopefuls, isn't she?"

"Yes. And Miss Crawford left the table abruptly after the announcement. I think I heard her say she'd forgotten something."

William tapped a finger against his arm. "And her mother looked rather smug, although doesn't she always?"

Henry's jaw tightened. "I can't believe we're actually considering this. That someone might ruin lives over ambition."

William raised a brow. "Have you met our peers?"

Henry let out a humorless laugh. "A fair point indeed."

They fell silent for a moment, the note sitting between them on the polished wood like a loaded weapon.

"We can't discount the servants either," William said eventually. "Any number of them might've overheard something over the past week. Or maybe someone bribed one to watch and report."

Henry tilted his head. "And if a servant told someone else, the note could have come from someone far removed from the actual eavesdropper."

"We'll need to watch everyone," William said. "Not just the obvious suspects."

Henry rested his elbows on the desk, briefly closing his eyes. He felt a headache coming on. "This is going to make me even more wary."

"Good. You need to have your wits about you because someone in this house wants to destroy you."

Henry looked down at the note, then back up at William. "Then let's make a list," he said, reaching for a pencil. "We can start with who was at breakfast, who overheard the announcement, who left early, who might benefit."

William nodded. "Let's get to work."

But half an hour later, they had little but a list of guests and servants that amounted to more or less every person in the house. If simple jealousy or advancement was the motive, it could be any one of the duke's guests.

Henry sighed. He would have to make time to speak with his mother and persuade her to be more forthright with him if they were to have any hope of uncovering the truth.

"I know you don't want to hear this—" William began cautiously.

Henry interrupted him, knowing what he was about to say. "You're going to ask me to call the betrothal off." It wasn't as though he wasn't thinking about it himself. Charlotte was in direct danger now.

"Not permanently. You'll break her heart," William said quickly. "And besides, I've gotten used to the idea of having you as a brother. But perhaps at least while Charlotte is here with this troublemaker in the house. I don't want her to be targeted."

The thought of once again causing Charlotte pain was like a dagger to his heart, but he didn't see a way to avoid it. "Let us go in search of her."

They found Charlotte standing at the edge of the terrace, the morning sun catching the loose strands of her hair and gilding them in gold. She was laughing softly at something Helena had just said, one gloved hand resting on the stone balustrade, the other clutching a small plate of berries. The ease in her manner and the gentle light in her eyes as she turned and saw him made what William had suggested seem all the more unbearable.

Henry cleared his throat as he approached, and all five young women turned. "Lady Charlotte," he said, schooling his face into something approaching calm. "Might I steal a moment of your time?"

She blinked in surprise, her cheeks coloring faintly. "Of course." Her tone was warm, if cautious, as she scanned his face. She passed her plate to Miranda and stepped toward him. "Is something the matter?"

Henry didn't answer her question until they were well away from the others and had stepped inside through one of the open doors leading to the long gallery. The quiet swallowed them, broken only by the distant tick of a clock and the faint rustle of trees in the wind.

He stopped beside one of the tall windows and turned to face her. "We've received another note."

Concern knitted her brow and her hands twisted together. "What does it say?"

Henry pulled the letter from the pocket of his coat and handed it to her. "It was slipped beneath the door to my office. I doubt that whoever wrote it was bluffing. They know, and they mean to act."

She scanned the hastily scribbled lines, and her lips parted slightly in shock. She lifted her gaze to meet his. "They want you to end the engagement."

"Yes," he said quietly. "Immediately."

She gave the note back to him with a steady hand, though her knuckles were white. "I must make a confession. I received a note too. It also asked me to call off the engagement."

Henry's heart squeezed. "When was this? And why didn't you mention it earlier?"

She dipped her head. "Yesterday. I was afraid that you might change your mind about marrying me if you knew." She glanced between Henry and William. "Is that what you now intend to do? Call it off?"

Henry exchanged a glance with William before speaking. "We believe the best course of action—difficult as it is—might be to feign an end to the engagement. At least for now. It may buy us time to investigate more thoroughly. To draw the blackmailer out."

Charlotte stared at him as if he'd struck her. "I feared as much. You want to lie to everyone and pretend we've ended things? After you have only just announced our betrothal?" As she said it, it made William's plan seem ludicrous.

He sighed, rubbing the back of his neck. "Not forever. Just until we can determine who is behind this. The timing of the note suggests they were present at breakfast. If we act quickly, we may catch them unawares."

Her eyes were bright with emotion, her chin tilted upward in that familiar, stubborn way he was coming to recognize. "And what would you have me do? Flounce into the drawing room in tears and announce that you've broken my heart?"

"Nothing so dramatic, Charlotte," William cut in, stepping forward now. "A discreet withdrawal, perhaps a quiet word shared with a few of the chattier mothers. Word would spread quickly without you having to stage a scene."

Charlotte crossed her arms. "So, I am to help spread gossip about myself?"

Henry flinched at the steel in her voice. "Charlotte, I don't ask this lightly."

"No, I rather think you do." She raised her chin once more. "You think I can be handled, moved about like a pawn. Do you think so little of me? You asked for my hand—

perhaps not with a ring, but with intention—and I gave you my heart. You said you would not marry me until the danger passed. I agreed to that. And now you wish to back away entirely."

"I wish to protect you," Henry said firmly. "To shield you from scandal and from harm. If we proceed as if all is well, we leave ourselves vulnerable to further manipulation."

"Then we face it together," she snapped. "I will not allow some shadowed coward to dictate the course of my life, nor my heart. You would not be protecting me, Henry. You would be abandoning me."

The accusation struck hard. He took a step toward her, lowering his voice. "Please, try to understand. If this becomes known, it will not only be my reputation ruined. It will be yours as well. They will say you were complicit. That you deceived society alongside me. I may never get a chance to wed you if this comes out first."

Charlotte shook her head. "Let them say those things." Her voice trembled. "I would rather be reviled for loving you honestly than praised for abandoning you out of fear."

William exhaled sharply and turned away, running a hand through his hair. "Charlotte, for heaven's sake, think this through. You're being so… stubborn."

She rounded on him, eyes blazing. "And you're being a coward. You say you care for me, and yet you side with fear every time. For the last time, I am not some fragile thing you must shelter. I have a mind of my own, and I have made it up. Must we go through all of this again? Was yesterday not enough? I will not agree to this plan. I'd rather tell everyone about the notes."

Silence fell again, thick and heavy.

Henry looked between them both, torn in two. William was right to be cautious, and yet, Henry could not keep playing with Charlotte's feelings. He sought to protect her, yet he was making her feel abandoned. They shouldn't start their lives together this way.

"You would rather risk everything," he asked slowly, "than take a step back, even if it is just for now?"

Charlotte's voice was quiet but unyielding. "Yes. Because taking a step back means we've already lost. You're giving them exactly what they want. This won't help you catch them at all. It will just embolden them to make more demands and play more games. We continue with the betrothal and draw them out that way. We can wed in secret if necessary, before it can be stopped."

He stared at her for a long moment. Then, without another word, he folded the letter and returned it to his coat pocket, giving William an apologetic shrug.

William shook his head incredulously. "This is utter madness."

"It may be," Charlotte replied, lifting her chin again. "But at least we are standing by our principles, not giving in to a blackmailer."

Henry wanted to pull her into his arms, press his lips to hers, and tell her she was extraordinary, that he'd never known anyone like her. But instead, he gave her a small nod.

"Very well," he said, the words catching in his throat. "No retraction. We proceed."

"Good." Charlotte's hands were still shaking, but she turned back toward the terrace with the grace of a queen.

Henry watched her go, equal parts admiration and dread coiling in his chest.

When she was gone, William groaned aloud and slumped into one of the chairs by the window. "You know, you used to be the sensible one."

Henry let out a laugh that held little humor. "I'm beginning to question that myself."

"What now?"

Henry looked out at the garden where the guests were

beginning to wander. "Now we start watching." He glanced at William. "And we pray we're not too late."

"And what about Charlotte?"

Henry stared at the door she had walked through and whispered, "God help me, I think I've just fallen in love with her all over again."

CHAPTER 27

THE DRAWING ROOM WAS WARM WITH SUNLIGHT AND laughter later that day when the Dowager Duchess of Arundel clapped her hands and declared, "I believe it is time for a game of charades!"

Charlotte, seated beside Miranda on a brocade settee in the drawing room, exchanged a glance with her friend. The suggestion drew a little interest—a few guests clearly wished for nothing more than to return to their needlework or books.

Regardless, the duchess's word was law in that room, and soon the furniture was rearranged, a makeshift performance space cleared, and everyone was being sorted into sides with light protest and good humor.

"Now," said the dowager, her voice carrying cheerfully, "as we have a newly betrothed couple among us, it seems only right that Lady Charlotte should go first."

A small, scattered round of applause followed, and Charlotte felt the blood rush to her cheeks. She stood slowly, smoothing her skirts with damp palms and trying not to catch Henry's eye. It was impossible not to feel every gaze in the room turning to her, particularly those of the unmarried ladies who now had every reason to wish her to humiliate herself.

Someone laughed lightly, and she wasn't entirely sure it was a friendly sound.

The box of prompts was passed to her, and she reached inside, her fingers brushing scraps of paper until one folded square came loose. She opened it, read the phrase—*riding sidesaddle*—and sighed. Not the worst, but hardly flattering.

Still, she moved to the open space with as much grace as she could muster and began. Her pantomime was met with a few quiet chuckles, several wrong guesses, and eventually a triumphant call of "Sidesaddle!" from William, who wore a self-satisfied grin, as though he'd just solved a naval code.

Charlotte curtsied and returned to her seat. Her heart was pounding more than the effort had warranted.

As she sat down, she noticed Adeline and Genevieve were seated a few places over, their heads bent together in murmured conversation. There was a sharpness to their glances, not aimed in her direction but past her, toward where Henry sat near the fireplace, enduring the attention of two particularly talkative debutantes.

Charlotte leaned closer to Adeline and whispered, "What's going on?"

Adeline, without looking at her, said under her breath, "Someone asked a rather pointed question during the portrait tour earlier. About the resemblance—or lack thereof —between Henry and the late duke."

Charlotte's stomach twisted sickeningly. She sat back slowly, forcing a smile as though she'd just heard some charming tidbit rather than what might be the first crack in a dam ready to burst.

Was it merely coincidence? Perhaps. Or perhaps not. The timing was too perfect, too suspicious. First the notes to both her and Henry, and now whispers about his parentage. Whoever was behind the blackmail wasn't idle.

She glanced at Henry. He was listening to something Miss Brighton was saying, but there was a tightness around his mouth she recognized. He wasn't enjoying himself.

Her instinct was to go to him, to warn him and to tell him that the whispers had already begun, but she hesitated. He was already so cautious, so hesitant about their engagement. If he thought the gossip had started in earnest, he might take it as another sign to abandon the whole thing.

It had been worrisome enough to tell him about the note in case he did so. She didn't want to test him again.

No, she decided. She couldn't risk that. She was determined to be his wife, no matter what happened.

Instead, she turned her attention to William. He was laughing at something Helena had said, his turn at charades drawing closer. She caught his eye and gave him a meaningful look, tilting her head toward the corridor.

He frowned slightly but nodded.

His name was called next, and he rose, rolled his eyes at the crowd for their dramatic pleasure, and then strode into the middle of the room. His charade was a rather absurd rendering of a foxhunt, complete with leaping and mock horn blowing, and it earned plenty of laughter—especially from the gentlemen who'd actually been on the hunt with him that morning.

As soon as the group called out the answer, Charlotte caught his arm.

"Walk with me," she murmured.

He followed her without protest, the two of them slipping out through the French doors and onto the stone terrace. From there, she led him along the edge of the garden until they were well out of earshot of the drawing room.

"All right," William said, hands in his pockets. "You've got that look, like you've uncovered a great plot."

She didn't smile. "Someone raised the issue of Henry's resemblance to the late duke during the portrait tour."

William stopped walking, his eyes widening. "Hell."

Charlotte grimaced. "Adeline told me. She overheard it."

"And this was today?" he asked.

She nodded.

He let out a slow breath. "It might be unrelated."

"You don't believe that."

"No, I don't," he admitted. "But I'd very much like to."

Charlotte wrapped her arms around herself, trying to stifle the anxiety that rose within her. "So would I. Do you know if Henry has broached the issue with his mother?"

He grimaced. "She remains tight-lipped on the matter but allows that it is possible a servant learned the truth."

"That isn't particularly helpful." She sighed. "I'm concerned. What if the blackmailer is starting to test the waters, seeing who'll notice the rumors, who'll whisper, and do his dirty work for him?"

William whistled under his breath. "This isn't good."

"No," Charlotte agreed softly. "It's not."

Charlotte returned to the drawing room with her thoughts still spinning. She tried to focus on the current round of charades. Genevieve was up now, pantomiming something with increasingly wild gestures, but Charlotte's attention kept drifting. The tightness in her chest refused to ease, no matter how many times she reminded herself to breathe.

She sat beside Adeline again, still half in a fog.

"From whom did you hear about the portrait?" she murmured, keeping her eyes fixed on Genevieve as if fully engrossed in the game.

Adeline didn't hesitate. "Miss Brighton mentioned it. Apparently someone asked why Lord Arundel doesn't resemble his father."

Charlotte's pulse quickened. "And did Miss Brighton say who asked?"

Adeline shook her head slightly. "No, only that she over-heard it."

Charlotte nodded, her lips pressed together. "Thank you."

Miss Brighton. Of course it would be her. Always watching, always listening; she was the gossip queen of the *ton*. Charlotte didn't know whether Miss Brighton had begun the whispering herself or was simply passing it along like a particularly eager carrier pigeon, but either way, it was information that needed tracing.

And fast.

She could hardly go up to Miss Brighton and demand answers. Not without drawing more attention to the subject of Henry's parentage. The last thing they needed now was more scrutiny.

A throbbing began to build behind her eyes. She rubbed at her temple lightly. Perhaps getting some air would help. She slipped out of her chair, leaned down, and whispered to the dowager duchess that she had a headache and would like to step out for a moment.

"Oh, of course, my lady," the duchess said with a wave of her hand, clearly more interested in the next round than in Charlotte's mild ailment. "Take as long as you need."

Grateful not to be pressed further, Charlotte exited through the double doors that led to the terrace and from there made her way around the side of the house. The afternoon sun was beginning to dip, casting long shadows across the lawn, and a soft breeze tugged at the loose tendrils of her hair.

She walked slowly at first, her slippered feet crunching softly on the gravel path that circled the great estate. The hedges loomed tall and manicured around her, and she let her hand trail along the cool, waxy leaves as she tried to make sense of what she'd heard.

Someone had commented on Henry's lack of resemblance to the late duke. That wasn't idle gossip. That was a direct threat. After all, what were the odds that this observation would come now, just after the announcement of their engagement?

Her thoughts were interrupted by the distant sound of hooves.

She frowned and slowed her pace, stepping quietly through the hedge until she reached the gravel drive at the front of the house. A black carriage was arriving at the base of the stairs. A tall man in a dark overcoat climbed inside, his face turned away.

But his gait. His posture. Even from behind, Charlotte's breath caught in her throat. She knew that man.

Sir Roger.

She crouched down instinctively, ducking behind a nearby yew bush, her heart hammering. She watched as the door was closed behind him and the driver flicked the reins. The carriage rolled down the drive and disappeared beyond the trees.

Her hand tightened around a branch, and she remained frozen for a long moment after the carriage had gone.

What on earth was he doing here?

He wasn't a guest. He hadn't been invited. And yet there he was, slinking away like a man who knew he shouldn't be seen.

She rose slowly, brushing the leaves from her skirts. The coincidence was too great to ignore. Sir Roger had no friends at Arundel Park, no social obligations that would bring him here. The only connection he had was to her, and, by extension, to her brother and Henry.

Could he be the one sending the letters?

She'd dismissed the idea before, thinking he hadn't the subtlety. But perhaps she'd underestimated him. If he were acting out of spite for being rejected, for being humiliated in front of society, it would make sense. And if it was money he wanted, what better way than to leverage a secret like Henry's?

The longer she thought on it, the more plausible it seemed. Although there remained an insurmountable question: How could he have discovered it?

She turned back toward the house, suddenly impatient to share this with someone—anyone who might take it seriously.

Henry. William. Even Felicity. Someone had to be told that Sir Roger had been on the grounds. She'd seen him with her own eyes, and it couldn't be a coincidence.

Her slippers scuffed hurriedly across the gravel, and she reentered the house through the rear entrance, heart thudding, hands trembling slightly.

They needed to know. And they needed to act.

She returned to the drawing room, trying not to rush despite the feeling of urgency in her chest. As she slipped back through the door, she found that the lively energy of the earlier charades had dissipated. The sofas had been rearranged and the crowd dispersed. Several ladies sat near the pianoforte now, speaking in low tones, while the men had largely migrated to the card tables in the adjoining room.

William was seated at one of them, holding a hand of cards and conversing with a young blond gentleman. Charlotte crossed the room, weaving past a group of young women chatting about a bonnet trimming demonstration, and stepped to his side.

"William," she said quietly, "can I borrow you again for a moment?"

He looked up from his cards, his expression immediately sharpening when he saw her face. "Of course," he said, tossing his hand down. "Gentlemen, I must fold. Duty calls."

The other players barely grumbled, nodding their understanding. William stood and followed Charlotte into the hallway without question.

"What is it? Has something else happened?" he asked once they were alone.

"I need to speak with both you and Henry. Now. It's important."

William didn't waste time asking why. He simply gestured for her to follow him. "I think he mentioned needing a moment to himself after charades. Likely in the library or his office. He lives in there."

They made their way down the corridor in silence, the echo of their footfalls on the marble floor almost loud in the stillness. Once they approached the office door, William knocked and pushed it open.

Henry was inside, standing by the window with one hand resting on the sill, looking out at the lengthening shadows of the late afternoon. He turned at the sound of the door.

"Charlotte," he said, surprised. "William."

"Sorry to disturb you," she said. "But I saw something you need to know."

Henry's brow furrowed, and he gestured for them both to come in. "What is it?"

She stepped into the room, taking a breath to steady herself. "I was outside just now, trying to clear my head, and I saw someone getting into a carriage out front. A man. From behind, he looked exactly like Sir Roger."

Henry straightened slightly. "Leonard? Here?"

"I think so," she said. "I can't be certain, but I swear it looked like him. And he left without anyone knowing. It didn't feel right."

William closed the door behind them with a quiet click. "Why the devil would Leonard be here? He hasn't any connection to the other guests, does he?"

"None that I know of," Henry replied.

Charlotte moved closer to the hearth, twisting her fingers together. "I thought perhaps he was behind the notes."

Henry blinked. "Because of you?"

"I don't know." She frowned. "Maybe. At first I thought it seemed ridiculous, but if he's angry about what happened between us—if he's holding a grudge—maybe this is his way of retaliating. Not by ruining me, but by threatening you. After all, one of the notes did come to me directly and whoever it is clearly wants the engagement ended."

William looked unconvinced. "You really think he'd go to such lengths just because you intervened between him and Charlotte?"

Henry's mouth quirked. "You underestimate how far a man might go to win someone he believes he's lost. If I thought I might lose you forever, I'm not sure I wouldn't consider desperate measures myself." He said the last to Charlotte, gazing deeply into her eyes.

That startled her, and she felt a faint flush creeping up her neck. She wasn't sure what to say to that, and William, sensing the sudden atmosphere, cleared his throat and stepped back.

"I'll make some quiet inquiries," he said. "If Leonard was on the grounds, someone must have seen something. A stable hand or a grounds servant perhaps. Someone would have noticed the carriage if nothing else."

Charlotte turned to him, grateful. "Thank you, brother."

"I'll let you know what I hear," he said, already heading for the door. "Keep an eye out yourselves. If he's involved in this, we need to find proof. Quickly."

And then he was gone, the door closing softly behind him.

Charlotte turned back to Henry. He was watching her thoughtfully, his gaze flickering over her face as though memorizing it.

"There must be more to this," she murmured. "With Leonard, I mean. He's here to ruin you."

"You truly don't think it's possible he's only here because he wants you back?" he asked softly.

She shook her head. "I don't think anyone would go to these lengths just to make me their wife."

Henry's expression changed slightly, but he said nothing.

Charlotte stepped forward just close enough for him to hear her lowered voice. "But I do think someone wants to hurt you. And I think Leonard's the sort of man who might enjoy that. Perhaps he is acting for someone?"

Henry's jaw tightened. "Then we'll find out if it's him."

She nodded. "Sooner rather than later."

They stood there for a moment, the quiet between them thick with unspoken things, before Henry broke the silence.

"Thank you," he said. "For telling me. For staying with me in spite of… everything."

Charlotte's lips curved into a small, private smile. "I think you're worth the risk."

The air had gone still, the gentle hush of the room pressing in around them. Somewhere, far off, she thought she heard the muted sounds of laughter from the parlor, the shuffle of footsteps and the crackle of the fire, but all of it was distant, irrelevant.

Henry was looking at her as though she were the only person left in the world.

"Charlotte," he said softly, his voice lower now, reverent. "I would go to any lengths. For you."

And then he stepped closer. Just one pace. But it was enough.

Her heart was racing, thudding hard against her ribs. She felt breathless, rooted to the spot, unable to look away from him. She searched his face, trying to make sense of his expression. Of the desperation, the longing, the fear, and the fierce affection that flickered there.

He reached for her slowly, giving her every chance to pull away. She didn't. She couldn't. Her hands lifted of their own accord, curling lightly around the lapels of his coat. She thought she might say something—warn him, or herself, against getting caught again—but the words stuck in her throat.

And then he kissed her.

It was not the hurried, spontaneous kiss by the lake. This was deliberate and certain. His mouth met hers with such intensity that it took her breath. One of his hands cupped the side of her face, his fingers threading through her hair as though he was afraid she might disappear if he didn't hold her close enough.

Charlotte leaned into him, her body melting against his. The kiss deepened, his other arm winding around her waist and drawing her into his chest, anchoring her. She kissed him back with every ounce of emotion she'd kept bottled up. Her fear, frustration, longing, and hope. It spilled out of her, pouring into a single, searing kiss.

The world fell away.

For one impossibly perfect moment, there was no black-mailer, no scandal, no future to fear. There was only Henry's mouth on hers, the strength of his arms around her, and the pounding of her own heartbeat in her ears.

When at last they parted, both of them breathless, he rested his forehead against hers.

"I love you," she whispered.

"I love you too, dear Charlotte."

Charlotte stood near the window of Henry's office, studying the way the late afternoon light caught the gleam of the polished floor and cast long shadows across the desk as she watched Henry reread the letter for what must have been the hundredth time. According to him, he had discovered the letter on his desk not an hour earlier.

There was tension in his shoulders and the tight line of his jaw. He looked up at last and passed the letter to her, his fingers brushing hers as he did so. She took it without a word, sinking into the chair beside William as she unfolded the page. The handwriting was messy, as though scrawled in haste, but the message was clear:

You have until the night of the ball to call off the wedding, or your mother's secret becomes the talk of London.

Charlotte's stomach twisted, but her hands were steady as she passed the letter to William.

"So, do you have news on Leonard?" she asked, turning her eyes toward him.

William nodded. "I've been asking around. He's been seen in the area on more than one occasion and at times that correspond with the letters. The day of the first letter, he was spotted buying paper and ink at the stationer's in the next town. One of the footmen saw him lingering near the east wing yesterday morning. And the worst part is... he's still telling people in Town that the two of you"—he nodded at Charlotte—"will be announcing your engagement soon."

Charlotte's mouth dropped open. "Even now? After everything?"

"It seems that news of the duke's engagement hasn't reached the gossip pages yet," William explained. "Or if it has, he's pretending he hasn't heard about it."

Henry leaned back in his chair, his eyes flashing with uncharacteristic fury. "He's desperate, then. If this letter is from him—and I believe it is—then he's running out of time, and he knows it."

Charlotte twisted her hands together in her lap. "So what do we do? Are we still going forward with this?"

Henry's eyes met hers, and for a long moment, he was silent. Then he spoke, his voice low. "Are you absolutely certain you want this, knowing what he's threatening?"

She rose from her chair, crossed to him, and settled her hand over his. "Yes, Henry. I was certain the moment I told you I'd take the risk. I'm not going to be bullied into giving up my life because of some man's bitterness. Please, let's have had enough of this constant questioning of my decision. I am yours."

He exhaled, and she could feel the fight drain out of him. "Then we go forward as planned. Safeguards are already in place. He will not set foot inside the ballroom—not tonight. Not ever. And if he does try, there will be footmen waiting to escort him to a room where he can explain himself."

William nodded. "I've spoken with the staff. No one will be admitted without a name on the guest list, and we've added guards near the doors and windows. Mother is circulating the story that thefts have been reported in the area so that the other guests don't question the extra precautions."

Charlotte exhaled, the knot in her chest loosening slightly. "That's good. There is nothing to fear."

She wasn't sure if she was trying to convince them or herself.

Henry gave her a small smile, then stood. "We should prepare. There's still the ball this evening to get through."

She left them there, the weight of what they faced still heavy, but somehow lighter now that the decision had been made.

Back in her chamber, the fire had been lit and the soft glow of candlelight flickered against the walls. Mary moved quietly around her, helping her into her gown of deep sapphire silk with embroidered detailing that caught the light with every movement. It was the most luxurious gown she owned, but surely the occasion of celebrating her betrothal called for it.

Her hair was pinned up in soft curls, a few left loose to frame her face, and she clasped the pearl-drop earrings her mother had insisted she wear.

Her friends were gathered outside her chamber as she emerged, each of them resplendent in their own gown. Helena's sharp grin was tempered by concern as she saw the frown on Charlotte's face. Miranda's hands were clasped in front of her, and Genevieve reached out to touch Charlotte's wrist gently.

Although her friends didn't know the full story, they knew Charlotte well enough to know there was trouble afoot.

"Ready?" Adeline asked.

Charlotte nodded. "As I'll ever be."

They descended the staircase together, six women strong, into the flickering candlelight of the ballroom. Charlotte walked across the room arm in arm with Felicity, scanning the gathering crowd with care.

Every smile, every glance, every murmured conversation

—she absorbed it all, searching for anything out of place. Somewhere in this very room, there could be a person who wished to tear apart her future. Someone in league with the despicable Sir Roger. She would not allow them to spoil her happiness.

The ballroom sparkled under the golden light of a dozen chandeliers, the polished floors gleamed like glass, and the guests moved in a flurry of silk and satin. The orchestra played a lively tune in the corner, warming up for the first dance. The scent of beeswax polish, flowers, and expensive perfume hung heavily in the air.

It was perfect, and the dowager duchess had done herself proud, but Charlotte felt anything but at ease. Even without the impending danger, she knew every eye would be upon her, and the thought made her palms clammy.

Henry appeared beside her, resplendent in deep navy. He bowed, a little smile playing at the corners of his mouth. "Shall we?"

Charlotte curtsied. "We shall."

With her hand in Henry's, her nerves receded. The waltz began, and he drew her into the circle of dancers. As he took her hand and placed his other lightly at her waist, a shiver slid down her spine. Not of nerves this time—but of anticipation. Of simple joy at his touch.

They moved together in elegant steps, effortlessly matching each other's rhythm. She was aware of the warmth of his hand, the closeness of his body, the intensity of his gaze. They didn't speak, not with words, but his eyes said everything. When he looked at her like that, as if she were the only person in the room, it was hard to remember that danger still lingered in the wings.

"You're beautiful," he murmured as they turned.

She blushed at his words, and he smiled then, not his usual guarded one, but something gentler. Something real that reminded her of the boy she had known years before.

When the dance ended, the room burst into polite applause, and they stepped back. Almost immediately, the dowager duchess appeared on Henry's other side. She looked every inch the pleased matriarch, her jewels glittering and her smile triumphant.

"Well," she said, her voice low and smug. "I suppose I must admit, this house party has proven more effective than I could have dreamed."

Charlotte blinked, unsure how to respond. Henry's expression was unreadable, though his lips thinned ever so slightly, in amusement or annoyance, Charlotte wasn't sure. Of course Henry's mother would claim their betrothal as her own triumph.

William stepped in with impeccable timing and bowed. "Sister, might I claim the next dance? I fear if I delay much longer, the matchmaking mamas may trample me on their way over."

She took his offered hand. "Of course."

Polite, brisk, and precisely on time, their dance was a contrast to the one before it. William led expertly, but his gaze kept darting around the room. He was clearly as wary as she had been earlier.

Halfway through the dance, he leaned in slightly. "You do realize," he said in a low voice, "that you and your little league of conspirators haven't been half as subtle as you think."

Charlotte startled, looking up at him in surprise. "What do you mean? Henry asked for us to try to keep those 'matchmaking mamas' away; you know this."

"I mean the whispering, the closed-door meetings, the quiet glances between you and Henry. Don't look so shocked. I may be a man, but I'm not blind. It's more than just protecting Henry, as your betrothal proves. You're all up to something, and I don't think it stops at this house party. What is it, a matchmaking club?"

She laughed despite herself. "I didn't think you noticed."

"Oh, I noticed," he said with a wink. "But I've decided I don't care. Not if it means we all get a happy ending out of this."

Her smile faltered slightly. "Let's hope we all do."

The dance ended, and they returned to the edge of the room, where Henry stood, speaking to a footman who had just arrived and was whispering something in his ear.

Henry stiffened. Charlotte saw the worry in his eyes.

"What is it?" Charlotte asked urgently, dread coiling in her stomach.

He turned toward her, his tone sharp. "Sir Roger is here. The footmen stopped him before he reached the ballroom. They've detained him near the east gallery."

William nodded. "We anticipated this. I'll distract your mother, and then we will go and question him."

Charlotte opened her mouth to offer her help, but before anyone could move, the doors at the far end of the ballroom creaked open.

A tall man stepped into the doorway.

Charlotte didn't recognize him—he was no one she had seen before, certainly not part of the household staff or any known guest. He stood straight and still, scanning the room with a gaze far too intent for comfort.

"Who is that?" she whispered, instinctively reaching for Henry's arm.

"I haven't a clue," Henry said, looking confused.

"But I have." The dowager duchess appeared at his side, clutching at her pearls, her face white. So softly her voice was almost imperceptible, she murmured, "It's *him*, Henry. Lord have mercy. I thought he was dead."

CHAPTER 29

THE MAN WALKED TOWARD THEM WITH SLOW, PURPOSEFUL steps. Henry studied him, his heart a thunderclap in his chest. Every inch of him was alert with an instinctive wariness hard-earned by years of pretending. Pretending not to carry the very secret that now threatened to burst from the shadows.

The man was tall and broad-shouldered, perhaps in his late fifties. His coat was modest but neatly pressed, and though his hair had silvered at the temples, the shade of brown was familiar. His eyes—the color of bark—were bright and searching. There was no trace of anger in his expression. If anything, he looked... hopeful. Eager. Almost afraid.

Henry's mother turned toward him and gripped his arm just hard enough for him to feel her nails.

"I don't understand what's happening." She sounded more lost than he'd ever heard her before. "I refuse to remain here for this. Whatever it is, it can't end well."

Before Henry could say a word, she was gone, sweeping past the crowd in a rustle of silk and jewels, her chin held high even as the color drained from her face and she ran away from the scandal she had helped create, leaving Henry, the victim of it all, to deal with it.

He didn't stop her.

"Your Grace," the man said when he reached him, his voice low and unsteady. "I received an invitation, but I wonder now if it was genuine. Might we speak somewhere private?"

Henry swallowed the rising tide of dread and gave a single nod. "Of course."

He could feel the eyes on them across the room—dozens of guests wondering who the man was and what he wanted of the duke. Curious whispering. Could they see a resemblance between them?

The music hadn't stopped, and yet the ballroom buzzed with energy that had nothing to do with the next dance. Charlotte stepped forward without a word and took Henry's arm. Her presence steadied him. William caught his eye and gave the faintest nod before turning toward the musicians, already taking on the responsibility of keeping the party from descending into chaos without needing to be asked.

Henry, Charlotte, and the man—*his father*—left the ballroom together and made for Henry's study. Once inside, Henry shut the door and locked it behind them.

He didn't offer anyone a drink.

He needed his head clear.

The man remained standing, glancing around the office as if it were something holy. "It's strange," he murmured. "To be here. I've passed this house a hundred times over the years, but never stepped inside."

Henry folded his arms. "You said you were invited?"

"I was," the man replied. "By someone claiming to be from your household. They said you were ready to meet me. That you'd arranged the whole thing and wanted it to be discreet."

"I didn't," Henry said, more sharply than intended. "I had no idea who you were until two minutes ago."

The man nodded slowly. "I realized that the moment I walked in. You looked like you'd seen a ghost. Which, I suppose... in a way... you had."

Charlotte stepped closer, standing just behind Henry's shoulder. She didn't speak, but he felt her anchoring presence like a lighthouse in the storm.

"Who are you?" Henry asked quietly.

The man's face creased with something between sadness and pride. "My name is Elias March. I own a modest shipping business now, but long ago I was an assistant steward to your grandfather—His Grace, the twelfth Duke of Arundel. I worked here on the estate. That was how I came to know your mother."

The air thickened.

"I was young," Elias continued. "Not stupid, but... optimistic. I was eager to prove myself. She was—well, you know what she's like. Beautiful. Clever. Terrifying, if I'm honest. We were both lonely, I think. And I was foolish."

Henry said nothing.

"When I learned she was with child, I went to her and asked if it might be mine," Elias said softly. "I wanted to support her as best I could, but she sent me away. She said it was handled, and there was no need for further contact. But I knew what it meant. I knew the duke—her husband—must have agreed to raise the child as his own. The way she worded it, I almost wondered if he'd known everything all along."

Henry nodded. His father *had*. Most likely, he'd masterminded the affair, and the duchess had simply followed his orders and manipulated poor Elias.

"I was devastated," Elias went on. "But I knew I would be unable to give either of you the life you deserved, and the duke could have ruined me if he wanted. Instead, he came to me soon after and offered me a cheque on the condition that I leave and never approach any of you again." He looked down, ashamed. "At the time, that was enough for me. I took the payment, and went."

Silence fell.

Henry stared at him, wondering what on earth to say.

Elias cleared his throat. "As the years passed, I wondered about you. I read what I could about your life. I even kept the painting from the papers when you became the new duke. You looked... proud. Serious. Like him, I thought. Like me."

There was a certain likeness between them. Even Henry could tell that at a glance.

Elias gave a shaky laugh. "I never dreamed we'd meet. Not until a few months ago."

Henry narrowed his eyes. "What changed?"

Elias hesitated. "I was drunk," he admitted. "In a tavern in London. I ran into the son of an old acquaintance, a Mr. Roger Leonard. I said too much. I let slip more than I should have."

Henry's jaw clenched.

"I thought he was just a man with a sympathetic ear," Elias said. "But now I see that he was using me to cause you harm."

Henry's eyes hardened. "He's behind a series of anonymous letters I've been receiving. He's threatening to expose us. You. Me. My mother."

Elias closed his eyes. "I'm sorry. I swear to you, I never wanted this. I never intended to ruin you."

"What *do* you want?" Henry asked, suddenly tired. "Why are you here?"

Elias straightened. "Only to tell you that I will never speak of this again. If anyone comes to me, I will deny it. I'll burn every letter I kept, every proof I ever had. You are the Duke of Arundel. No one else. He raised you as his son and accepted you as his heir. I agreed to that at the time, knowing it was best for you. Why would I want to take that away now? Going away and staying quiet was my gift to you. The only one I could give."

The words sat heavy between them.

"I'd like...." Elias paused. "I'd like to get to know you, if you're willing. I know it's a lot to ask. But I'm not here to claim anything. I'm not here for money. I only—well, I only hoped you might like to know me too."

Henry looked at Charlotte, whose gaze was soft with empathy. She nodded once, encouraging him

"I'll think about it," Henry murmured. "That's the best I can do right now."

Elias's shoulders sagged in relief. He reached into his coat, pulled out a card, and offered it. "This is where I'm staying. Just a small inn in the village. I won't linger. I just wanted you to know I'm here and that I have no ill will toward you."

Henry took the card but didn't look at it before he slipped it into his coat pocket.

"Thank you for hearing me out," Elias said. "And congratulations. She is a very pretty girl." He nodded at Charlotte, who gave him a flattered smile.

With that, Elias March let himself out. The door clicked shut behind him.

Henry stood still for a long moment, staring at the place where the man had been.

"Well," he said quietly. "That was something."

Charlotte came to his side and slipped her hand into his. "Are you all right, my love?"

"I don't know." He was rather stunned by the events of the day.

"Do you want him in your life?"

"I don't know that either," Henry said honestly. "It's strange. I thought if I ever came face to face with him, I'd be angry. Feel betrayed. But mostly I'm just... tired. And a little sad."

Charlotte squeezed his hand. "You don't have to decide anything right away."

He turned toward her, his face softening. "No. But thank you for being here."

"Always." She slipped her arm through his as they left the study to return to the ballroom.

Henry's thoughts buzzed with everything still unresolved, but the relief he felt was real. Tangible. A weight lifted off his chest that had settled there when he was barely old enough to understand it.

Charlotte leaned closer as they walked. "We're safe," she whispered. "He said he'll deny everything. No one will hear the truth from him. We don't have to worry anymore. Without his evidence, it's nothing but a salacious rumor cooked up by Sir Roger. This means we're free to be together without fear of scandal."

Henry stopped in his tracks as her words hit him. A flicker of lamplight danced across her cheek as she turned to face him. For the first time in days, maybe weeks, he felt something other than dread. Something warmer, brighter, more alive.

He dipped his head and kissed her.

Not cautiously this time. Not with any restraint. He kissed her like a man who had thought he would lose everything, only to find it again in the shape of the woman before him. Her arms slipped around his neck, and he held her close, anchoring himself to her. Tasting her, burying his face in her hair.

When they pulled apart, she was breathless, smiling softly.

"Come," he said, threading his fingers through hers. "Let's go finish this."

The room where Sir Roger was being held was small and sparsely furnished, more of a storage room than a cell. Two Arundel footmen stood guard at the door, arms folded and expressions grim. Henry gave them a nod, and they stepped aside to let him and Charlotte pass.

Sir Roger sat in a chair in the center of the room, his legs sprawled out and his arms crossed defiantly, but the way he chewed on his lower lip gave away his nerves. He looked like a man who had been caught but wasn't sure yet what crime he'd been charged with.

Henry shut the door behind them. "Sir Roger," he said coolly. "I think you know why we're here."

"I have my suspicions," Leonard drawled. "Though I must say, you've gone to an awful lot of trouble. A bit dramatic, don't you think?"

Charlotte stiffened beside Henry, but he kept his tone even. "You spoke to Elias March. He told you something he shouldn't have."

Leonard shrugged, one side of his mouth hitching up slyly. "Men say foolish things when they've had too much brandy and not enough sense."

"And then you used that information," Henry said, "to orchestrate a campaign of blackmail. To keep me from marrying the woman I love."

Leonard smirked. "Blackmail? Oh, come now. I never sent a single note. Never lifted a pen. I told someone, that's all. What they did with the information wasn't my business."

"So you know about the notes. Strange, if you had nothing to do with it. Who did you tell?"

Leonard flushed guiltily, knowing he had been caught out. "The Fairchilds. You remember Miss Harriet Fairchild, I assume? Pretty girl. You were alone with her in the garden not long ago."

Henry's stomach dropped. Of course. The note directing him to the grotto, the scene staged with Harriet. It had all been a trap. He had seen the outline of it; only now could he put it all together.

"They wanted a match," Leonard went on. "They figured if you got caught alone with her, they could steer you into a marriage without ever having to say why. No need to spoil the arrangement with scandal. Clever, really."

"You stood by and let them do it."

Leonard grinned. "I didn't want you. I wanted her." His eyes flicked to Charlotte, and Henry nearly took a step forward.

"She looked at you like a man dying of thirst looks at a glass of water," Leonard said nastily. "No matter what I did, she wouldn't even see me. You had everything I wanted."

"And now you have nothing," Henry said quietly. "I've spoken to Elias. He will deny all knowledge of these rumors about being my father. Including to the Fairchilds. No one will believe *you* over a duke. If you continue, I'll see you in court for slander."

Leonard's grin faded.

"I'm having you escorted from the premises," Henry continued. "You will not come near Lady Charlotte again. Not in town. Not at any ball, any gathering, or any shop on Bond Street. If I so much as hear your name spoken in her presence, I will meet you at dawn. And we both know," he added coldly, "no matter how much you love hunting, you're a miserable shot."

Leonard paled but nodded his assent. He'd clearly realized he could go no further.

Henry opened the door and motioned to the waiting servants. "Show Sir Roger out. Please make sure he understands that he is not to return. Ever."

They stepped inside, flanking Leonard without a word. He rose stiffly, and for a moment, it seemed he might protest —but then he saw Henry's expression and thought better of it.

He turned to Charlotte. "You're making a mistake, you know. Men like him don't change. He'll ruin you eventually."

Charlotte met his gaze with steel in her eyes. "Get out."

Leonard was gone within moments.

Henry exhaled.

"What now?" Charlotte asked.

Henry turned toward her. "Now we confront the Fairchilds. We'll make it clear their game is over. That whatever they thought they might gain has slipped through their fingers. As far as they're concerned, Sir Roger was lying to them. I'll have them banished from the house, ordered to never speak of this again unless they wish to be arrested for blackmail."

"And then?" she prompted, her tone teasing.

"And then," he said with a small smile, "we go back to the ball and celebrate our betrothal. Smile for the crowd. Pretend none of this happened. And I'll have to consider what I want to do about... my father."

Charlotte swayed closer. "You'll figure it out."

"But before any of that..." Henry took a step toward her, reaching for her hand again. "Before I think about anything else at all—I want to celebrate being free."

She tilted her face toward his, expectant.

He kissed her.

A kiss full of victory and promise, and something deeper still—something fragile but certain. The kind of kiss that tasted like beginnings and the end of fear.

In the quiet room, with shadows curling around them and the ghosts of secrets starting to fade, Charlotte let herself believe—for the first time since all this had begun—that perhaps, just perhaps, they were going to be all right.

CHAPTER 30

London
August 1813

THE SCENT OF BEESWAX POLISH AND OLD STONE FILLED THE church, mingling with the delicate perfume of the bouquets clutched by her bridesmaids as they made their way inside. Charlotte clung lightly to William's arm, her heart fluttering like a trapped bird.

"You're shaking," William murmured in her ear.

"I'm not," she lied, clutching her bouquet a little tighter.

He leaned in, a rare softness in his voice. "You're sure, then? Last chance to make a run for it."

Charlotte laughed, the sound barely audible beneath the organ's swell. "Very sure," she whispered back. "Now hush, or I'll trip just to spite you."

Felicity and Miranda moved gracefully ahead of her down the aisle, pale gowns catching the light, their matching smiles steady and composed. Charlotte followed, and suddenly hundreds of eyes were on her. She kept her chin up, but the weight of all that expectation pressed heavily against her chest.

Until she saw him.

Henry stood at the end of the aisle, tall and impossibly handsome in his dark coat, his expression unreadable to anyone but her. But she saw it—the flicker of awe, the softness, the way his breath caught as she stepped closer. The world around her blurred into silence. There was only him.

As they approached, she noticed a man seated inconspicuously in the back pew, hair touched with silver and posture a little too upright for a disinterested guest.

Henry's father.

He gave her a small, respectful smile, and she returned it. He and Henry had been getting to know each other over the past few weeks, and Charlotte had been included in that. Elias was a good man, and his face as he watched her and his son glowed with pride.

The dowager duchess had taken a while to come to terms both with the fact he was alive and with the prospect of having him in their lives. Apparently, the late duke had never told her about the money he had given Elias and had informed her some months after Henry's birth that Elias had perished in the course of his new career at sea.

Fortunately, she seemed to be warming to him. Charlotte suspected that shock and embarrassment had made her cold toward him in the beginning but that might change with time.

William stopped just short of the altar and looked down at her, all mischief gone from his face. "You're certain," he said again, very quietly.

"I am," she replied.

He let out a breath, then took her hand and placed it in Henry's. His fingers closed around hers, steady and warm.

"You look like a dream," Henry murmured. "Are you ready?"

She nodded, breathless.

The ceremony passed in a blur. Vows exchanged. Rings

slipped into place. Her heart, she was certain, had never beat so loudly.

When they emerged into the sunlight outside, the cheers of the crowd seemed far away. Henry bent his head toward her, his lips brushing her ear.

"You're mine now, Duchess of Arundel."

"And you're mine," she said, unable to stop the smile from overtaking her face.

They took a carriage to her family's home for the wedding breakfast, which was a blur of toasts, laughter, and far too many speeches. Charlotte nodded and tried to be gracious, but her mind was elsewhere—on the promise of privacy, of quiet, of being alone with her husband. She was excited but nervous.

What if she did something wrong?

She knew the bare bones of what happened between a man and woman on their wedding night, but that was all. And none of her friends were married, so she couldn't ask for their help.

No, she realized, *she* would be the one they would come to for advice.

At last, the carriage rolled them away from her former home and toward Henry's London townhouse. As the streets passed by in a haze, her hand stayed firmly clasped in his the whole time.

When they arrived, the staff stood lined up, all tidy smiles and welcoming bows. Charlotte did her best to seem composed, offering kind words and polite thank-yous. Henry made quick introductions, his arm a firm, reassuring weight around her waist.

As soon as the last of the formalities was seen to, he swept her up into his arms without preamble.

"Henry!" she gasped, half laughing, half scandalized.

"Tradition," he said with a grin. "Don't tell me you expect me to let you walk upstairs on your wedding night."

She looped her arms around his neck, heart thudding wildly. "Only if you promise not to drop me."

"I would never," he murmured, voice suddenly low and serious. "Never, Charlotte."

He carried her through the threshold of their room and set her down gently. The curtains were already drawn. It all felt surreal.

He touched her face, thumb brushing the curve of her cheek. "I love you," he said simply.

"I know," she whispered. "I love you too."

She trembled, both nervous and desirous as he pulled her toward him and started to kiss her gently. Her lips parted of their own accord, and she let out a small gasp as his tongue probed hers and his hands slid around the back of her dress, untying the laces of her bodice.

"Turn around," he said, his voice sounding rougher than usual, his eyes dark with desire.

Charlotte did as she was bid, her chest fluttering as she felt him deftly loosen her dress, and then it fell to her feet leaving her in her shift. She turned around to face him, stepping out of the mass of lace and silk to stand in front of him. Her nipples strained against the thin cotton of her shift, and she fought the impulse to cover them with her hands. Henry's eyes travelled over the silhouette of her body, and his breath sounded ragged in his throat.

"You're so beautiful, Charlotte."

He reached for her hair then, pulling out the pins so that the weight of it fell around her shoulders and into his hands. He ran his fingers through it slowly, then suddenly groaned and pulled her to him, nuzzling her neck and collarbone.

"God, my love, I need you." He sighed against her neck, nibbling the soft skin at the hollow of her throat, and Charlotte gasped as a ripple of desire went through her. Her gasp became a moan as his lips traced a trail down to the tops of her breasts, pushing her shift down over her shoulders and arms as he did so.

By the time it reached her waist and he took one of her nipples in his mouth, she had forgotten her nerves. She arched against him, one hand buried in his hair.

"Henry…" She panted, heat pooling between her thighs as his tongue circled her nipple and he cupped her breasts with his hands. A need she had never experienced before curled in the pit of her stomach. Her anxieties were gone.

She wanted him. All of him.

Yet she wasn't prepared for him lowering himself onto his knees as he kissed down her stomach. As he reached her sex, she shuddered, and his face flushed as he brought his mouth to her, his tongue flicking over the secret nub between her thighs.

She pressed her hand to her mouth as her sense of propriety warred with the gnawing need; part of her wanted him to stop, the other—much louder—wanted him never to stop.

Waves of sensation coursed through her body as he continued to taste her, slipping a finger gently inside her. There was a slight resistance, and then her body accepted him. She balled her fingers in his hair, feeling her thighs tremble and heat travel through her body as she gasped his name.

Then he got to his feet and began to quickly discard his clothes, pulling at his collar with impatience. With one hand he took one of hers and laid it on the laces of his breeches. Charlotte bit her lip, her nerves returning.

"I… I don't know what to do," she whispered even as she helped relieve him of his breeches while he stripped off his shirt, revealing a muscular chest and taut, hard stomach. He had broad shoulders and rippling biceps and a smattering of dark hair across his chest, and at the sight of him, she bit her lip again, drinking him in.

He was hers. Her husband.

Henry guided her hand inside his breeches, wrapping her hand around him. The skin of the shaft was warm and velvety soft against her palm, but it felt both firm and long in her hand, and she had a moment of apprehension at the thought of fitting his length inside her. She squeezed, experimenting with moving her hand along him, and he responded with a deep groan.

"Did I do something wrong?" She stopped moving, worried she'd hurt him.

He shook his head, his eyes closed and his head thrown back. "No, Charlotte," he said in that ragged voice. "No, that's perfect. I love your touch."

Her insides warmed at that, and she continued to touch him, exploring the feel of him until he groaned again and grabbed her wrist. "Stop, or I'll be finished before I can even get inside you."

"Is that bad?"

He opened his eyes, smiling at her with a mischievous twinkle in his eye. "No, my love, it's very, very good."

In one swoop he picked her up and laid her on the bed, then knelt again between her thighs.

As he lowered his mouth to her again, Charlotte felt the urgency of her need take over. She widened her legs further, pressing her hips into him as he gripped the soft flesh of her thighs. She moaned as he paused and then ran his tongue over her again, butterfly light, teasing her until she whimpered with need.

She rocked against his mouth, gasping as he slipped a finger inside her again, she clenched around him in response, her insides tightening with pleasure as he began to move it inside her, making a fluttering motion that made her gasp in delight. Her whole body was one exposed nerve ending, raw and aching.

Then Henry raised his head to look up at her.

"I want to see you climax for me, Charlotte," he said in a deep, rough voice, his eyes so darkened with desire, they were almost black. He kissed the skin where her thighs met her body. "I love the taste and smell of you," he murmured. "I love knowing you're mine. My wife."

Charlotte ran a hand through his hair as he put his mouth upon her once more, and she tipped her head back, surrendering herself to the moment as he again started to tease her with his tongue.

She whimpered with longing and gripped his hair, writhing against him. Henry pushed his fingers deeper inside, increasing his rhythm and pace until she could feel waves of pleasure building within her, every inch of her skin on fire with longing, any capacity for coherent thought beyond her.

Then her ecstasy hit, wave after wave of pleasure crashing over her, flooding her body with sensation from head to toe. She heard herself cry out as though from a long way away and then felt a rush of wetness between her thighs.

"Henry," she gasped, her tone urgent, tugging him toward her. With a wicked smile he climbed up between her legs, positioning himself over her on the bed. She lifted her legs and wrapped them around his hips as he looked down at her, his eyes suddenly soft.

"Are you ready, my love?" he asked softly.

As if there could possibly be any doubt.

"Yes," she whispered, and he began to gently push himself inside her. There was another sharp sting, but it was over as quickly as it appeared, to be replaced only with an aching need to have him fully inside her. She arched her back, pulling him into her.

"I don't want to hurt you." He ran a hand through her hair. It looked as though it was taking all of his self-control to hold back, and it gave her a throb of pleasure to see the effect she had on him.

"It doesn't hurt," she protested, bucking her hips wantonly toward him, but he slid himself inside her impossibly slowly until she felt filled by him, stretched by him. Only when she had gotten used to the sensation and her body was relaxed around him did he start to move inside her, his breath hot against her neck.

Charlotte gripped his firm backside, feeling his muscles contract as he moved inside her. She tipped her head back as he squeezed the nape of her neck and nibbled at her throat again.

"Charlotte," he groaned, and his movements quickened and deepened, his back slicked with sweat. His whole body tensed as he thrust deeply inside her and he shuddered as his own climax came. He moaned her name over and over.

Then he exhaled, long and low, before laying his head next to hers on the pillow, shuddering as his pleasure subsided. Then he rolled off her, leaving her bereft for a moment until he pulled her into his arms, kissing the top of her head. Her limbs were warm and heavy, and she was utterly content.

"You're trembling," he said softly.

"So are you," she replied, smiling into his chest. "That was amazing."

"This is only the beginning," he whispered, kissing her again. "I hope you're ready for forever."

THE END

EXCERPT FROM THE DUKE'S INCONVENIENT BRIDE

London,
October, 1819

Vaughan Stanhope, the Duke of Ashford, had never wanted a wife. Unfortunately, one could not get heirs without a wife, and without an heir, his title would pass to his bullying cousin, Reginald, and his brood of entitled brats.

Thus, here he was, in his best carriage, bedecked in his finest evening wear, and accompanied by his long-suffering friend, Andrew Drake, the Earl of Longley, on the way to a ball.

"I always knew you'd be the first of us to find a wife," Longley said, glancing out of the window as they arrived outside the Earl of Wembley's townhouse.

Vaughan scoffed and resisted the urge to look for himself. He was anxious enough without laying eyes on the crush of society that would no doubt be turning up tonight.

"Yes. After growing up with such a splendid example of matrimonial bliss, how could I possibly resist?"

Longley rolled his eyes. "Not because of your awful parents. Purely to spite that loathsome jackanapes, Reginald."

"Ah, yes. Him."

"Darling Reggie" as Vaughan's dearly departed mother had called him, had spent years tormenting him behind their parents' backs. Calling him names, mocking his shyness, and telling everyone who'd listen what a joke it was that he'd one day be a duke.

"He is the reason we're here, is he not?" Longley asked.

"In a roundabout way." At that moment, the carriage came to a stop. The door opened, and Vaughan climbed out, only too eager to be free of the conversation.

They made their way up the stone steps to the house's main entrance and stepped inside the foyer, where they were met by their hosts.

"Your Grace." The Earl of Wembley greeted Vaughan with a nod, then turned to Longley. "Lord Longley. Welcome to Wembley House."

"Felicitations. It seems as if you have a success on your hands," Longley said, and Vaughan shot him a look of gratitude for taking the lead. He was so much better in social situations than Vaughan was. Longley took the countess's hand and bowed over it. "My lady."

"Lord Longley," the countess demurred, then smiled slyly at Vaughan. "Your Grace, please allow me to introduce my eldest daughter, Lady Henrietta."

Vaughan acknowledged the girl with a tilt of his head. "Lady Henrietta. It's an honor to make your acquaintance."

Lady Henrietta's blond curls bounced as she angled her head back to look up at him, a friendly smile on her face. "The honor is all mine, Your Grace."

He glanced at Longley, who discreetly bumped him in the ribs with his elbow.

"I hope you will save me a dance," Vaughan said, the words difficult to get out past the lump in his throat. Still, this was what he was here for. To find a wife. Lady Henrietta was both pretty and suitable in terms of her connections. He could do worse.

"I would be delighted." She offered him her dance card and he filled a spot.

"We must move along," Longley urged as more guests arrived behind them. "Until later, Lady Henrietta."

They moved into the ballroom, which was massive, with high ceilings, white walls gilded with gold, and a polished wooden floor. It was also packed. Vaughan grew warmer, and not only from the mass of bodies pressing in around him. He and Longley seemed to have attracted a lot of attention with their arrival. Many young misses glanced their way, while their mothers studied the men more openly.

Heat prickled at the back of Vaughan's neck. He had the unmistakable feeling that he was being hunted. He drew in a shaky breath, his nostrils filling with the scent of the shrubbery somebody had felt the need to drag inside. He shrugged, trying to shake off the sensation of his skin being too tight for his body.

"Your Grace." A redheaded woman appeared in front of him with two younger ladies in tow. "Ah, and Lord Longley too." She looked like the cat that had eaten the canary.

"Lady Bowling," Vaughan replied, glancing over to make sure Longley hadn't beaten a rapid escape. His friend may be kind enough to have accompanied him tonight, but he had no desire for a wife of his own.

"May I present my daughter, Lady Esther, and her cousin, Miss Rose Hawthorne. They are new to society this season."

Vaughan blinked at the girls, one of whom wore a ridiculous feather construction in her hair, and the other of whom seemed to have been cinched so tightly into her ball gown that she might pass out at any moment.

"Charmed," Longley said, covering for Vaughan's hesitation. "I daren't hope that either of you lovely ladies have any space on your dance cards for His Grace or myself?"

The cards were proffered with much giggling and glee, and Vaughan dutifully added his name to each. They bid farewell to the group but had only made it another five paces before they were intercepted yet again.

By the time they reached the stairs leading to the upper balcony that overlooked the ballroom, Vaughan felt as if he hadn't drawn in a full breath for hours. A male voice called his name, but fearing yet another introduction to an eligible lady, he hurried up the stairs with Longley trailing behind him.

"Good lord, Ashford," Longley puffed as he drew even with Vaughan at the top of the stairs. "You're far less likely to find a wife up here than you were down there."

Vaughan surveyed the throng below, his pulse pounding madly in his temples. Even several feet above the revelry, he could hear the giggles, the inane chatter, and felt gazes following him.

"I did not realize it would be so…." He waved his hands, searching for a suitable descriptor. "Intense."

Longley chuckled. "'Tis the biggest ball of the season so far, which means every marriageable miss is seeking to make an impression. The fact that you are an unmarried duke, who has apparently decided to rectify your lack of a wife, makes you the plumpest catch here tonight."

Vaughan snorted. "You make me sound like a grouse."

"To the mamas of unwed young women, you might as well be."

Vaughan shook his head. "There must be a better way to find a wife."

Longley shrugged. "If you find one quickly, you won't have to subject yourself to many of these ghastly affairs. How many dances have you scheduled?"

"Almost half of them." His tone was morose. He enjoyed dancing, but not in cramped quarters such as this, and especially not with so many eyes on him.

Longley leaned on the balustrade. Vaughan followed his example, gazing out over the shining jewels of the ton.

"What do you want in a wife?" Longley asked. "Perhaps we can hasten the matter by being selective about the ladies to whom you offer your remaining dances."

Vaughan nodded. That made sense. "She must be well-mannered and respectable." His duchess would need to be able to smooth over his own occasional social missteps. "She does not have to be wealthy or from a titled family."

He pursed his lips, trying to quiet his thoughts, but it was difficult with the ruckus below. "She would ideally be popular and able to entertain herself, as I don't intend to spend much time together after we are wed."

There was a moment of silence, and then Longley asked, "Are you truly sure you wish to do this?"

Being Lady Violet Carlisle's twin sometimes made Emma feel invisible. Especially on nights such as these, when gentlemen were practically getting into fisticuffs to determine who would have the honor of dancing with Violet whilst seeming not to notice Emma at all. It made it difficult for Emma to find a man to fall in love with when they all wanted her sister.

With a sigh, Emma shrank back against the wall beside the refreshments table, watching as Violet spun across the dance floor on the arm of a viscount. She surveyed the gathering, searching for her mother, but her attention was halted by the sight of the square-jawed and remarkably well-built Earl of Longley, who seemed to be making his way directly to her.

Emma straightened, pushing her shoulders back and smiling in welcome. She had always liked the earl. Not only was he handsome, but he was also clever and kind. Perhaps he would spare her from another evening spent as a wall-flower by asking her to dance.

"Lady Emma," he said, stopping in front of her. "You look well tonight."

She dropped into a curtsey. "As do you, my lord."

When she rose, he gestured toward the dance floor.

"Do you know when Lady Violet will next be free? I have someone to whom I'd like to introduce her."

Emma's heart sank. Of course the earl had not come over here to see her. As always, it was her sister whose company was desired.

"I believe she is free in two dances' time, my lord."

"Very good. My thanks, Lady Emma." He sketched a quick bow and left.

Emma turned to the table beside her and poured herself a drink. She sipped the lemonade and eyed the tiny pastries and cakes set out nearby. They had not eaten dinner prior to departing from Carlisle House because their mother had wanted them to look slim in their gowns.

Unfortunately, being hungry made Emma lethargic, which meant she lagged even further behind Violet in the beauty department than usual. She edged closer to the table and reached for a pastry, slipping it into her hand and quickly raising it to her lips. She glanced around, checking whether anyone had noticed, but of course, nobody was looking at her.

Nobody ever was.

She took another pastry and spied one of her acquaintances dancing with her new husband. Their heads were ducked close together, their gazes locked on each other. Emma sighed. They looked as though they were aware of no one else in the room.

How she wanted that.

Emma sipped her lemonade, wishing it were laced with something stronger. Something that would make the evening more tolerable. It wasn't that she didn't like balls. She rather thought she'd enjoy them if she weren't such a wallflower.

"Emma!"

Emma flinched and spun around. Her mother, Lady Carlisle, was making a beeline toward her around the edge of the ballroom, past the row of chairs where the spinsters and chaperones sat, drawing even with the refreshments table. Her eyebrows had climbed impressively high and her eyes were narrow as she appraised her erstwhile daughter.

"What on earth are you doing all the way over here?" her mother demanded. "Nobody will ask you to dance if you do not remain near the dancing."

Emma pursed her lips. She thought there were likely other, more pressing reasons she was not asked to dance, but far be it for her to say so.

"Sorry, Mother. I shall return with you momentarily."

She tried to finish her lemonade, but Lady Carlisle plucked the glass from her hand and put it on the table.

Emma sighed. "Very well."

Lady Carlisle took Emma by the arm and guided her back into the fray. Emma nodded at an acquaintance of hers who was, likewise, not particularly popular with the males of the aristocracy.

"Doesn't Violet look brilliant tonight?" Lady Carlisle asked, watching her other daughter with such pride stamped across her face that Emma had to look away. It was difficult to bear the knowledge that she never brought her mother the same level of joy.

"She does," Emma agreed because it was true. Violet sparkled tonight, as she did every night. The song ended, and there was a brief pause before the next one began. Violet was making her way toward them across the dance floor on the arm of a handsome gentleman Emma did not recognize.

The music started again, and Emma tapped her foot,

wishing somebody would ask her to dance. Even an elderly bachelor or a homely one would do. She did so love to dance.

"Mother," Violet said as they drew near. "This is Mr. Bently."

"Cousin to the Earl of Longley," Mr. Bently added—presumably to make himself look like a better catch to the Carlisle matriarch.

"He's quite a dashing dancer," Violet exclaimed.

Emma felt a pang of envy. She tried not to be jealous of Violet, but sometimes it was difficult.

"Lady Carlisle." The voice came from behind Emma and startled them all. Emma's hand flew to her chest as she turned toward it.

Lord Longley smiled broadly. He tipped his head. "Lady Emma. Lady Violet. Bently."

"Lord Longley." Violet's smile was beatific. Lord Longley was on her shortlist of prospective husbands. While Emma wanted to find a connection before she married, Violet was much more pragmatic. A title and a fortune would do nicely for her.

Lord Longley waited for the greetings to finish and then gestured to the man beside him, an austere-looking fellow with an immaculately tailored waistcoat, dark hair, and eyes the color of the sky on a cloudy morning.

"Please allow me to introduce you to my good friend, the Duke of Ashford."

Emma heard her mother's quick intake of breath. Violet was more subtle, but her eyes still widened. Emma didn't know why they were surprised. She wasn't. If the rumors were to be believed, the duke was looking for a bride, and Violet would make a remarkable duchess.

There was a chorus of "Your Graces" followed by curtsey-ing, during which Emma surreptitiously watched the duke. His eyes were unusual and quite stunning, but he didn't have the same amiable air about him that Lord Longley did. In fact, while his mouth twitched slightly during the introduction, he didn't even smile.

When Emma found a husband, she'd want one who smiled regularly and laughed easily.

"A pleasure." The Duke of Ashford's voice was cool and cultured. He reminded Emma of what she imagined the character of Mr. Darcy from the novel she was reading would sound like. He turned to Violet. "Lady Violet, may I have this dance?"

Violet fluttered her eyelashes—dark, unlike Emma's overly pale ones—and smiled. "It would be an honor."

She took his hand and allowed him to lead her away. As soon as Violet left, Mr. Bently made his excuses, and the earl melted away into the crowd.

"Would you believe it?" Lady Carlisle asked, hushed but excited. "A duke."

"They look lovely together," Emma said. The duke had an intriguing dark handsomeness about him that did not appeal to her, but she knew many young ladies would go crazy for it. In conjunction with Violet's pale blond hair, strawberries-and-cream complexion, and dark eyebrows and eyelashes, they were a striking pair.

The song picked up, and Emma's foot tapped as she watched the dancers.

"Oh, Emma, please stop that," her mother snapped.

Emma scowled, but stilled her foot. All she wanted was to dance. And perhaps to eat a few more of those pastries.

When the dance finished, the duke returned Violet to them. His expression gave nothing away, but Violet appeared to be in raptures.

"His Grace is truly accomplished at the cotillion," she said.

The duke seemed to shrink an inch, and Emma frowned. She'd have expected him to either preen at the comment or not acknowledge it at all.

"It was a delightful dance," he said with all the enthusiasm Emma saved for when her governess had made her practice her sums as a girl.

He turned to Emma, and those pale gray eyes met hers. He hesitated, actually pausing to look at her, whereas many people simply swept straight over her. His lips parted, and anticipation fizzed in her stomach. Would he ask her to dance too?

ABOUT THE AUTHORS

Jayne Rivers adores regency romance books, especially those by Sarah MacLean and Julia Quinn. She writes feel-good stories with heroines she'd love to befriend and heroes she'd love to sweep her off her feet—if she weren't married, of course.

Maggie Kent is a former teacher from the UK with a passion for creative writing and introducing diversity into publishing. She also writes romance under other pen names.

www.ingramcontent.com/pod-product-compliance
Lightning Source LLC
Chambersburg PA
CBHW061219310726
48971CB00007B/1873